Praise for awar s
"darkly compelling"* para es

CAPTURED BY MOONLIGHT

"These lovers have much to overcome, including their own self-sabotaging character traits. Gideon adds new clues and layers to her world while placing her protagonists in terrible danger, both physically and emotionally. A terrific series that thankfully leaves the opportunity open for future exploration!"

—*Romantic Times**

"Exhilarating adventure . . . and extremely erotic sex."

—Fresh Fiction

"*Captured by Moonlight* is profoundly moving as emotional challenges endlessly crop up amid the perilous danger."

—Single Titles

"As good as if not better than its predecessors. . . . Gideon has written the perfect paranormal romances."

—Romance Junkies

"A deliciously complex novel full of love and devotion, personal angst and paranormal intrigue. I highly recommend it."

—Night Owl Reviews

CHASED BY MOONLIGHT

"Gideon does a terrific job with her world-building as her characters and readers discover dark and hidden secrets."

—*Romantic Times*

"Another dynamic thriller in this series filled with exciting drama and erotic romance. . . . This book will keep your senses alert and the blood pounding."

—Fresh Fiction

"An outstanding romance overflowing with emotional issues and innovative supernatural elements."

—Single Titles

"The boiling-hot duo of Max Savoie and Charlotte Caissie returns, and the thrill-ride just keeps getting better. . . . This series is a must read!"

—Bitten by Books

MASKED BY MOONLIGHT

"A paranormal romance series with intriguing characters and zippy action. . . . Gideon masters the tension required to keep her complex and engaging story moving."

—*Publishers Weekly* (starred review)

"Definitely a series to keep an eye on!"

—*Romantic Times*

"Sizzling . . . dark and compelling!"

—Susan Sizemore, *New York Times* bestselling author

"Vivid, dark, and memorable. . . . I couldn't put it down."

—Janet Chapman, *New York Times* bestselling author

"The reader won't find more excitement anywhere."

—Fresh Fiction

"Brilliantly spellbinding with fascinating supernatural aspects, heated passions, and unanticipated dangers."

—Single Titles

"An exceptional read. It will have the reader laughing one minute, crying the next. It's a compelling story and a tremendous first book in Gideon's new series."

—Reader to Reader, NewandUsedBooks.com

"Darkness and danger never seemed more appealing. Gideon's paranormal world comes alive with dynamic characters and seductive werewolf lore. A must read!"

—*ParaNormal Romance Reviews*

These titles are also available as eBooks

NANCY GIDEON

Bound by Moonlight

POCKET STAR BOOKS
New York   London   Toronto   Sydney

Pocket Star Books
A Division of Simon & Schuster, Inc.
1230 Avenue of the Americas
New York, NY 10020

This book is a work of fiction. Names, characters, places, and incidents either are products of the author's imagination or are used fictitiously. Any resemblance to actual events or locales or persons, living or dead, is entirely coincidental.

First Pocket Star Books paperback edition August 2011

POCKET STAR BOOKS and colophon are registered trademarks of Simon & Schuster, Inc.

For information about special discounts for bulk purchases, please contact Simon & Schuster Special Sales at 1-866-506-1949 or business@simonandschuster.com.

The Simon & Schuster Speakers Bureau can bring authors to your live event. For more information or to book an event contact the Simon & Schuster Speakers Bureau at 1-866-248-3049 or visit our website at www.simonspeakers.com.

Cover design by Min Choi
Cover art by Craig White

Manufactured in the United States of America

10 9 8 7 6 5 4 3 2 1

ISBN 978-1-4391-9948-0
ISBN 978-1-4391-9952-7 (ebook)

For my fabulous editor,
Micki Nuding.
Thanks for believing!

Bound by Moonlight

Prologue

C'MON. C'MON.

She shifted from one foot to the other and scowled through the grated front window, unable to see anything in the dark, uninviting interior.

It's not like I don't have better things to do at the butt crack of dawn.

She checked the luminous dial on her cartoon character wristwatch, a silly gift from her father she couldn't make herself toss away. It was the only thing from her past she'd hung on to. Everything else belonged to her new incarnation: Kikki Valentine, exotic dancer and reluctant temporary prostitute. Temporary because as soon as she had the money put aside, she'd enroll in a real school for dance and the past few months would just be a bad dream. At least that was the plan. But, lately, things weren't going in the direction they were supposed to.

Lately, she'd been questioning a lot of things that had seemed like a good idea at the time.

She didn't mind the life so much. It was hard, but she was tough. You gotta pay your dues, her daddy had always said, and this was a school with some pretty hard knocks. But weird shit was going on lately, the whispers passing from one girl to another. They were scared, and fear was like an STD. It spread everywhere if unchecked.

Some of the girls were even talking about getting away while they could.

But if she caved now and gave up her dreams, what would she have except more of the same dead end?

She'd always been the rebel, too impatient to wait for chances to come her way. Not the smart one, like her brother. Not the sweet one, like her sister. She was the one who was just a little harder to love, her mama had told her after one of many arguments. The others were praised for their academics and good behavior. That left her the *all-time* fuckup.

From the time she was a toddler, she'd wanted to dance. She wanted to be center stage, a star so bright no one could look away.

Rhythm beat in her blood, motion stirred through her soul. Music seduced her body the way a lover never could. She'd mastered pop-'n'-lock in grade school, was mimicking the steps in *Dirty Dancing, Simply Ballroom, Step Up, Save the Last Dance,* and *Stomp the Yard* as a preteen. At thirteen, she was sneaking into clubs with a fake ID just to dance, until she got caught.

She'd never fit into the home scene, anyway. Too many rules and regs. But lately she'd been thinking about maybe giving the folks and school another chance. Probably because of the weird shit.

She paced in front of the clinic, her feet pinched by her new boots, then tried the door again. Cupping her hands by her eyes to lessen the glare, she peered inside. No lights were on, just the familiar soft fluorescent glow. Damn, where was the doc? If she didn't hurry she'd miss her bus, and she couldn't afford a cab.

Maybe she could call home, just this once. They'd come get her. She was sure of it.

She straightened and glanced about her gritty surroundings. It looked like a scene from one of those end-of-the-world movies. Steam roiling out of the alleyways, swirls of white over oppressive gray, the empty streets bled dry of all life. In the grainy light she could see her reflection in the grated window: a cold, frightened little girl with teased auburn hair, hiding behind heavy makeup and garish clothes. Alone.

Then she heard a noise from around the corner of the building. The doctor—good.

"About damned time."

She dropped her cigarette and ground it out under the toe of her platform boot, then stepped off the curb to check the alley. A vehicle was parked at the far end, squat and dark in the shadows and mist. She started walking toward it. She should have gone to the side door instead of waiting out front like an idiot.

Suddenly the headlights came on, bright and blinding. Shielding her eyes, she kept walking. "Hey, Doc, it's me, Kikki. Turn those off, will ya?"

She heard the low purr of the engine coming to life, and stones crunched as the car moved toward her at a slow, stalking pace.

She froze, then started backing toward the street, hearing the girls' whispers warning her to be careful, warning of the danger. She scrambled and ran, darting to the safety of the sidewalk. She fumbled in her purse, looking for her pepper spray.

The car edged into view, turning onto the street to stop in front of her. Then the passenger window slowly rolled down.

She exhaled a shaky breath. Probably just a john looking for some early action. She straightened, cocking her hip and tossing her head. Maybe he'd be willing to give her a ride to the bus station if she threw in a little extra. These new boots were *not* made for walking.

"Hey there. Lookin' for a party?" she asked.

She started toward the car with an exaggerated roll of her hips to begin the bartering. The door opened. The figure bent toward her, and she started to smile.

"You nearly scared me to death, turning on the headlights like that. What—"

Strong fingers gripped her upper arm, pulling her inside the car before she could think to struggle. Her temple hit the door molding, making everything go bright and glittery like the New Orleans nightlife she loved. A sharp sting at the base of her throat, a flare of burning heat. Then nothing.

The door closed and the car moved in no hurry into the morning mists.

One

ONE GLANCE TOLD Charlotte Caissie what she'd feared from the start. The situation was high risk and potentially dangerous.

She visually swept the area, studying the scene with a cop's attention to detail. The press were everywhere, seeking scraps to tantalize the public's hunger for information. The more sensational, the better.

She scowled, wishing she had the authority to make the vultures scatter. Unfortunately, she wasn't here in an official capacity, couldn't brush them off with a flick of her badge. *What the hell am I doing here?*

The most controversial criminal figure in New Orleans stepped out of a sleek, dark town car, coming toward her with lethal grace and fixed intensity. A shiver rode across her skin. *This* was why she was here. Max Savoie had taken the place of crime kingpin Jimmy Legere, his dead mentor, with frightening competence and control. He'd built his reputation as Jimmy's unflinchingly loyal enforcer upon tales of gruesome deeds. Rumors, because no one really had a clue as to who—or *what*—Max really was. Except her.

Savoie, with his dark, forbidding looks and ferocious silences, had become her obsession. A smaller prize wouldn't have drawn her out into this terrifying arena. Less important stakes wouldn't bring her to the most daunting endeavor of her career without backup. She cursed him under her breath, yet was unable to take her eyes off him.

Sleek, powerful, and deadly, he still provoked all her senses the same way he had eight years ago, when she'd seen him walk handcuffed through the station as if nothing could touch him.

Tonight he was the sophisticated image of a wealthy businessman, but tailored Armani couldn't disguise his harshly cut features. A bristle of dark hair arranged by the drag of fingers, the solemn black brows above eyes like pale, impenetrable jade, added to his ruthless mystique.

Unblinking, unsmiling, he stepped right inside her guarded circle of personal space, and offered his arm. "Ready?"

Her hesitation brought no change to his expression. "If you want to get back into your cab, I'll understand. I would be the last one to fault you for it." He softly added, "Coward."

Her spine stiffened. "I said I'd come with you, and I'll stick it out."

"Heroically spoken."

"Now's not a smart time to be amused at my expense," she growled. "I'm only doing this for you."

"I know." He lifted her hand, pressing her palm to his freshly shaven cheek. "And that means everything to me. You mean everything to me."

She swallowed hard, her fingertips tenderly stroking his jaw.

He leaned down slowly, making her breath catch,

her eyes flutter shut. At the sound of his quiet chuckle, they flashed open again.

"You're trying to distract me, *cher*. It won't work. I'm not leaving."

She shoved away from him to glare at the gauntlet before them. "Give me one reason why I put up with you."

He smiled, heat kindling in his gaze. "Because you know that while everyone here is admiring how beautiful you look in that dress, I'll be anticipating how beautiful you'll look as I'm taking it off you."

She eyed him thoughtfully. "Damned good reason. Okay, let's get this over with."

"Your enthusiasm is underwhelming, but the reward of seeing you naked will sustain me."

She laughed and finally relaxed as her hand rested in the crook of his elbow. "Let the bastards do their worst. I'm ready for them."

"Spoken like one of NOLA's finest. Chin up, *sha*. Don't let them see what frauds we are. The tough homicide cop and her mobster-beast boyfriend milling with the city's best. Shall we?"

She hesitated, then said, "I love you, Max."

His breath hitched as if she'd shot a round into his chest. Then his free hand slid over hers and pressed lightly. "That sustains me, too."

And together they breached the society that shunned them.

She'd say one thing for her least favorite politician. Simon Cummings sure knew how to throw a wingding. He'd pulled strings all over the Crescent City to commandeer the streets surrounding Jackson Square for his block-party-style fund-raiser. The pre-ticketed event promised plenty of good PR for those contributing to the launch of his new foundation. Security was high to separate the curious from the guests and to protect the celebs from being mobbed by fans.

Charlotte groaned as they were approached by one of the off-duty cops hired to keep things under control. Donner, from Robbery. His smooth, dark face betrayed no emotion as his palm slapped against Max's shirt-front.

"Sorry. Private party."

"Sorry. Invited."

Without breaking from the man's challenging glare, Max carefully reached into his jacket, keeping one hand visible, and produced the embossed card. When the officer refused to look at it, he tapped it with one finger.

"That would be me."

"I know who you are," Donner snarled. "*What* you are."

"And I believe you know my date. Who and what she is."

Donner's gaze flickered to acknowledge her. "Caissie."

"Donner. Are you finished, or are you going to piss me off even more by asking to see my identification, too?"

He stepped aside with a grim, "Have a nice evening."

"Like that's going to happen now," she muttered to herself.

The instant they entered the roped-off area, the press swarmed them. Each garnered headlines on their own, but stepping out as a couple for the first time in public, they were media magnets. Scowling, Cee Cee fielded the rapid-fire questions with a crisp, "No comment." Max never spared them a glance as he towed her into the fray, until Karen Crawford planted her microphone in his face. Before the Terror of Tabloid Journalism could begin her barrage, Cee Cee pushed between them.

"Back off, Crawford. I'm not on the clock and I don't have to be polite."

Her nemesis arched a penciled-in brow. Refusing to let age force her out of her youth-obsessed profession, Crawford now relied on pure shock value to sell herself. Her questions were precisely lobbed grenades. "Detective, this is a glamorous look for you. Obviously you're enjoying the spoils of Jimmy Legere's ill-gotten fortune."

Direct hit.

"I buy my own clothes, Ms. Crawford. A job that you give very little credit to pays for them."

"I hadn't credited you with having good taste." Crafty eyes swept over her escort. "Until recently."

Max's arm curled protectively about Cee Cee's waist, protecting the reporter. "Ladies, play nice. This is a charity event, after all." He smiled at the newswoman. "You're looking very elegant yourself, Ms. Crawford. Putting our faces under your byline along with your lies must have paid you well."

She grinned like a shark. "Not as well as an exclusive would."

"Dream on, Crawford," Cee Cee growled. "The only thing exclusive about him is me."

The reporter chuckled. "Can I quote you? At five

hundred dollars per ticket, you've come out as a couple in a big way."

Cee Cee gaped up at Max. "Five—"

He gave her a warning squeeze and answered the reporter. "It's an important cause to both of us. Let's focus there, can we?"

Crawford pounced on the opportunity. "Important why?"

"We both lost our mamas when we were young. We were lucky to have good, strong influences step in to raise us. Others aren't that fortunate."

"The Cummings Foundation targets homeless or exploited children," Crawford pressed. "I know the detective owes much of her rearing to Father Furness and St. Bartholomew's. But when Jimmy Legere took you in, wouldn't you consider that more exploitation than salvation?"

His eyes went flat and cold. "No. 'Cuse us, please." He propelled Cee Cee forward, making her hurry in her four-inch heels to keep up with his long strides.

He was here to make a statement, and when Max set his mind to something he was as subtle as a bulldozer: get out of his way or get plowed under. And she was crazy enough to ride shotgun as he strode into the limelight.

At first glance, Michael Furness appeared more a man given to spirits than the spiritual. His big, coarse figure should have appeared imposing behind the clerical collar, but something in his eyes and smile showed an inner compassion that reached out to the lost and those in need. He'd founded a small church in a rundown neighborhood and opened its doors to all. They flocked to him, those of bruised heart and soul and body, and he gathered them close. Charlotte had considered St. Bart's home while her top cop father was working the streets undercover. She and her best friend, Mary Kate Malone, who was the light yang to her dark yin, grew up inside the humble embrace of kindness and care, Mary Kate an orphan, Cee Cee left on her own. She owed the priest more than she could ever express, and Max knew it. Which is why he headed straight for that calm man of God, in spite of—or because of—who was standing next to him.

Father Furness stood on the steps of St. Louis Cathedral speaking with NOPD chief Byron Atcliff.

"I was hoping Max would bring you," the priest murmured in a surprisingly gentle baritone as he swallowed her in his embrace. "It's good to see you, Lottie. And Max." He put out a big hand. "I wish you'd let me give you the proper accolades for what you've given to the church."

"No thanks needed, Father. I wish there was more I could have done."

Furness patted his hand and released it before Max grew uncomfortable enough to tug away. Praise made him restless, so the priest doled it out in small doses.

"Looks like you'll have no trouble raising the rest of what you need." Cee Cee glanced around at the crowd. "A lot of deep pockets here looking for good press."

"And speaking of deep pockets, I see one I need to fleece." Father Furness winked at her. "For a good cause, of course. Come see me, Lottie."

She promised she would, but they both knew she probably wouldn't unless work brought her to his door. He gave her another hug and left her to deal with the two very opposite, and at the moment confrontational, men who meant the world to her.

Byron Atcliff was more than just Cee Cee's superior. She'd practically grown up on the seat of the squad car between him and her father when they were partners on the force. A wiry man, as relentless as Furness was forgiving, Atcliff despised crime in any form. And in his eyes, Savoie was its bold embodiment.

As police chief, he worried over the career of his most decorated detective because of her association with Max. As her godfather, he fretted over the happiness of his best friend's only child.

He regarded Charlotte with a disapproving frown as she pushed her unacceptable escort in front of him. To his credit, Savoie met his gun-barrel glare without flinching.

"Uncle Byron," Cee Cee said, trying to soften him up as she linked her arm through the rigid figure's at her side, "Max Savoie. Max, Chief Byron Atcliff."

"I believe we know one another by reputation," Max said.

"Yes, we do," Atcliff returned just as stiffly. No hand was offered. None was expected, considering Atcliff had spent his career trying to put Savoie and those like him in prison. Or the morgue.

Atcliff was about to turn away when he caught Cee Cee's flinty stare, calling him on his promise that he'd give the man behind the mobster a fair chance. And Atcliff prided himself on being fair, even when it choked him.

Scowling, he pinned Savoie with a stabbing glance.

"Father Furness tells me you've almost single-handedly been responsible for the rebuilding of St. Bart's."

"The father was exaggerating to make me more palatable in your eyes."

That unexpected honesty didn't throw Atcliff off. If anything, it made the chief sink his teeth in deeper. "The money Jimmy Legere spread around for charity was fertilizer. He hoped it would grow a good opinion to cover the stink of what he was. What are you spreading, Savoie?"

Max remained unblinking for a long, lethal moment, then he offered a narrow smile. "I don't have much of a green thumb."

Atcliff snorted. "You've managed to grow on my goddaughter. You harm her career, I'll cut you off at the ground like chokeweed."

"Understood."

"I'm not in favor of this relationship," the older man continued. "I can't say I approve of you parading it around."

"Good thing for me your opinion isn't the one that matters most."

At the coolly mocking tone, Atcliff warned, "You break her heart, I'll pull you out by the roots."

Cee Cee stepped between them with an exasperated, "Would you two stand down? Uncle Byron, Max is my choice. Deal with it. Max, you will respect his right to be pissed off about it. Clear?"

They gauged one another again.

"Take care of her and stay out from under my feet professionally, and I won't have a problem with you, Savoie."

"I'll stay out of your way unless you push that professional foot into our personal lives again. Then I'd have to make myself your problem. In a big way."

Atcliff assessed the arrogant man who'd somehow managed to snag the heart of Tommy Caissie's daughter. Did he have the steadfastness Cee Cee could depend upon, the strength to support her, and the wisdom to protect the best damned thing he'd ever have? Savoie wasn't someone he'd enjoy seeing across the dinner table at holiday time. He doubted they'd ever make easy small talk while fishing off his boat together. But he was Charlotte's choice, and Savoie didn't give an inch when it came to claiming that.

And there was nothing wrong with a little arrogance.

Chief Byron Atcliff allowed a grim smile. "Understood."

"THAT WENT WELL."

Max had no comment as they followed the movement of the crowd around the Square.

Booths fronting the Pontalba offered handcrafted items from area artisans, donated for the cause: exquisite jewelry, paintings, one-of-a-kind and vintage clothing, as well as accent pieces in metal, glass, and ceramic with price tags only the rich could afford. Not much of a shopper, Cee Cee kept her attention on Max. She noticed his silence and distraction and followed his stare to the source: Karen Crawford.

"Max, she's a cold, soulless bitch from hell. You know better than to talk to her."

He stopped. "Do you agree with her?"

Cee Cee laughed. "I hate to think I'd agree with Crawford on whether it's night or day."

His unblinking gaze wouldn't let her off the hook.

"Oh, for fu— Do we have to do this now?"

"Is it the timing or the topic you find so objectionable?"

She put a hand on one hip. "What I find objectionable is the fact that you haven't told me how you like my shoes."

He continued to glare at her.

Come on, Savoie. You know you want to look.

He held for another admirable moment. Then he glanced down, checking out the navy blue heels barely held in place by a serpentine twist of shantung winding over the top of her foot. She smiled to herself as a low growl vibrated from him.

"Like them?" She pivoted her foot on the pointed toe to show off all the views.

He took a harsh breath. "I'm going to suck on your toes after I take them off you."

"Good. Then that's money well spent."

Max shook off his lustful fascination and regarded her once again with that insistent silence, waiting for his answer.

She sighed. "Okay. Do I think Jimmy used you? Yes. You know it's one of the things I hated most about him. Do I think he loved you and cared for you and raised you like a father would? Yes, damn him, he did. So I have to be grateful to him for that, which annoys me to no end. But whatchu gonna do?"

He put his arms around her. "I'm sorry, *cher*. I didn't mean to spoil our evening by being disagreeable." He sighed heavily. "We don't belong here with them. Maybe we should just go home."

She shook her head. "Screw them, Max. We're here for Father Furness and St. Bart's and all those kids he's helping. So let's go spend an obscene amount of Jimmy's ill-gotten gains on something that will do some good. Besides, you promised there'd be dancing. Don't you want the chance to grope me in front of all these repressed, upscale folks?"

She felt the slow curve of his smile against her temple. Laughing, he curled an arm about her shoulders.

There was a time when she would have thrown off that possessive gesture as too personal for a public venue. But tonight was all about him.

Low, bluesy music from the far side of the Square reached them over the sound of the crowd. Piquant smells from the food booths tantalized upon the spring air. They wandered from booth to booth, awareness of one another sizzling like the fryers serving up catfish and hush puppies. It was nice—that simmering sense of belonging to each other, of comfortable closeness and anticipation for two people who had never belonged anywhere.

Max stopped at one of the tables. He turned to her, his expression somber as he lifted a creamy string of pearls. "I'd like to see you in these."

"And probably nothing else," she teased.

He didn't smile. His mood was strange as he laid the long rope about her neck, looping it a second time to admire the way the pearls glowed against her skin. "Would you wear them for me?"

She touched them tentatively. An extravagant

gift from someone who rarely gave them. Unless she counted her car and the treasured flowers reduced to petals kept in a bowl at their bedside. He wasn't a creature of impulse, which made her wonder about the significance of the perfect beads.

"They're beautiful. Thank you."

He counted out an alarming stack of bills to the woman behind the cash box, then took Cee Cee's hand to lead her along the crowded street. He didn't look around, his focus set grimly on his purpose: to be seen.

Where he walked, attention followed, forcing him to take a narrow road of behavior and consequence.

He controlled an empire built on a foundation of crime and violence. He ruled a hidden clan of creatures like him, who existed in secret behind a veil of superstition and danger. And balancing those obligations was his absolute devotion to the one person who could tear down both worlds: Charlotte. She owned him heart and tarnished soul.

And she would not fail him.

Two

"Mr. Savoie. Detective Caissie. You got my invitation."

They looked around at the soft greeting to see Noreen Cummings and her daughter. Both were blonde and lovely and scarred, one externally, one emotionally, by traumatic events tied to Max.

He took the fragile hand offered him in a gentle grip. "Mrs. Cummings, you're looking far better than the last time I saw you."

She'd been in the hospital, torn and stitched from a brutal attack reporters had tried to link to his dark reputation. Truth hadn't been a big concern while building their salacious story, and no apologies came when it proved to be pure fiction—except from this woman who'd lost the most.

Slender fingers tightened about his with a show of strength. That didn't surprise him. He knew she was strong.

Her smile was bittersweet. "I want to thank you again for your visit. It brought me . . . great comfort. This is my daughter, Janet. I have you to thank for her safety."

More praise he didn't deserve. He'd done nothing to protect her; circumstances and a sharp blade wielded by another had removed the threat.

"Miss Cummings. I heard you speak on your father's behalf at a fund-raiser some time ago. You were very passionate. It impressed me."

The young woman nodded her thanks. "I'm strictly behind the scenes now."

Max and Noreen exchanged a glance. *Good*, his stare conveyed. *Keep her safe. Keep her away from attention.*

Cee Cee watched with curiosity. She hadn't known Max was acquainted with Cummings's wife. She extended her hand to Noreen. The last time they'd spoken, the elegant woman had condemned her for her relationship with Max, which was understandable at the time. "This is a wonderful thing your husband is doing for the children of our community."

A firm clasp. "Actually, it's my project. I'm just letting Simon have the glory. I imagine you and I both do what we can in our own ways."

Cee Cee nodded. She liked the gutsy woman who wore her loss and her scars so proudly. Though Simon Cummings's character was suspect, his wife made up for it abundantly.

Then he was there, slick smile, hard eyes, quick to surround his wife and daughter with shielding arms.

"Detective. Savoie. Surprised to see the two of you circulating with the crème of New Orleans." The smooth drawl of contempt earned Cummings a sharp look from his wife, but his focus was on Max. And that look was deadly.

"My money's as green as anyone's, as you well know," Max said with an equally chilly smile. "And my motives are more pure than many." He reached into the inside pocket of his jacket, then extended an envelope. "A contribution from LEI. For the good of the community."

Cummings's features tightened, and for a moment Cee Cee thought he might rip up the donation and throw it into Max's face. Then the pop of a camera flash made his political façade slide into place as he accepted it.

"The community thanks you for your generosity." He tucked the envelope away, his attitude unmistakable. Max may have forced him into taking his stained money and doing business with him, but Cummings wasn't about to be social. "Darlin's, we need to keep moving."

Noreen bestowed a regretful look upon them. "Good to see you both. Beautiful pearls."

Cee Cee touched them. "Thank you. A gift,"

Her gaze slid up to Max, who had eyes only for the departing Cummings. Eyes that were fierce and dangerous. A tug on his arm brought him to heel but in no way tamed his mood. He was rigid with animosity and . . . something else. Something he hadn't shared with her.

Cee Cee finally broke the silence. "If you despise him so much, why are you working with him?"

"Business makes for strange bedfellows. Keeps your enemies closer."

"A Jimmy Legereism, if ever I heard one."

He didn't smile. "He had something I wanted and I had something he needed. Neither of us has to like it."

"He's dangerous and powerful, Max. Don't underestimate him."

"So am I. And I don't plan to."

She kept her hand on his sleeve as he stalked through the glamorous company, a barely leashed predator whose similarity to them went only as deep as his tailor. If they knew what truly lurked beneath the sheen of civility, they would run screaming in terror.

But Max knew how to blend so they wouldn't guess what Charlotte knew. The first lesson his mother had ever taught him was that humans destroyed what they didn't understand.

As she and Max moved among them, people stepped back, eyes averted, voices dropping to a whisper. She knew what they were saying.

What the hell is he doing here?

. . . heard he killed men for Jimmy Legere . . . ate their hearts.

She should lose her shield. A police detective with the likes of him . . .

They live together in that mobster fortress out on River Road.

Cee Cee's chin went up a notch. She was used to barbs from the press and she didn't care about gossip. But she cared about Max—and for some reason, the impression these people held mattered to him.

He made no excuses for his past. He'd been an expert at wielding fear while prowling the shadowed streets like the shiver of a bad dream, alone and dreaded. This game of diplomacy and appearances was new to him, enduring the stares and whispers so he could push his way in to establish himself where he wasn't wanted.

And damn, if she wasn't proud of him.

They'd gone full circle about the Square and Max paused to gaze at the crowd with that unnervingly still focus.

"Well, I think I've managed to intimidate and annoy just about everyone by being here. My goals have been achieved. If you've finished rubbing your exquisite taste in clothing and men in their faces, I'll take you home and attend to your very sexy feet—along with any other desires you might have."

Oh, baby.

She backed down her racing motor, letting passion rumble at a rough idle. "I want to dance with you first. I want to squeeze your exceptionally fine ass in front of all these snotty people."

That got the flicker of a grin. "Such noble aspirations, Detective. How could I not comply?"

A local band was doing an excellent job on a variety of cover songs. Strands of tiny lights crisscrossed above the couples dancing on the street. One hand on her waist, the other engulfing hers, Max moved her in long, graceful steps to the Cajun waltz "*La Vulse des Chère Bébé.*" As the sweeping tempo of the music and the heat of his touch worked magic upon her mood, Cee Cee forgot the cameras, the whispers. There was only Max, and the way she'd felt dancing with him barefoot on his lawn among his feral clan.

Gazing up at him, her heart in her eyes, she smiled. He smiled back, a slow, sexy curve that promised her everything she'd been looking for. Those watching covertly got a quick glimpse of what went on between them behind closed doors, between smooth sheets.

Max's smile widened into a grin when her hand grabbed the seat of his trousers for a firm squeeze.

When the band eased into the bluesy ballad "That's How Strong My Love Is," Charlotte sighed—until she felt a vibration stir between their bodies.

"Is that you or me?" he murmured.

"Me. Dammit."

He stopped so she could retrieve her cell phone from her tiny handbag.

"Caissie."

As she listened, Max felt tension gather in her long, strong body.

"I take it our evening is over," he commented as she closed her phone.

"I'm sorry, baby."

His knuckles brushed her cheek. "It's all right." Damn, this wasn't how he'd wanted their night to end.

"Babineau is picking me up over by Café du Monde. Don't wait up. This looks to be an all-nighter."

"I'll wait."

Max walked her through the crowd, his pride in who she was and where she was going evident in his strut. His woman. His warrior mate.

His arm cinched possessively about her waist when he saw her partner, Alain Babineau, leaning against his car. Babineau, who was cover-model good-looking, and had shared a romantic moment with Charlotte in the past. A moment she refused to discuss.

The hairs at Max's nape rose as Babineau sent Cee Cee an appreciative whistle.

"Woo wee. If I'd known the crime scene was gonna be formal, I'da worn my other jacket."

"Stuff it, Babs."

The detective's gaze met Max's in shared hostility. "Savoie. Sorry for the interruption." He didn't look sorry. "I'll see she gets back to you in one piece."

"She doesn't need your help for that."

Pleased by his growly confidence, Cee Cee turned into Max's arms. "I'll be careful. I wouldn't want anyone but you to wrinkle my dress."

Max kissed her, a hard, tongue-to-tonsils kiss. As he claimed her mouth, he fixed Babineau with a cold, unblinking warning. *Mine.*

With a final nip at her bottom lip, Max shrugged out of his suit coat and slipped it about her shoulders. His scent and heat wrapped her up like an embrace.

"Thanks for the dance, Detective."

"Thanks for letting me show you off, Savoie."

He stepped back and let her go, watching her slide her arms into his coat sleeves as she demanded an update from her partner. Then she climbed into the car, consumed by her job.

But as Babineau pulled away she turned to raise two fingers to Max, sending a kiss his way.

THE GIRL HAD been left behind a Dumpster, like garbage.

Anger simmering at the casual contempt of that gesture, Cee Cee asked, "Same as before?"

Joey Boucher straightened from his crouch after taking one more picture. "Same ole, same ole. Our boy is a creature of nasty habits." The young officer turned, then stared at Cee Cee, amazement slackening his homely face. "No one told me we were supposed to dress up. How come no one told me we were supposed to wear our good clothes?"

"Shut up, Boucher, or I'll stick the toe of these very nice shoes someplace very unpleasant. Now, talk murder to me."

Wisely, he got right to business. "Looks to be the same pattern. Underage hooker. He snatches her up, hangs on to her for a month, does all those sick-bastard things to her in some hidey-hole, then dumps her here and kills her."

"Why kill her here?" Cee Cee mused aloud. "Why not just dump the body? That's safer, easier to transport."

Boucher shrugged. "Who the hell knows?"

"He knows. There's a reason."

"If he's sticking to pattern," Babineau said, "he'll already have his next plaything picked up."

"Out with the old, in with the new." Cee Cee cursed softly as she angled to get a look at the body. Even prepared, it gave her an ugly jolt. Violent death was never pretty.

Just a baby, probably fifteen, sixteen, blonde, petite, probably attractive . . . before the life she led got a hold of tender flesh and perverted it on that hard, hard road. Someone's daughter. Someone's sister. Someone's friend. Used, abused, and discarded as if she were nothing, as if less than human. The image of another girl was there before Cee Cee could push it away, blonde, laughing, full of the joy of living.

She shoved to her feet. "Any witnesses?"

Boucher shook his head. "The plant is shut down. No one around. No watchman. An alarm system to keep folks out of the building, but nothing to secure the perimeter."

"How long has she been here?"

"At least twenty-four. Dovion's on his way. He'll give us a TOD window."

She glanced around, sizing up the area. Industrial, bustling during the day, but a ghost town at night with production cut back because of the economy.

"Who called it in?"

"Sanitation. Spotted her from his truck. I've taken his statement. He didn't see anything but the body. That was more than enough," the young detective muttered with empathy.

Yeah, it was. The sight would haunt the man forever. It was always more than just the dead who were victimized.

Babineau observed the body up close, his handsome features expressionless. A trick of the trade, not to get involved. "Multiple stab wounds to the neck and chest. No signs of struggle, at least here. Ligature marks on wrists and ankles. Evidence of torture, sexual trauma, starvation." His façade broke for an instant. "Poor kid. Hell of a way to go." He started to reach for the lids of her open eyes, but caught himself. He stood and met Cee Cee's steady gaze. "You *know* he's already got the next one."

"So let's go find out who's missing."

Babineau gave her attire a slow assessment. "Darlin', you're not exactly dressed for Pussy Patrol." He shot a quelling glance at Boucher, who'd snickered. "I'll do a sweep of the streets while you wait on Dovion's initial. This is number three. Maybe if the working girls get scared enough, they'll be more forthcoming. We're due for a break."

Cee Cee wasn't that optimistic. The pros didn't give up info on their usual customers. It was bad for business.

But then, so was murder.

Three

MAX HEARD HER come in just before midnight.

When Babineau's car came through the security gates, it took him a minute to smooth down his bristling tension as Charlotte's words stabbed through his memory.

Alain Babineau and I were lovers.

That was before him, and her partner was married now. Charlotte was his. But Max didn't want to share her even with the past.

It was hard to pretend to be civilized when instinct demanded he tear out Babineau's throat.

The car paused briefly at the mansion's front steps. The front door opened and closed, and Max relaxed.

He waited a minute. Two. Then ten. She didn't come upstairs.

He padded downstairs to the silent first floor of the sprawling house, reaching out for her with his senses.

She sat in the dark parlor, on the sofa where she'd once lounged naked after they'd made love. She sat with her feet drawn up on the cushions, arms about her knees, swallowed up in his coat as she stared out into the night. He could taste her sadness and her tears.

Why hadn't she come to him for comfort?

He stood in the shadowed hall, just looking at her.

She took his breath every time. Strong, sexy, and exotic with her curvy lines, dark, daring eyes, and sleek tawny skin, she was his every desire. He'd ached for her for years, knowing he could never have her. Twelve long celibate years. She was worth every minute of the wait as they'd pursued each other for very different purposes. She'd wanted to put him inside a jail. He'd wanted to put himself inside her.

She seemed quite content with his winning that round.

She still wore the dress and those shoes that made his tongue want to roll out. She was the best-looking woman he'd ever seen, whether in skinny jeans and a snug-to-the-edge-of-indecent tank top or one of his silk shirts. She was lush and blatant in her sexuality, with a *Don't get too close, I bite* attitude that made the animal inside him roar to life.

Tonight she'd tamed her short, spiky dark hair into a sleek curve, and toned down the bold colors that usually lined her eyes and lips to make them soft and sensual. Her sophisticated sheath was every bit as elegant as any worn by the Crescent City's elite. Alternating swirls of filmy fabric iced with bands of midnight-blue satin skimmed her body, hinting at her perfection. The sheer hem fluttered about her knees, covering gorgeous legs she normally left bare. And then those shoes. He swallowed the growl that thickened in his throat.

Knowing that she'd gone to such lengths to provide him with the image of success and quality she thought he wanted to be seen with humbled him. He didn't care how she chose to wrap the package. She was the gift he treasured.

Charlotte turned suddenly and saw him there. The creamy glow of the pearls about her neck quieted his lusty emotions into something deeper, something almost frighteningly intense.

"Everything all right?" he asked softly.

She nodded as if the quick squaring of her shoulders could erase the shimmer of dampness on her cheeks. "Just wanted some time alone to think through a new case."

A not-so-subtle suggestion that he get lost. But she'd have to be a lot more direct to get rid him.

"Bad?"

"They're all bad," she shot back, as if he didn't understand exactly what she went through every time she leaned over the shell of a life not lived to the fullest. He could feel her anger and frustration welling up inside her like a scream pushing to get out.

"Tell me."

"This has nothing to do with you, Savoie." Prickly, provoking, insultingly so. "Not everything in the criminal universe revolves around your place in my life. I can't do my job with you whining for my attention every second. I probably should have just gone home."

Gone home? This was her home. *Their* home.

She was deliberately jabbing his buttons, goading him to argue so she could push him away. That's when he realized how scared she was that he'd see beyond her bluster to the pain she was trying to hide.

Silly female. She knew him better than that.

"Just forget I'm here, then."

With that cool drawl, he crossed to where she huddled behind her thorny hedge of wariness. Objection and resentment glittered in her glare as he sat on the couch.

She exhaled. "Whatever." With that terse statement, she turned to stare at the window—at his reflection. "Suit yourself."

"I usually do." Then a bit stiffer. "I never whine."

An aggravated sigh. "Yes, you do."

"When?"

He sounded so offended, she couldn't restrain a faint smile. "When you want sex."

"Well, I'm not whining now. And I've wanted to hump you like a horny dog since you drew my attention to those shoes several hours ago."

Her lips quivered, then firmed. "Stop it, Max."

"Stop what?"

"Making me laugh. You're so damned irritating."

She rubbed her fingertips along his jaw, the gesture tender if distracted. "You can't help me with this, Max. My worries, my job, my problem."

"I won't get in your way, Detective."

She regarded him suspiciously, not reassured by his bland face. "Just sit here with me."

"I can do that."

Cee Cee closed her eyes, trying to focus on the case without raising the tearing memories. Usually it was enough to remind herself this was why she did the job—because it *was* personal. But this girl's suffering duplicated her own too chillingly. When would she get beyond that ancient history?

Max's thumb soothingly rode the ridge of her toes, his heat warming her flesh. His other hand cupped her heel and lifted her foot into his lap, where he began to undo the strap about her ankle. Then he eased off her shoe and started to massage her foot with both hands. She eyed him cautiously, but he appeared totally absorbed. The stern set of her features softened as the moment became less about her. She nudged his hip with the toe of her other shoe.

"I didn't mean to snap at you."

"Too late to apologize. You've already wounded me beyond my ability to recover."

"It's not like *you're* never disagreeable."

"If I snapped at *you,* Detective, you'd be missing a limb."

She could hear the smirk in his tone, so she pushed him. "You promised there'd be toe sucking."

"So I did. I live to serve."

He pulled her other foot into his lap and removed her shoe in a delicate striptease while she kneaded his shirt with her bared toes. She could feel his heart pound beneath them.

When he lifted his head, his eyes glowed, golden.

He lifted her foot to his face, rubbing his cheek against its high arch. His eyes closed and her breath caught as he pressed a kiss to the sensitive curve, then shivered at the slow stroke of his tongue. His hands were rubbing her calf. With her knees bent, her dress pooled down the length of her long, toned legs, inviting his touch to follow.

He nipped at the ball of her foot, then at the fleshy pad of her big toe. Cee Cee was simmering by the time he drew that slender toe into his mouth.

Then he reared back abruptly. "You have blood on your feet, Detective."

"Oh, geez. I'm sorry. It must be from the crime scene. I should have showered when I came in."

He didn't release her, sniffing her instead. "Was your crime scene in the bayou?"

Cee Cee's thoughts sharpened. "No. Why?"

"I can smell it on you." He sampled the blood again, rolling it on his tongue. "Female. She was drugged."

Cee Cee stared at him. "You can tell all that? What else?"

"Only that. Not much here to go on."

"Get your shoes, baby. There's someplace we need to go."

After he left the room, she pulled out her cell. "Dev, have you started on that Jane Doe that just came in? Good. Don't touch a thing."

THEY COULD HEAR the drama of "Masquerade" from *Phantom of the Opera* wafting down the sterile corridors long before Cee Cee pushed open the doors to the medical examiner's domain. Devlin Dovion was a Broadway fanatic, a Jerry Garcia look-alike, and the best damn body man she'd ever met over a Y incision.

He blinked at her and whistled. "If I'd known it was a formal evening, I would have worn my tuxedo tee shirt. Hey, Max. She got you out on a field trip?" He waved them to the table. "*Mi casa es su casa.*"

Max liked the ME because even knowing who he was, Dovion accepted his place in Cee Cee's life. Now that Dev understood *what* he was, one of the few humans who did, Max was a bit more leery. Lately Dovion regarded him more as something under a slide to be studied; Max hadn't thought the loss of a potential friendship would disappoint him so.

When he saw the body on the table, Max realized why they'd made this midnight run to the bowels of the hospital. The dead girl eerily resembled Cee Cee's best friend, Mary Kate Malone, as she'd looked when Max had rescued the battered girl from a warehouse twelve years ago, along with her fierce companion, a teenage Charlotte Caissie.

Cee Cee approached the table with professional detachment. "Are we dealing with the same killer?"

"No question about it." Dovion gestured to the similarities. "Same type of restraints, the chemical burns on the skin, signs of repeated, prolonged torture, and depravation. Of course, that's not official until I roll up my sleeves. She's probably a working girl. If she's ever been processed, you should have an ID pretty quick." He gave her a shrewd look. "You here working some kind of angle?"

"I guess you could say that. Could I get a minute alone with her?"

His shaggy brows lifted.

Her tone grew impatient. "We won't contaminate anything."

"We?" He glanced at Max, who appeared equally surprised. "Nothing kinky."

Cee Cee's scowl sent him backing away with hands lifted.

"I can give you ten while I grab a cup of coffee."

"Thanks, Dev."

Once they were alone, Cee Cee nodded toward the corpse. "Well? What can you tell me about her?"

Max blinked. "She's dead, Detective. I don't understand what you expect me to do."

"Back at the house, you told me you didn't have enough to go on." She gestured to the body. "What can you tell me about where she's been, who she's been with?"

He recoiled. "Charlotte, I'm not a scientist."

"Science hasn't told us a damned thing. What do your instincts tell you?"

His resistance redoubled. "I thought you didn't need or want my help with your work."

She *had* just thrown that at him, but frustration made her push into touchy areas. Areas uncomfortably similar to an exploitation of their relationship. "A good cop uses all her resources."

He was quick to latch onto that. "Uses? Is that what I am now? A resource to be used?"

This wasn't where she wanted to go with him. Not with her time so limited. Tamping down her impatience, she reached out to take his hand. His gaze grew suspicious but he didn't pull away.

"You have special talents, Max. You can't expect me to pretend otherwise. I've gone to psychics and psychotics to solve my cases, so why not shape-shifters? You can use your abilities to help the next poor girl's family sleep at night. Will you do that? Please?"

Max studied her features for a long moment, seeing only sincerity and the passion to help others that made him love her madly. Still, comforting strangers wasn't enough reason to risk exposure of what he was. His abilities were carefully guarded, used only to serve and protect himself and those few he cared for.

But to help Charlotte sleep at night, he was willing to do just about anything.

He moved beside the table, then drew in a tentative breath. Cleaning solution, harsh and acrid, burnt his nose. He started to pull back, then saw Cee Cee's hopeful gaze.

Damn.

He bent close to snuffle along the body, sifting through the abundant smells, discarding those of Charlotte and her fellow officers, of garbage and warehouse and morgue. Searching deeper with his highly refined senses, he separated the strands of scent into delicate threads.

There. He drew in the unmistakable aroma of the swamps, thick, stagnant, and damp. Tension cramped in his belly because he knew this place, these smells, and his memories were dark and horrible.

"Max, what is it?"

The concern in Charlotte's voice gave him the strength to continue, to resist the uncomfortable associations. He closed his eyes and breathed in the subtle hints that clung to this poor soul.

"Rubber. Feathers. Salt water . . . not like the Gulf. An aquarium. Birds."

"What kind of birds? Parakeets, pigeons?"

He ignored the intrusion of her voice and investigated the pungent scent. "Barnyard. Chickens? Does that make any sense?"

He felt her move closer. "Like some kind of voodoo shit? What else? Anything else?"

He'd reached the bend of an elbow and his brow furrowed at the medicinal bite. "Drugs of some kind.

Can't tell if they were given to her or they were done by her choice. Strong and recent. Sex . . . not by choice. Sweat and fear." His tone tightened as those things rolled over him, through him.

"Any sense of him, of who did this to her?"

"No. Nothing . . . Wait. Sweet."

"What? What is it?"

"Cologne. Sweet." He was up by her neck, easing along the side of her face, her hair.

And then a trace, just a whisper, but to him, as identifying as a fingerprint. The killer had touched her hair with an unprotected hand.

Max opened his eyes to find himself staring down into the girl's filmy gaze, and he paused.

Was anything left of her final sights behind those dead eyes?

He'd only read someone once, but it was one of his own, not a human. Not a corpse. But with the power of Charlotte's belief driving him, he leaned closer to the girl until they were almost nose-to-nose, he focusing and gazing deep, letting himself fall until all sense of self faded away, and awareness exploded all around him.

"Max?"

Cee Cee caught his arm as he jumped away from the table, stumbling back wildly. His face was wax pale and slick with sweat, his pupils so dilated his eyes seemed a solid black.

Frightened, she asked, "Max, are you okay? Baby, are you all right?"

She had him by the elbows when his knees gave, easing him down to the floor where he sat gasping, disoriented, scaring the shit out of her. She palmed his cold cheeks, forcing his lolling head up so she could hold his glassy stare.

"Max, look at me. Look at me, baby. There. There you are. Geez, you scared the shit out of me. You okay now? You okay?"

"Charlotte?" His pupils shrank down. He blinked and fixed upon her worried features. "I'm all right. Just got a little light-headed."

His reassuring smile was too wobbly for her to be convinced. But before she could ask more questions he leaned into her, resting his forehead on her shoulder while she stroked his hair, shivering so hard his teeth chattered. She said nothing, just holding him until he relaxed.

What the hell happened?

"I knew it," Dovion announced as he came back into the room. "Hanky-panky the minute my back is turned."

"It must have been the music," Cee Cee retorted as she gave Max a quick squeeze and eased him back. His color was better, his expression normal. His gaze avoided hers.

She took the hand Dovion put down to her. It amazed her that such a huge paw could do such delicate work, and be so gentle. He'd been like a father to her when her own wasn't around, and was just as protective. And suspicious.

"So you gonna tell me what the two of you are up to?"

She relayed what Max had told her without attributing the source. "I'm looking for any trace that involves the bayou. Also rubber, feathers, salt water aquariums, or chickens."

He chuckled. "And you said it wasn't something kinky. Not that I, a happily married man, the father of three girls and new grandfather, would know anything about that."

Cee Cee snorted, then grew serious. "I'm looking for where he might take them. Somewhere in the swamps, where he can take his time." She was rolling now, her mind latching onto the killer instead of identifying with the victims. It made her a lethal battering ram against a solid door, eager to split wood with sheer force.

"Think he's already got another one?" the ME asked.

"Babineau's checking on it. Follow up on those things for me. Maybe we'll get lucky."

But it wasn't luck. It was because of Max Savoie, and whatever strange extrasensory methods he'd used.

He'd gotten to his feet and was back in control now, expressionless. Hiding whatever he'd just experienced from her—or from himself. Gratitude and a purely selfish desire growled through her, for her uniquely resourceful mate.

But it was more than Max. It was the hunt. Her adrenaline was pumping, a euphoric high that surged as a case unfolded. Her blood hummed with it, her senses were sharp as razors, a feeling Max would understand. He was a predator who knew the thrill of running a scent to its satisfying end. And if even one detail he'd told her helped her solve this case faster, *he* was going to get *so* lucky.

"I'll let you get back to work, Dev. I want your report—"

"An hour ago," he finished with a grin. "When I have it, you'll have it. Enjoy the rest of your night. Looks like it started out as something special."

Cee Cee smiled. That's exactly how she planned for it to end.

The staff lot was almost empty at two A.M. Her borrowed car sat in heavy shadow. Max walked silently beside her, edgy, probably waiting for her to spring all sorts of invasive questions on him. But that wasn't what she intended to jump him with.

He slid into the passenger side of the big vehicle, looking up in surprise when, instead of going to the driver's door, Cee Cee climbed in with him, stepping one knee over his thighs, her skirt hiking high as she settled on his lap. Gripping the seatback with her hands, she bracketed his head between her forearms.

"Thank you." Her voice was a husky breath of reward.

"Wouldn't you rather thank me in the comfort of our home?"

"No, I really wouldn't."

She swooped down for a kiss, warming his lips beneath the urgent slide of her own. Her tongue thrust aggressively into his mouth, lapping up his heat, savoring his unique taste. She felt him breathe in her scent so it bathed his senses, letting it flush away the stench of death and memory. She smiled at his helpless rumble of surrender.

His palms skimmed under her dress, thumbs hooking in the side strings of her panties, drawing them down. She leaned back to wiggle out of them, her fanny perched on the glove box for balance.

After pulling her underwear over her shoes, Max gave them a careless toss. The scrap of silk caught on the rearview mirror to dangle like a graduate's tassel.

Her hands were busy with the fastening of his pants, then got busier once she'd freed him. Max rose masterfully to the occasion, consumed by his desire for her, not caring that they were in a parking lot in full view of whoever might wander by.

Let 'em look. Let 'em envy.

Gripping the globes of her rump, he guided her down onto him with a growled, "Make yourself at home, *sha.*"

For a moment, there was nothing but heat and Charlotte. Her hoarse, shaky breaths excited his passions. Her reckless need fired his. Max closed his eyes as her lips brushed across them. He began moving her on top of him in a quick, hard rhythm as she kissed his cheeks, his chin, his throat, licking, nipping, whispering his name in a hurried mantra. Tension and anticipation coiled through him.

At the sound of her husky moan, his eyes opened and fixed upon the string of pearls rocking in front of his face—distracting him, mesmerizing him into seeing something else.

Pearls stained by blood, dropping in slow motion from their broken string into dank, dark waters.

Then everything he'd taken from that dead girl's psyche, everything he'd felt of her last minutes of life, came back with a hard, breath-stealing punch of horror. There were no sights, because her eyes had been covered. But her senses had been screamingly alive: the pangs of starvation wrenching through her belly, the bite of fear and panic, the stench of the swamp overwhelming him like that sweet, sweet scent.

No! Please, don't! Her desperate cries.

Don't leave me! Please don't leave me here alone! His own cry from a time he tried to keep to bad dreams.

He shuddered violently as Charlotte came, lost in a nightmare that ripped through his soul, a nightmare fed by fear and hunger and impossible sorrow.

By the horror of a child watching his mother slain before his eyes.

Four

MAX COULDN'T SLEEP.

Cee Cee lay beside him, breathing easy.

He'd dreamed of her for so long, the reality of her soft and naked next to him sometimes took him by surprise upon waking. He'd find himself fearing it was just some cruel trick, that she wasn't really there. So he'd carefully sniff at her hair, cautiously taste her warm skin, slowly curl himself around her as if expecting her to leap away in alarm. The sound of her contented sigh, the feel of her snuggling into him, were every prayer of a lonely life answered.

Now he lay awake in the early dawn studying the scars marring her shoulder. His bite, marks that claimed her for his own. He'd been out of his mind for her, out of control. She'd pushed him to it, goaded him into throwing off the human guise he wore to become the beast that lived inside, to prove to them both that she was strong enough to be his match, and he'd taken her with the primitive violence of his kind. He'd feared she'd regret it, surrendering herself to something so foreign, so different from what she was. But she said no, and he believed her. Except on nights like this when old worries haunted him, whispering through his soul with a chill.

He traced those vicious marks with his fingertips. What would it mean, this bonding of their two spirits, this blending of their two kinds? How would it change what they were, what they'd found with one another?

Max didn't understand their new bond. He didn't know how to use it, just as he was unfamiliar with many of the skills lying dormant inside him. He'd had no one to teach him, to show him, until Rollo—his greedy, opportunistic father—slipped briefly into his life with some precious information and a few dire warnings. That he was rare and valuable, one of a kind—and in danger because of it. His bonding to Charlotte made him even more of an oddity because, to his knowledge, no other human woman had ever survived it.

Now she shared special abilities with him: a physical ability to heal herself that had saved her life. A mental communication of feelings and thoughts that had saved his. She wanted to explore it more, but he'd pulled back behind the shielding his mother had taught him. Afraid of what she might discover, afraid of what she'd awaken, he prevented her from reaching out to him, from touching his mind and his experiences.

He was afraid it would make her a target.

She murmured in her sleep, rolling onto her side. Her luscious rump pushed against him, wiggling to get comfortable until he placed a hand on her hip to still the provocative movements.

Even in her sleep, she drove him wild.

How selfish to thrust her into danger just to soothe his aching heart, to calm his raging needs.

Would she now be hunted just as he was, the human mate of the Shifter king?

He eased out of bed to dress in the misty half light. He'd pulled on jeans and was taking a sweatshirt out of his drawer when unexpected movement at the edge of the dresser caught the corner of his eye. A rattle of sound made him hop back in alarm, stifling a startled yelp as he sought the potential danger.

On the floorboards, coiled where they had fallen, was the string of pearls he'd given Charlotte.

He started to reach down for them, but his toes curled under, his muscles pulled taut. A low, instinctive growl rippled out of him as he sensed threat where there seemed to be none. He snuffled the air just in case.

His breathing grew tight as panic strangled him. Hot dampness welled up from a dark place deep inside him, flooding his eyes, skewing his vision, changing the beads into the shadow of something else.

A small sound escaped him, breaking his trance.

Jumpy, anxious, he took a few quick steps back and gave the area a wide berth on his way to the door. Out in the hall he swallowed the acidic taste of fear and put on his sweatshirt, grateful for the fleecy warmth against his goose-bumped skin.

Then, he hurried downstairs and outside, running from what he didn't want to recall, from secrets his mind had buried but which wouldn't rest quietly.

His housekeeper Helen found him on the side porch, tense and inwardly trembling in one of the wicker chairs. Helen had served Jimmy, and now him, with an efficiency that bordered on telepathic.

"Beautiful morning. It's going to be a warm one," she said quietly, never sure if he'd respond.

"Do you remember where Jimmy and your Sam said they found me?" Max asked abruptly.

Helen's composed features betrayed none of her surprise. Max never spoke of the past. Until his policewoman, he'd barely spoken at all. She continued putting place mats and glasses out for two, pouring his juice before she answered.

"I believe it was over near Rayne."

"Tell me."

"What do you want to know?"

"Everything."

His tone was adamant, but something in his eyes made her hesitate. She began matter-of-factly, while inside her heart went soft with sympathy. "You were just a little thing, four, maybe five years old. You'd been out there for days, just you and your poor mama."

"Did you . . . did you see my mama?"

"Yes." How could she ever forget? They'd brought her out of the swamps in the trunk of Jimmy's big town car. He'd never been able to get the smell out of it— that hot, ripe, putrid stink of decay. The same stench that clung to the little boy even after they'd scrubbed his skin raw.

"Did you see what happened to her?"

"She'd been shot. I don't think she suffered, Max." Not like he did, both then and now.

His gaze flickered away. He swallowed hard. "I don't remember much. Jimmy wouldn't talk about it. But I have dreams sometimes."

Yes. His screams and eerie howling cries had kept the household up nights for almost a year after Jimmy brought him home. She hadn't known he still had them. "Just dreams," she told him with a comforting certainty.

"You think so?" His gaze lifted to hers, huge green eyes flooding up in unimaginable anguish. The eyes of that little lost boy.

"Yes, I do. Jimmy was right to keep the past in the past. He always knew what was best where you were concerned. They're just dreams. Don't let them pull you back." Back into madness.

She took a step toward him, and because he didn't automatically draw back the way he usually did, she slipped an arm about his shoulders and gathered him close. Her own eyes welled up as she stroked his dark head. He'd never let her hold or comfort him as a child, though she'd longed to. Back then, she'd wanted a child so desperately. But Jimmy was the only one young Max would let near him. Such a strange, somber boy with his unnatural quiet and haunting sorrow. Even now, even as he leaned into her, he was so still.

"Do I smell coffee?"

They moved away from each other as Cee Cee stepped out onto the porch. Helen immediately filled her cup and nodded good morning. The sight of the police detective making herself at home in Jimmy Legere's house no longer seemed a sort of blasphemy. Not when Max's expression brightened enough to vanquish the shadows the second he saw her.

"Breakfast, Detective?" she asked.

Cee Cee took the coffee cup in one hand and Max's chin in the other. "No, thanks. I've got everything I need for the moment." She bent to kiss him as if she could survive on the taste of him alone.

"Morning, baby," she murmured against his lips as Helen tactfully withdrew. Cee Cee laughed as he pulled her onto his lap without spilling a drop from her cup.

She was wearing one of his tee shirts and a pair of gym shorts. His palm roamed the long stretch of her legs as he tucked her bare feet up beside him in the chair. She buried her face in his dark hair as he nibbled on her kneecap. He was the only thing she'd go for before her kick start of caffeine. And she went for him in a big way.

"You should have stayed in bed a bit longer," she whispered. "I woke up with a need to ride you hard."

"Yeah?" He looked up at her, brows lifted. "And where did you want that ride to take you?"

"To work," she grumbled, "since I no longer have a car."

He made an unsympathetic sound. "It's not like you have to hitchhike."

"Yeah, but I have to listen to the guys' bullshit after your driver opens the limo door for me like I was royalty."

Max cupped the back of her head to tip her face up to his. His eyes glowed with hot intensity. "You are royalty. You are my queen."

She gave an unregal snort. "And where, pray tell, is my kingdom?"

He placed her palm flat upon his chest. "You rule my heart."

"So you've decided to subjugate yourself to my royal whims without argument. I like this job."

"I don't believe that's quite what I said."

She chuckled and leaned back against his shoulder, smiling as she sipped her coffee. "It's good to be queen."

They relaxed with one another for a long, contented moment, then she felt him tense as Alain Babineau joined them on the porch.

"Morning."

"Help yourself to some coffee, Alain. What brings you all the way out here?" Cee Cee asked without changing her indolent pose.

"Thought I'd give you a lift in."

A growl vibrated silently through Max. She patted his rough cheek. *Down, boy.* "Thanks."

Her partner dropped the morning paper on the table as he settled into a chair. "You made the news."

She reached for it. "I hope they got my good side."

"A rather flattering shot of me, don't you think?" Max commented as he saw the prominent photo in an article on last night's event. It showed them dancing, with her hand very obviously copping a feel of his butt.

Babineau cleared his throat as if to get out an unpleasant taste. "Tina wants you two over for lunch tomorrow." He added grimly, "She said no excuses. She wants to say thanks, and the boy's been asking to see Max."

"What time?" Max asked.

Babineau met his gaze with thinly veiled distaste. "Noon. It's going to be outside, real informal." No need to get up close and friendly.

"Am I supposed to bring something?" Cee Cee asked in horror. "Like some kind of Jell-O salad thing?"

Babineau laughed. "No, don't make us suffer that. Tina's got it all under control."

Tina, the perfect woman, wife, and mother. "At least we can talk about the case," Cee Cee said.

"Ah, no. She made me promise no shop talk."

"What the hell are we going to talk about, then?" Her dismay echoed his.

"Polite things that civilized people discuss," Max asserted. "I'm sure we can think of something."

She eyed Max doubtfully, picturing a long, horrid silence in which they gobbled up the food and snuck out as fast as possible.

She turned the topic to something more agreeable. "What did you find out on the street?"

Babineau's gaze touched on Max. "We can talk about it on the way in."

"I want to know now. Come on up with me. You can fill me in while I change."

She was off his lap and the two of them had gone inside before objection hit Max between the eyes like the slug of a SIG Sauer. She was taking Babineau upstairs to his bedroom—*their* bedroom. And she was going to get dressed just as comfortably as you please in front of a man who wasn't sharing that bed with her.

Alain Babineau and I were lovers.

Images of them together filled his mind, and for a moment he was plunged back into the hot madness that plagued him the weeks before he and Charlotte had bonded. That same dark, furious need to claim and guard her as his own snarled through him with teeth-bared possessiveness, startling him with its intensity and his inability to just shake it off.

He'd been taught only one way to deal with a threat that came into his yard. And for a moment, he considered killing Alain Babineau as if it were a rational solution.

"SO, WHAT'S THE story?"

Babineau hesitated just inside the room, trying not to look at the big unmade bed. Savoie's bed, where he'd been sleeping skin to skin with Charlotte.

"Like I figured," he began, awkward at first, then falling into the familiar pattern, "no one is eager to give anything up to the cops. I tapped a couple of my usuals, asked them to sniff around. We'll see where it goes."

Cee Cee snagged a pair of black jeans out of a dresser and carried them into the bathroom, leaving the door open so they could continue their conversation.

Babineau watched her reflection as she stepped out of the shorts and wiggled into the stretch denim. She had the most amazing legs he'd ever seen. That hadn't changed.

"Dovion should have a report for us this morning," she continued, rummaging through her makeup bag. "We need to stop there first. Hopefully they've ID'd the vic by now and we'll have some photos to circulate."

"There's something we need to talk about first."

"Yeah? What's that?" When he hesitated, she called out, "Don't be shy. Spill it."

"Ceece, the guys were wondering . . ."

"What?"

"What to do about Savoie."

Her head poked out of the bathroom, her eyes narrowed dangerously. "What do you mean, 'do' about him?"

"It's been bothering us. All of us. We didn't want to say anything until you were back to one hundred percent." His hand raked through his sandy blond hair, his bewildered relief over her amazingly quick recovery evident. Then his expression tightened. "It's not like we can forget what we saw him do. What we saw him . . . turn into."

"Your point?" she snapped out, anger covering her sudden leap of alarm.

"Ceece, I don't know what to tell them. I don't know what the hell he is. What do you want me to say?"

Charlotte felt blindsided, though she should have seen it coming. She'd been aware of Max's world long enough to accept it without the doubt and confusion she saw in her partner's eyes.

He had seen what Max was. How he reacted to that information had to be carefully controlled before any damage was done.

Her response was forceful and fierce. "You tell them that Max Savoie saved your son when no one else could have. You tell them that I owe him my life several times over. You tell them that if they have a problem with him, they'd better bring it to me first. And they'd better keep their mouths shut about what they think they saw."

"Think?" His tone said there was no mistake about what took place before their shocked eyes. "Or what— they'll end up in an alley minus throats and hearts?"

"No!" She had to get them to see Max as an ally, not as a monster. There was nothing natural about Max, but that didn't necessarily make him a threat.

"No, Alain," she continued with an exasperated laugh, as if the very thought of violence was ridiculous. "He would never harm them. But I'm not going to let them"—*or you*—"harm him, either."

Cee Cee watched her calm, rational partner trying to make sense of the unbelievable.

"Did he kill Cummings's daughter?" Babineau asked.

"No. It was another of his kind."

"Another?" He latched onto what she hadn't meant to give away, then anxiousness jumped in his eyes. "There are *more* of them here? How many more?"

She grew guarded and vague. "Max protects them, I protect him. That's all you need to know."

"There are these . . . these creatures prowling our streets, and you don't think I need to know? What *are* they? How are we supposed to act around him, now that we know?" His chiseled jaw worked for a long moment before he got right to it. "How can you—be with him, now that you know?"

She went stiff with outrage as she saw his disgust. "Excuse me?"

"He's not human, Cee Cee. He's a fucking animal that kills and eats those who get in his way. He's—I feel like I'm going nuts, just saying it—a loup-garou, or some damned thing like that. How can you be okay with that?"

"Answer him, Charlotte. How can you stand to have something like me touch you?"

Babineau had a healthy respect for Max Savoie the mobster, but the figure circling behind him with smooth, lupine grace scared the spit dry in his mouth.

He, two other detectives, and his son had watched Savoie physically shape-shift, had seen him rip the beating heart from another's chest and devour it. Had stood in stunned horror as he'd latched onto an exposed neck with huge sharp teeth to slash through tendon and cords in a fountain of blood.

And he'd said nothing, because he'd also seen Savoie take two bullets to the chest to rescue his stepson, Oscar. He and Joey Boucher and Junior Hammond had gone back into the swamp later that day to tidy up the mess left behind, but none of them had felt good about it. None of them rested easy.

They'd all shivered at night to think that something like Savoie was out there.

And there were *more*.

Alain's nape crawled just being in the same room as him.

Max didn't bother to disguise his preternatural power, that quicksilver speed and sleekness of his species, letting Babineau see him as those of his kind did: a cruel force of nature, destructive, deadly, unstoppable. He growled low in his chest as he stalked up behind Cee Cee to slip his arm about her middle. As he rubbed his cheek against hers, his eyes glittered with hot gold and ruby flashes. As his tongue drew a long damp line up her neck, her hand lifted to cradle the side of his face. He smiled at Babineau with teeth as sharp as the point he was making.

"I'd be very, very careful if I were you, Detective Babineau. You have no idea what you're dealing with. I control more than Jimmy Legere's interests in this city. If any hint of what you saw leaks out, I'd hate to think what that would unleash upon you and your friends."

He stepped away from Cee Cee to select a crisp white shirt from his closet. Louis Vuitton, for the up-yours attitude spoiling through him. He stripped off his sweatshirt, letting Babineau see the hard strength of his body and the scars on it. Deep tears in his upper arm. The pucker of bullet wounds; two to the chest with one exiting the back, and one to the stomach. Fatal shots no *man* could have survived.

"Leave my house, Detective. You can wait for Charlotte in your car."

As Babineau began to turn, Max continued, "We'll be there tomorrow at noon. I wouldn't want to disappoint your wife or your son—my brother."

Babineau's expression hardened at that reminder. He spun and was gone.

Then there was just Cee Cee and her fierce glare.

"Are you quite finished with all the big dog posturing, or do you plan to piss on me to stake your claim a little more dramatically?"

He proceeded up his shirt buttons. "What do you want from me, Charlotte? He comes into my house, insults me, threatens those I care for, and I'm supposed to do nothing?" He grabbed a jacket with enough violence to send the coat hanger flying. "You know what I am, and now so do *they*. How am I supposed to be comfortable with that? They could crush everything I value with one careless word."

"I'll talk to them."

He was far from comforted. "Sure. Smooth it over like it was nothing more than a social blunder. *Talk*."

He flung the jacket onto the bed and peeled down his jeans.

For a moment she said nothing. Even knowing what he was, she continued to think of him as a man. He looked human. He sounded arrogantly, maddeningly, like an everyday, testosterone-fueled male of her species. If she got closer to him she'd smell man next to the pulse at his throat, she'd taste man all hot and salty when she took him in her mouth, she'd feel man as her palms moved over him in restless appreciation. When she parted her lips beneath his, she wouldn't be thinking of creature feature monsters.

But that didn't change the fact that he wasn't a human male. Something else flickered behind his unblinking stare. Something different, something other. Something more.

And it was this difference that drew her, not the sameness he tried to project.

She loved him and trusted him with all that she was precisely because he *wasn't* a man. Men had failed her, harmed her, betrayed her. They didn't possess the singular, all-consuming sense of loyalty intrinsic in Max Savoie. When they said *forever* they meant until next month, next week, next commercial, next orgasm.

When Max said it, he meant for eternity.

He'd been raised to mimic humans, but what prowled through him was wild and unpredictable. Max didn't look at things the same way she did. He didn't react to the same circumstances with socially acceptable actions. And it would be foolish and dangerous to assume she knew what he was thinking at any given moment.

So she asked him.

"How would *you* handle it, Max? Would you kill them to keep them silent?"

"Yes."

She took a step back before he gripped her elbows to hold her in place.

"That's what everything I am tells me to do. To eliminate the threat quickly, completely, without thought or conscience. To come at them from the shadows and end their lives, before they take mine and threaten the safety of all I've sworn to protect. It's what I am, Charlotte."

"But it's not *all* you are, Max." Her need to believe that glimmered in her eyes.

"Only because of you, *sha*. Otherwise they'd be dead right now, and I'd be safe." His thumbs brushed across her cheeks. "I stop myself from doing what I should because I love you and it would hurt you. It would make you look at me differently, and I won't take that risk. Not ever."

She made a soft sound.

"But you have to understand, Charlotte. This involves all my kind, Oscar, and even you—because you know and have said nothing. It's a secret truth that will damage all of us should it become known. Are you willing to take that risk with these men?"

Her eyes cleared. Her chin lifted. "Yes."

He said nothing for a long beat, then told her, "Finish up. I'll walk you down."

He went out onto the porch with her, wearing the sleek guise of a powerful businessman. His glance touched on Babineau in his car before he turned to Cee

Cee. His hands brushed over the sleeves of her long raincoat, the gesture intimate and sheltering. His lips touched her brow and he asked with quiet intensity, "If the risk becomes unacceptable you will tell me, won't you, *cher*?"

"Yes." Soft, firm. Enough for the moment.

"Be careful on the streets."

"Be careful in your meetings."

They shared smiles.

He wanted to grab her up for a passionate display, almost more than he wanted to tip that car with the pretty boy detective inside over onto its roof.

"Max?"

As his brows raised in question, she whipped her arms around his neck and planted her mouth on his hard. Then she whispered against his lips, "I plan to take that rough ride tonight. Be ready."

He smiled. "Thanks for the warning. I'll pace myself today at work."

He watched her jog down the steps to the car, while the cold beast inside weighed the risks he'd spoken of.

And found them unacceptable.

Five

THEY RODE INTO the city in silence. Alain stewed in his pride and outrage, while Cee Cee sank into somber reflection.

He'd been partnered with Cee Cee for years. They'd had each other's backs, covered each other's asses, and held each other's head over a toilet more than once. They'd agreed to disagree, and had gone toe-to-toe, on many an issue.

But never, ever, had they had doubts about the other's ability to do the job—to be there, to hold the line, to take a bullet if necessary.

The minute she'd stood over a mangled corpse and covered up for Max Savoie, all that had changed. And now she was asking *them* to sweep up after him as well.

The job and her coworkers were no longer her first priority. And Alain resented the hell out of it.

It was Savoie, the spooky hit man—Jimmy Legere's ferocious pit bull, who'd broken his chain to stand over the city's throat with sharp bared teeth. Mobster, monster, he was exactly what Babineau protected decent folks from.

It had nothing to do with the snarky way Savoie had once turned to him to ask, "Can I call you Daddy?"

"Hey!" Cee Cee's shout cut into his moody thoughts. "That's our turn. Dovion's first."

Babineau hauled on the wheel, sending his economy import into a skidding turn.

Gripping the dash and the—*oh, shit*—handle above her door, Cee Cee scolded, "I don't care what's got your panties wedged up your ass, pull 'em out and pay attention."

Something inside him snapped. "Oh, so you're the only one who can corner on sidewalls, hanging on to gravity by the fingernails, Ms. Big Balls. If you think you're going to neuter me so I'll roll over and beg like your boyfriend, what you've got up *your* ass ain't your silky drawers."

She grabbed the wheel and yanked hard, forcing him to stand on the brakes or go up over the curb.

Babineau slammed out of the car to stalk across the street.

Putting up her hand as a stop sign, Cee Cee ran after him, tugging him to a halt on a triangular traffic island.

"What the hell has gotten into you, Babs?" she shouted, furious and alarmed. Her heart was beating like crazy as she wondered what possessed him to pull such a stunt, yet she was afraid to find out.

Her partner turned on her with bulletlike fury. "Don't you mean what the hell have *you* let get into *you*? Why don't you stop pretending to be a cop, and go whelp his puppies under a porch someplace."

Her adrenaline-fueled punch connected squarely and had him seeing stars.

Shocked and furious, she snapped, "Whatever little

macho hissy fit you have with Savoie, get the fuck over it. You don't have any say over who I invite into my personal life."

"I do when it slops over onto the job," he retorted, wiping the blood under his nose. "He's got you concealing evidence, making false statements, and looking the other way while he goes all 'Monster Mash.' He's a criminal, a killer, and . . . and I don't even *know* what the hell else. But whatever it is, I sure as hell don't want it at my table with my family."

She gaped at him, her pulse pounding in her ears, battering her judgment. "Is that what this is about? Your white-freaking-bread suburban family? So it's okay to let Max throw himself off a causeway full of bullet holes to save them for you, but he's not good enough to sit at your crappy little table? And you preach fire and brimstone about me in his bed, but it's okay when you're taking the same thing into *yours*?"

Alain Babineau's face went slack—and in that explosive second, Charlotte realized what irreparable harm she'd just done.

He knew his stepson was the product of a rape Tina never spoke of, and he'd assumed her attacker was a Shifter. It had obviously never occurred to him that what made Oscar so different came from *both* sides of the family, and it hit him like a flaming meteorite.

"Oh, hell," she muttered miserably as she fished in her coat for a wad of tissues. He took them in a shaky hand to swipe the blood from his face, his eyes glassy. She took a tight breath. "Maybe it's time I got a new partner."

He crumpled the stained tissues in his fist and said coldly, "No one else will work with you."

He walked back to the abandoned car and waited stiffly behind the wheel for her to join him.

And an hour and a half later he sat still and uncommunicative at the morning briefing, his nose obviously swollen, while Cee Cee relayed what they'd learned from Devlin Dovion.

"Marjorie Cole, sixteen. Reported missing by her mother in Corydon, Iowa, eighteen months ago. Whatever she thought she'd find down here in the Big Easy, I doubt that she found it dancing at a strip club. Was picked up in a drug sweep three months ago, and got her prints on file.

"We need to know everything that took that kid from singing in her Pentecostal church choir to turning tricks. We need to know who she saw, personally and professionally, from the time she worked her last shift until she had a garbageman puking up his po' boy."

"I'll take the strip club," Junior Hammond offered with a leering grin. He was a squat bully of a man who could have changed uniforms from NOPD to neo-Nazi without any major alterations in character. But he'd fit right in where he asked to go.

"Take Boucher with you."

"Awww, that's no fun." He gave the young officer a poke in the ribs that was a little too sharp to be playful. "One look at his fresh face and they'll clam up tight."

"One look at his fresh face and they won't be thinking cop, they'll be thinking quick cash," Cee Cee countered, earning Joey's grateful nod. "The press is now calling our boy the 'Tides That Bind' killer, since he keeps them for a cycle of the moon before discarding them. If that has some significance out in Woo Woo World, we need to know about it. He had this one for a full cycle, just like the two before her. We don't have IDs on them so let's focus on Miss Cole. Babineau has the stats. He'll answer your questions while I talk to the next of kin. Let's get this guy."

Cee Cee waited to catch Hammond and Boucher at the door, motioning them to join her off to the side.

"Thanks for the confidence," Boucher began, fairly quaking with excitement and pride.

"I want you guys to meet me at Newton's tonight at nine-thirty," Cee Cee ordered.

Hammond groaned. "Shit, Caissie, the pole dancing action will just be going full throttle."

"I'm sure you'll get more than an eyeful between now and then." She patted Junior's beefy arm. "Make sure Joey has plenty of dollar bills. Bring back info, not something communicable."

Hammond wrapped an arm about the younger man's shoulders. "C'mon, kid. Let's go pop your cherry. Got any ones on you? Where do you bank?"

AFTER AN HOUR pummeling the speed bag brought no relief from his restlessness, Max took to the pavement. He'd spent a deskbound morning unable to concentrate through the anxious fog clouding his mind. Time to suck in some fresh air and burn off his aggression and fear with a good run.

He took the level path between the streetcar rails that cut through the Garden District, his pace brisk.

The sun was warm on his head and, aside from walking tour clusters and hurrying students, he had the just-past-lunch hour to himself. He matched the tempo of his running shoes to his heartbeats and refused to think of anything else. Not easy when he was sure disaster was racing up behind him in the form of a posse led by Alain Babineau.

Breathe. Don't think.

Gradually he became aware of a matching set of footfalls on the other track. Solid, even, untiring, like his own. He didn't glance over, letting his senses reach out instead. Nothing unusual. Just another jogger out enjoying the day.

He increased his stride.

And so did the other runner.

It was just the challenge he needed to clear his head.

He took the turn into Audubon Park and, once hidden within the leafy lanes, Max let the beast he'd kept bottled up go. His movements blurred, making him almost invisible to the human eye as he raced beneath the shaded nave of oaks. He heard the shadowing steps right behind him, never faltering.

His breathing quickened from excitement. Another of his kind—had to be. Yet, he picked up no trace, no scent, no sign from this mysterious other who now pursued him. No Shifter that he knew had the ability to mask their presence, to conceal the glimmer of their psyche.

After cornering to the left around a sharp turn, Max came to an abrupt stop and whirled to face his challenger. The other dodged by without breaking stride and sped on. There was no way to identify the figure wearing large dark glasses and a baggy black sweatsuit with concealing hood. But now Max knew what, if not who, he was dealing with.

His pulse shuddered in alarm and anticipation.

Someone like him—a pureblood, or close to it. A Tracker sent down from the north for a purpose as hidden as his face.

The second Max started after the other Shifter, the agile figure darted off the path. Grinning ferociously at the thought of some rugged competition, Max plunged through the thicket of dazzling fuchsia azaleas, sending petals fluttering in a bright pink rain as he gave chase.

Up steep hills and through thorny hedges that tore his flesh, over impossibly high rock walls and into pretty streams, he pushed himself until his lungs burned and his muscles cramped. Still he couldn't close the distance between them. He'd never had anyone best him, ever, at anything!

They came to a deep culvert that split the path into a T. Max gathered his strength, certain the shadowy figure would have to slow to make the sharp turn. Instead, without breaking stride, one sneakered foot went up onto the rail edging the gully and pushed off with a fluid motion, clearing the distance of close to twenty feet with a jaw-dropping hang time.

Max would never have attempted such a jump, wouldn't have thought it possible. But fueled by the competitive chase, he went up and over, concentrating on the other side. Time suspended itself as he stretched in defiance of gravity, to touch down lightly on the opposite rail. He grinned. *Learn something new every day.*

His pulse quickened with excitement. This was someone who could teach him about his unknown abilities. Someone who had knowledge and skill, whether friend or foe.

The chase took on new meaning.

They approached two buildings set a sidewalk's width apart, with a brick wall creating a dead end. Again, Max's certainty that he had the other Shifter trapped was met with a stunning contradiction in physics. Unable to go through, the other went up, bouncing from wall to wall off powerful legs to the roof three floors above.

Amazed, Max hesitated, losing the momentum needed to replicate the climb, forcing him to go around the building. He spotted the lithe figure coming down the fire escape—not taking the zigzagging steps, but swinging straight down from level to level like a child's Slinky springing down a stairway.

Racing forward, Max was stunned when his target avoided interception by running onto a good-sized pond. *Onto.* Max stared, dumfounded, as his adversary ran across the surface, barely making a ripple.

How was it done? He had to know!

By the time he rounded the pond he'd lost sight of his opponent, who'd gone over a grassy knoll into a landscape of flowering bushes. Giving chase, Max burst through a tangle of rhododendrons to find himself on a collision course with two women and their baby strollers. He hurdled the first to the astonishment of the twin tots inside, then had to cut sharply to the right to avoid the second. By the time he recovered his balance, the mysterious Shifter was gone, leaving him to placate two outraged mamas.

And leaving him to wonder if the encounter had

been a coy getting-to-know-you ritual or a test of dominant strength that he'd just failed.

Alain Babineau was no longer the greatest threat to those he loved.

THERE WAS NOTHING worse than watching a mother's face as the sheet was pulled down from her child for identification.

Cee Cee threw down her Jack and water and signaled for another, wondering how many it would take to erase the bitter taste from her mouth, and pain from her soul.

It was more than a wailing Iowa housewife weighing on her thoughts.

Anger at Babineau was easier to handle than the guilt underneath it. She'd had no right to out Tina as one of Max's kind. What she'd done was inexcusable. Babineau had blindsided her with the puppies crack, startling her into a vicious defense that shamed her as much as it wounded him.

Definitely not one of her finest moments.

As she started on her second glass, Hammond and Boucher entered the bar.

Newton's, founded by former desk sergeant Isaiah Newton when an auto accident led to his early retirement, was always filled with off-duty cops and companions in the medical and emergency fields. Dark wood, dartboards, and honky-tonk and heavy metal in the jukebox created a haven to unwind in, to ease back into normal life.

The two men headed to her table at the wave of her hand. Boucher was all bright-eyed; Hammond sported lipstick stains and had a feather boa looped about his neck.

"Have fun on your boys' night out?"

Hammond grinned. "A good time was had by all." The smug look on his face was faintly disgusting.

Cee Cee turned to the blushing Boucher as he took a seat. "Whatchu know, Joey?"

"Miss Cole worked there for about five months, waitressing at first, then moving to the stage." Only the tenderhearted rookie would sound so respectful when recounting the life of a stripper and whore as if she were still that choir soloist. "The girls liked her. The clients liked her. The management wanted to keep her on, but she developed a pharmaceutical problem and they had to turn her out."

"Turned her out doing tricks," Hammond added.

"She was on the street for about a month and a half."

"Who's stable was she out of?" No one worked independently in that neighborhood. Too dangerous with all the predators, from customers to rival street-walkers and their pimps.

"Manny Blu's. That's the unofficial word."

Cee Cee leaned back in her chair. "Good old Manny," she mused.

Her father in Homicide and the fellows in Vice had been after Blu for decades. But like Jimmy Legere, Carmen Blutafino had a nonstick coating. Jimmy had relied on shrewdness, Max, and damn good attorneys. Blutafino hid behind missing witnesses, payoffs, and brute force. The same slime with rougher packaging. She'd love to somehow tie him into her case.

She ordered a beer for Boucher and a scotch for Hammond, then listened as they laid out what they'd learned, processing it thoroughly as her gaze lingered on Junior's feathered boa.

"This may sound strange, but does the club have an aquarium?"

They blinked at her.

"Never mind." She tossed back the last of her drink. "This is off the clock, guys," she began, and took a deep breath. "We need to talk about Max Savoie."

Boucher looked uncomfortable. Hammond stared at her boldly. "What about him? Other than the fact that he hides his illegal activities behind a designer suit these days, is some kind of fuckin' werewolf, and gets away with both because he's playing Hide the Sausage with you."

"Keep your voice down, asshole," Cee Cee gritted out as she checked the surrounding tables to see if his words had carried above the hammering music and raucous conversations. No one seemed to be paying him any attention.

Hammond's hard eyes gleamed. "Calling me an asshole ain't exactly the best way to get me to cover up for your boyfriend. You might try being a little nicer."

She leaned across the table. "Listen to me, and listen good. I don't do favors for anyone. I'm only bringing this up because I don't particularly want to find your empty head four feet away from the rest of your body and have to explain it to the brass."

"If you're trying to threaten me—"

"No. I'm telling you to wise up. You have no idea

what you saw, and how many innocent lives could be affected by you opening your big mouth. I'm not trying to protect myself or Savoie. I'm suggesting you consider Joey and Babs, along with your own fat ass."

Boucher went pale at her meaning, but Hammond got even more belligerent. "He's not going to take down cops. He's not that stupid."

"He isn't stupid at all. But you are, if you think grabbing a few headlines is worth the lives you'll put in danger."

He rocked back in his chair. "I always wanted to do an 'On the Scene with Karen Crawford' interview. I bet she'd be willing to pay plenty to get goods like this. And maybe even put out."

"Listen here, you—"

His hands slapped down on the table, bringing attention their way. "*You* listen, you hard-assed bitch. You've been breaking my balls since day one and I'm sick of it. I don't care if you and the chief are all cozy— if I spill what I know, your career is gone. *Gone*. And so is that creature feature character you're shacking up with. So you think about that, and get ready to listen to what I have to say when I get back from taking a leak."

He shoved up from the table, and elbowed his way to the back of the bar while Cee Cee sat rigid and ice cold in her chair. Not going well. Unless he changed his tune drastically on his return, she was going to have to seriously consider him an unacceptable risk. But could she live with that outcome?

Could she afford to do nothing?

"He really is an asshole," Joey Boucher summed

up mildly after a number of awkward minutes passed. "Maybe I'd better go after him."

"Maybe you'd better," Cee Cee agreed quietly.

Hammond held the future of those she'd promised to protect in his meaty hands, and he knew it.

JUNIOR HAMMOND PUSHED open Newton's rear door and stepped out into the alley. The men's room was too crowded and his bladder couldn't wait.

The weak glow of the mercury light over the back door reached only a short distance through the gathering evening fog. The uneven bricks underfoot glistened with puddles, and he cursed as he caught his toe on one and fell against a ripely scented Dumpster.

Then he heard something.

Squinting blearily toward the heavy shadows, he saw no movement—but something was creeping around just out of sight. Something bigger than the usual rat or stray dog . . . probably just a couple of bums. If they gave him any shit, he'd run 'em in. Right now he *had* to pee.

Practically dancing with urgency, he ducked behind the Dumpster to relieve himself. He was fumbling to undo his belt when he heard low growls that vibrated with menace.

Dozens of them.

He whirled around to see faint shapes slinking through the mist, their movements unnaturally fluid and quick. Eyes glowed, way too high to belong to a dog. Drawing nearer, huddled packlike, sinister in their caution, predatory in their patience.

He turned to find the other end of the alley blocked

by more of the unearthly beasts. His breathing caught, than panted out raggedly. He knew what they were, and what they'd come to do.

Kill him.

His bladder let go as he grabbed for his gun, his sweaty hand almost dropping it in his hurry. The pistol was snatched away. One of them was at his back, close enough for him to feel its hot breath on the back of his neck.

He lurched forward, stumbling into the center of the alley, trying to tear through the effects of liquor and fear to think of how to save himself. Terrifying figures cast shadows that were half man, half . . . something else.

Unarmed, he squared up to face whatever was coming. Bad enough to go out with a stained crotch; he wasn't about to bite it on his knees.

"Come on," he shouted at the beasts that encircled him but came no closer. "What are you waiting for?"

It wasn't what. It was who.

The ring of feral creatures parted, not to give him an escape, but to provide a purposefully dramatic entry.

The swirl of his long black raincoat swept away the ribbons of fog. He approached with an unhurried stride, the rhythmic swagger filled with arrogance and lethal control. Hammond knew who it was even before he could see the hard angles of his face, even before the dim light glinted ruby red off his unblinking eyes.

Savoie.

Not sure if he should laugh in relief or start begging, Hammond waited, trembling as the animals closed ranks behind their leader. Savoie came to a stop and regarded the quaking detective with barely disguised contempt. When he didn't come closer, Hammond grew more bold in self-defense.

"You can't get away with killing a cop."

Silence, then a low drawl. "I can get away with pretty much anything I choose. But I'm not going to kill you, Detective. I promised Charlotte I'd give her a chance to talk sense into you. She believes you can be reasoned with—but you and I know that's not going to happen. Let me lay this out simply so that you'll understand your options. You can agree to keep what you saw to yourself, and you can go home and clean yourself up. Or you can spit in my face, and I walk away."

"Then what happens?"

A flash of sharp teeth. "There won't be enough left of you to flavor a bowl of gumbo."

Soft, hungry snarls sounded from all around him. The movements grew restless, pacing, aggressive. Only Savoie was still. Savoie, who scared him more than any of the others because they moved at his command.

"I think I'd like to go home and clean up."

Savoie continued to look at him with that flat, penetrating stare. "Should you have a change of heart— say, when you've showered away the stink of your fear and get your manly courage back—you might think about speaking to a certain reporter just out of spite. Think carefully. Because there will always be someone not of your kind close enough to hear whatever comes out of your mouth. Always. And they won't have to check with me before they make sure those words are your last. Understood?"

A jerky nod.

"Oh, and I would prefer you not mention this little discussion to Charlotte. Let her think it was your idea to be sensible. And don't call her a hard-assed bitch again. It makes me disagreeable."

He moved in so quickly that they were nose-to-nose before the detective could blink. Savoie's eyes blazed hot with their unnatural light, and his tone ripped as sharply as his teeth could.

"You mess with Charlotte, you're history. You mess with me, you're lunch. Now go away." When Hammond was slow to react, Max roared, "Go!"

He ran, slipping on the wet bricks as he pushed through the thick press of Savoie's preternatural pack. He held back screams as he felt their teeth snapping at his neck, their claws ripping at his clothes. Once free of them he sprinted to his car, jumping in and racing away as if the hounds of hell were after him.

Because he feared if he even glanced over his shoulder, they would be.

"IF YOU'RE LOOKING for Detective Hammond, he's gone."

Joey Boucher jumped at the quiet words spoken from the dark alley. "Gone, as in dead?" he ventured, swallowing hard at the sight of Max Savoie separating from the mists.

"Gone, as in ran for his life. He forgot this."

Boucher took the service pistol, feeling comforted by its solid weight in his palm, even though its bullets couldn't harm the figure before him. He tucked it in his coat. "He's an asshole. I would have enjoyed watching him scramble."

Max chuckled softly. "You're a good policeman, Boucher. Are you a smart one?"

"Yes, sir. I like to think so. You put it on the line to rescue Babineau's little boy. I won't forget that. Detective Caissie has always been fair to me, and gave me a hand up when she didn't have to. I won't forget that, either."

Max smiled. "Watch her back for me, Joey. Can I trust you to do that?"

"Yes, sir. What shall I tell her about Hammond?"

A wide show of teeth. "Tell her he had an unexpected accident and had to run home to change his trousers."

Boucher laughed out loud and glanced toward the end of the alley. Hammond's car was gone. "Damn, I would like to have seen that."

When he turned back, Savoie was gone.

Six

MAX WAS SITTING on the front porch glider when Charlotte came wearily up the steps. She made a bee-line for him, straddled him with her knees, and buried her face against his shoulder. Her arms curled about his neck, almost desperately tight. "I've had a monumentally crappy day."

"I'm sorry. Want to tell me about it?"

"I will. Not just yet."

He nuzzled her hair, his lips swiping her brow. "Then tell me what I can do for you to improve the hours left in it."

She didn't have to consider. "I need you naked under me."

"Right here on the porch?"

His amused but willing tone made her smile. "As quickly as you can get us behind a closed door would be fine."

"I can do that for you."

He rose, carrying her easily with her arms and legs wrapped around him into the darkened house and up the wide stairs. She slid down when he shut the door to his bedroom behind them, but she didn't step away. He simply held her, waiting for her to set the pace and the mood.

She started down the buttons to his shirt, touching, caressing, kissing his chest as she bared it, moving him back toward the bed. She palmed the hard swell of his shoulders and arms, exploring the familiar, tough terrain. She knew him intimately: all the intriguing strengths, the rough burr of his evening whiskers, the springy dark hair on his pectorals, thinning to a tease down his taut abdomen and thickening again where his zipper parted to release his already engorged sex. She stroked him there, her own arousal building at his eagerness for her.

She pushed him down onto the mattress, his pants tangled about his ankles. She nipped at his chin, his shoulder, his chest, sharp little bites that had his breath quickening. When his hands came up for her, she pressed them back to the sheets. He kept them there, letting her have control while he watched her, glittering eyes heavy-lidded.

She continued to taste him with her mouth, her teeth, her tongue, moving down over the quiver of his flat belly, skimming the jut of his hip bone, tormenting the sensitive flesh of his inner thighs. And all the while he waited, stiff as a two-stage rocket anticipating lift-off, rumbling when she started down his legs instead of triggering a countdown.

She untied his shoes, slipping them off with his socks and trousers. He had large, surprisingly elegant feet. She could feel his pulse in the curve of the arch, the way it jumped when she tugged at his toes with her teeth.

"Let me know if there's anything you'd like me to do," he offered.

"Just lie there," she purred. "I'm using you for sex. Relax and enjoy it."

"I'll try." She heard the smile in his voice.

As she worked her way up, his body tensed, taut as a guy wire. She meant to put his self-control to the test, focusing on that to distract herself from her anxious mood. And Max Savoie, in all his naked splendor, was infinitely distracting.

Her mate. Her love. Hers alone.

He trembled as her mouth slid over him, a slow, tormenting stroke down one side and up the other. The swirl of her tongue had his hands twisting in the sheets.

The taste of him, the heat of him, had her moaning softly and he answered with a groan of her name. "Charlotte. Charlotte, let me have you."

"The having is all mine, my king. Deal with it. No whining."

She sucked him in hard, covering the length of him she couldn't take with one hand, simulating the movement of her mouth until his hips helplessly took up the rhythm.

"If you're going to take that ride, *sha*," he grated, "climb aboard now. Right now."

She didn't relent, rolling the taut weight of him in her other hand until the persuasive torture had his mind swirling. Pressure pounded hot and heavy, but still he hung on, fighting against the explosive pleasure.

Finally she whispered, "Let me have you, Max. Let go, baby." A coaxing squeeze, and he was gone.

We have liftoff.

He didn't move as she settled beside him on the bed. Rubbing her palm over his chest, she felt his jackhammering pulse slow down. The long slant of his eyes opened just enough to meet hers and his mouth stretched into a lazy curve.

"I don't know about your day, but mine just improved by about five hundred percent." He caught her hand, nudging his cheek into it, holding it there as he continued to doze contentedly.

Cee Cee rested her head on his shoulder, wishing she could enjoy this tender moment as completely as he did. She couldn't.

"Max . . ."

He kissed her palm. "Tell me."

She took a breath and then exhaled. "I did something today I shouldn't have. Something foolish and awful. I wish I could take it back, but I don't know how."

"Why do I get the feeling this involves your partner?"

She noticed how carefully neutral his voice was. "Don't get all pissy on me, Savoie. Not now."

Max took a deep, controlled breath. "Go ahead."

"We had an argument in the car this morning. He said some things, so I said some things. And . . . oh, hell, I told him Tina was a Shifter, too."

Max went completely still. He stared at her, unblinking.

"I didn't mean to. He just got me so mad, going on about my poor judgment and his perfect life and . . . and I just said it."

"How could you do such a thing?"

If he'd yelled at her she could have worked up a defensive temper. But the quiet disbelief in his tone had her quaking. He drew back, releasing her hand, his expression so shocked, so horribly injured.

"It was mean and careless, but what he said hurt me— Max?"

He'd rolled out of the bed away from her and went to the balcony doors that opened to the night. Silhouetted against the darkness with his hands laced over the top of his head, he stood motionless for long, anxious moments. Nothing could have surprised her more than his soft chuckle.

"Max?"

"Here I've been sweating the fact that our secrets are in the hands of strangers, and it's your jealousy over your lover's happy home life that destroys us all. Don't you see the irony there?" Silence, then: "Was that what this was about? Softening me up before telling me how you betrayed us?"

The starkness in his voice brought a swift, gutting fear. *Betrayed* was such a strong, ugly word. But the *us* brought his entire world into the consequences of her selfish act.

"No." *Not intentionally.* "You know better than that." An impatient pride clawed its way up over the shame. "How much harm could it have done? Alain already knows what you are. He loves Tina and Oscar. He won't do anything to harm his family."

"Unless that family becomes as much an abomination to him as I am."

She hadn't thought of that. And now she could think of nothing else.

"What have you done?" Max continued. "You have no idea how vulnerable we are, how fragile our existence is in your Upright world."

His words pushed a frightening gulf of difference between them.

"I'm sorry. Okay? I'm sorry. I'll make it right. I'll talk to Babineau; you can talk to Tina. We can fix it. I didn't mean to make trouble for them, Max, or for any of you. I didn't." Her voice choked off. There wasn't any more she could say, because it wasn't just about Alain and his wife. It was about what she'd done to Max. The one possibly unforgivable thing.

She wanted to run to him, to fling herself on him to beg for forgiveness. But begging wasn't her style, and at the moment she didn't think forgiving was his.

"Maybe I should go. I'll only make things worse if I stay." Her tone of offhanded aggravation was fairly successful. "I'll want to keep explaining, and it'll just muck things up more."

She paused, waiting for him to tell her to stay. When he didn't, the enormity of it hit her. What if he couldn't forgive her? What if she'd shattered his trust and become an unacceptable risk herself?

At one time, her insecurities would have had her slinking away rather than testing that awful truth. But no more. She walked over to him and wrapped him in a slow, binding embrace.

"I'm sorry, Max," she whispered, her cheek pressed to his shoulder. "It was careless, and it won't happen again."

His hands covered hers, squeezing gently. "I know, *sha*, I know. And tomorrow we'll fix things. Together."

She let him coax her back to bed, let him undress her. He held her fiercely, but she tucked her head when he went to kiss her because she could feel the distance mingling with the desire. The distance that came with a threat. A liability. He had to be thinking that. She was.

Puppies.

Oddly, it hadn't hit her until that moment just how unnatural their relationship was. She lay awake for a long time, studying him in his uneasy slumber. Her lover. Her one and only. Who wasn't human, no matter what appearances told her. She reached out to soothe her palm across his furrowed brow, whispering, "It's all right, baby. I'm here." And his fretful movements stilled.

When finally she slept, she dreamed of screaming through the pangs of giving birth. But what she delivered wasn't a normal child. It was a litter of Shifter pups with Max's green eyes.

DEEP IN THE balcony's shadows, a figure watched the sleeping couple through impassive eyes.

Rumors had depicted Max Savoie into mythic proportions: untouchable, indestructible, undefeatable. But that wasn't really the case. A male protecting a vulnerable female became vulnerable himself. It made him dangerous, true, but also weak. Only the weak gave in to emotion.

A few fierce slashes, and they'd both be dead with no drama or fuss. Not inventive or satisfying to the reputation, and also not what the employer had paid for. There were always rules to get in the way. And rules couldn't be broken without consequences.

Dispassionate eyes gleamed with impatience. Now that a way had been discovered, all that was left was for the right time to present itself.

That time wasn't now, but soon.

And like a whisper, the assassin faded into the darkness.

THE NEXT MORNING, Cee Cee was surprised to find a message on her phone from Junior Hammond apologizing for his behavior the night before, and even more stunned by his anxious assurance that he could be trusted to keep Max's secret. His insistence that she share his pledge with Max made her suspicious, but she had more immediate concerns to deal with.

She'd screwed up majorly, had damaged the things Max valued most: trust and family. And she'd done so out of no good reason but spite.

Time to face the music.

She made a conscious effort to appear harmless as she dressed for the Babineaus'. Instead of what he called her hookerwear, she slipped on a sleeveless shirtwaist dress of navy blue with white polka dots. The princess seams, fabric-covered belt, and soft pleats made her feel uncomfortably domestic. She'd bought it to wear during her trip to California when she'd laid her long-absent mother to rest. Navy slingbacks and a headband to keep her hair under control had her looking at a stranger in the mirror. If Max thought so too, he didn't voice his opinion.

He was silent as he pulled on slouchy cargo pants and a black polo shirt, along with his favored red high-tops. No snooty Armani for him, no racy cleav-

age for her. They looked the perfect sedate couple.
For added support, she draped the pearls Max had
given her around her neck, then scowled at her reflection.

"I look like I belong in a fifties TV show."

Max, lacing his shoes, paused. He replied without
intonation. "You look beautiful. And you belong to
me."

Say that like you mean it. She smiled grimly. "Ken
and Barbie off to visit the family."

"Who?"

"Never mind."

As she drove Legere's conservative black Mercedes,
Max remained closed off in his own thoughts, probably worrying over how to undo the harm she'd done.
She wasn't good at apologies; confrontation was her
way of dealing with difficulties. But this was going to
require some finesse, some ass-kissing.

She shook off the image of Alain Babineau's shock
when he learned the truth. And she tried to convince
herself that she hadn't irreparably ruined his future
just because his callous jibe had punctured her dream
of leading a normal life with Max. Because Max was
right: she *did* envy what she had never had. Stability, a
front lawn, competency in the kitchen, a husband who
only turned a bit grumpy if the channel was switched
from the ball game, and mostly, the miracle of her own
child.

None of those things lessened what she felt for
Max. They were old dreams, ghosts from a life she'd
never been allowed to lead.

She parked the posh car in front of the Babineaus'

cul-de-sac castle. It was modest in size, with shut-
ters, a basketball hoop, and a carport, and Babineau
regarded his home with pride. He constantly talked
about things like trimming hedges, cutting grass, put-
tying windows, and fitting the toilet with a universal
wax ring. Who in their right mind wanted to fuss with
mundane tasks when there was takeout and the main-
tenance and lawn-care services of apartment living?
Yet those conveniences never made her glow with sat-
isfaction the way Alain did after defeating some garden pest.

"Are we going to go in, or wait until they come out
for us?"

She glanced at Max in surprise, then sighed. "I suppose it's too late to just sneak off."

His expression went flat. "Far too late." And he
was out the car door before she could comment.

Soberly, she got out on the driver's side and saw
Oscar Babineau flying down the driveway.

"Max! Hey, Max!"

The skinny ten-year-old flung himself on Max, who
hugged the boy up to him, spinning about with the
whip of centrifugal force. The sunburst of pleasure on
his face gave Cee Cee uncomfortable pause. It was the
way she used to catch him looking at her.

"Heya, Oz. You been behaving?"

"Mama won't let me do anything else."

Max grinned and set the boy down. "Your mama's
a smart woman. You listen to her."

"Hey, Detective Caissie. You fixin' to go to
church?"

"Why?"

"You're all dressed up."

Cee Cee managed to smile. "It was this or my Kevlar."

Oscar laughed. "You look real pretty. Don't you think she looks pretty, Max?"

He stared at her with unnerving intensity. "Yes, I do." He started for the house, making her hurry to catch up so that they'd reach the side door as a unified front. Where Tina and the explosive situation Cee Cee had created were waiting.

"There you are. Come on in."

Though Tina's smile was warm with welcome, Cee Cee tensed as the door opened.

Max's palm fit to the curve of her spine. His touch was light as his fingers spread wide and pushed her forward, announcing dryly, "Ken and Barbie are here for lunch."

Oscar grabbed Max's hand the instant he cleared the threshold. "C'mon, I want to show you my room."

Max gave the two ladies an apologetic look and allowed himself to be towed away.

Tina chuckled and shook her head. "Boys. Alain's in his study. Why don't you go tell him you're here."

Nothing had cast a cloud over Tina's sunny disposition. Maybe Alain hadn't said anything to her. Could she be that lucky?

Alain Babineau's study was a tiny third bedroom where he housed a battered desk and a ratty sofa from his bachelor days. He kept his gun safe and his paperwork in it, and this morning she felt like she was intruding upon a badger in its lair. He leaned back in his creaky office chair to regard her through narrowed eyes.

"Surprised you had the balls to show up here."

"Having balls has never been my problem. Having brains is."

"If you expect an argument from me, you won't get one." He turned back to his computer and clicked off a map of the warehouse district where they'd found their latest vic. "How'd things go with the mom?" His voice was very neutral.

She leaned against the doorjamb. "Brutal. Good kid, good family. Dumbshit boyfriend convinced her to go on a road trip with him. Dumb because she was a minor, shit because he lost all their money about an hour after they got into town, and pushed her into working that club to support the both of them."

"Nice guy. Where is he now?"

"Skipped for Vegas with another stripper."

"What a sweetheart."

"Yeah. From there, it's the same old story. Girl too proud to call for bus fare to get home. Tries to put money away, ends up putting it into her arm, and turns up on a slab. Mom's made arrangements to take her back to Iowa when Dovion gives the okay."

Babineau sighed. "Parenting is hell." The layers in that couldn't go unaddressed.

"Oscar's a good kid, Alain."

He turned on her, his expression fierce, voice ripping with anger. "I don't need *you* to tell me what my boy is. Or what my wife is. I think I'd know those things better than you and your fancy-ass, cop-killing, four-legged boyfriend."

Retaliatory words were immediately on her lips, but a quiet voice from behind her said, "Mr. Fancy-Ass Cop-Killing Four-Legged Boyfriend thinks it's time we took this outside."

Seven

BABINEAU SURGED UP, his chair careening into a stack of magazines, sending them sliding across the floor. "*Way* past time."

Max curled an arm about Cee Cee to lift her out of the doorway. His stare burned into the other man's while his tone was conversational.

"Tell Tina we'll be back in a minute." Without looking around to see the boy approach, he said, "Oz, go help your mama."

"But, Max—"

"Do as you're told," Babineau snapped, earning a sullen poke of the boy's bottom lip and an unmistakable stiffening of Max's posture as Oscar mumbled, "Awright."

Babineau pushed past Cee Cee and his adopted son to lead the way out onto his little eight-square deck off the living room. A foldout camping table with built-in seats was set up under a faded umbrella. A far stretch from the cool verandas and wicker furniture out on River Road.

"You've no call to talk to the boy like that," Max began.

Babineau rocked back on his heels, hands clenching at his side. "I'll talk to him any way I like. He's my son."

"He's my blood."

"That doesn't give you any rights here in my home. And if you think different, I'll toss you to the curb."

Max's stare was icy. "Don't put a hand on me unless you want this to get uncivilized in a hurry, Detective."

"What the hell is civilized about what you are?"

"Nothing. Remember that. The only reason you're still alive is Charlotte. So be careful not to get on her bad side."

"I'll pass along a friendly warning to *you*, bub. Cee Cee is cop all the way around, no matter *what* side of her you get up on in the morning. And I'd know."

Maybe not the smartest thing to say to a man who was not human, with dangerously possessive animal tendencies.

When Max refused to be goaded into a response, Babineau paced to the steps leading down into his yard and dropped onto the top one. His temper lost out to anguish.

"Is what she said true? Are Tina and Oscar . . . like you?"

"Oscar, yes. There are those who would go to any lengths to have him."

"Like those creatures that snatched him from school."

"Yes. He needs to be protected. You need to understand the danger he's in."

"He's my boy, and I can take care of him without your interference."

"No, you can't."

Babineau didn't argue. He was thinking about

those seven sleek beings who'd kidnapped Oscar. That it was Max who rescued him, taking bullets that miraculously didn't kill him. He was seeing those red flaming eyes, the fangs and claws. And the way Max tore through those who would harm his boy in a way he never could.

"What would you suggest?" he asked heavily.

"That he come to stay with me. The estate has security. He'd be safe."

"And he'd grow up behind those walls just like you did, separated from life. A damned freak."

Max didn't answer right away. When he did, his reply was quiet. "It's not what I would have wanted for him."

"It's not what I want at all. Dammit, and damn you for bringing this down on us."

"I didn't bring it. They didn't even know about me."

"Who wants him?"

"I don't know."

"What are they?"

"I'm not sure."

"Well, aren't you just full of helpful information."

"He's your son. I can't tell you what to do."

"Damn straight."

"But you can't keep me out of his life, either. He needs someone to teach him how to use his skills to protect himself."

"So you want to introduce my kid to all your shaggy pals?"

"No. The fewer who know what he is, the better. Some secrets are meant to be kept for the good of all. You might want to impress that upon Hammond and

Boucher. Jimmy hid me from notice for good reason. I didn't know what I was until my father found me and told me."

"Your father?"

"Oscar's father. He's dead now, so I can't find out any more from him."

"Oscar's father. Tina's . . . what?"

"I don't know. I didn't know Oscar and I were related until after our father died. I don't know the details. I'm not sure Tina does, either."

"We knew there was something wrong with the boy, but thought it was something like ADD. But Tina—" His voice broke. "She's not human? They're not human? How could she hide something like this from me?"

For a moment Max saw not a threat, but a man whose heart was shattered. "Probably because she doesn't know."

The sliding door opened behind them.

"Hey, you two, wash up. We're about ready to eat," Tina said.

And as Babineau went inside, Max noted how he went out of his way not to brush against the woman he'd married.

THE SUN WAS warm, the breeze light, the food ample and satisfying. Oscar and Tina kept up a steady banter with Max, while Alain and Cee Cee were mostly quiet. The only topic they could safely talk about, work, had been placed off-limits.

Max made his move, asking Tina, "What's Oscar doing over his school break this summer?"

"We haven't thought about it yet."

Oscar perked up, all ears.

"I've been thinking about inviting him to stay out at the house. That'd give you two some time alone, too. Would you like that, Ozzy?"

Oscar bounced in his lawn chair. "Could I? We could do things together like you promised. And Giles and Pete can teach me about cars and engines and stuff."

Max's gaze lifted, cool and calculated. "We'd have to make sure it was okay with your father."

Babineau met that steady stare without betraying the fury roaring through him. What could he say without coming off like the villain? "It's a ways off, Oscar. I thought we were planning to do some stuff together, just you and me?"

Oscar blinked at him, too young to cloak his disappointment. "Oh, yeah."

"There are a lot of weeks in the summer. No reason you can't do both." Max smiled, the clever diplomat.

"We can talk about it later," Tina decided, changing the volatile subject by telling Cee Cee, "What beautiful pearls."

Cee Cee touched them, flustered by the sudden compliment. "Oh, thanks. Max bought them for me."

She could swear she heard her partner's teeth grind across the table.

They were clearing the dishes when a distinctive roar caught Cee Cee's attention. She leaned over the kitchen sink to look out the window and gave a whistle.

"Man oh man, will you look at that hot baby."

Tina looked at the bright orange car rumbling down the street, perplexed when it turned into the driveway to sit idling. "That's no one we know."

Max settled his hands at Cee Cee's waist. "Sounds like a 1969 Yenko Camaro 427. Only two hundred others ever made."

She turned, her gaze bright with excitement.

He smiled. "Go see if you like it, *sha.*"

With an uncharacteristic squeal, she raced outside. Giles St. Clair, Max's burly bodyguard, had climbed out and was polishing the chrome side-view mirror with his shirttail. Before Max made it to the front steps, the hood was up and the two of them were under it as Giles pointed out the Corvette big-block V-8 that had been swapped out for the factory engine, along with the heavy-duty hardware and performance upgrades. The sight of her polka-dot-clad rump in the girlie dress and high heels as she leaned into the engine compartment sent a supercharged rush of lustful pleasure through him.

"She's a lucky woman," Tina commented, standing at his side.

"No," he disagreed softly. "I'm the lucky one."

"Wow! What a great car!" Oscar ran down the drive to be greeted by Giles's boisterous, "Hey, sport. Got something for you, too. Go on and grab it out of the backseat."

Oscar reached in to pull out a bulky box. "Wow, a radio-controlled car. And it looks just like this one!"

"Ever driven one of those before?" Giles asked.

He shook his head, all wide-eyed.

"C'mon. It's all charged up. I'll bet we can get it running the bases at the school."

Oscar looked up toward the porch. "Can we, Mama?"

"Go ahead."

While Giles crossed the street with Oscar bounding at his side, Max went down the drive to where Cee Cee was waiting.

"Like it, Det—"

She threw an arm about his neck and hauled him down for a deep, tongue-thrusting kiss that melted into a lot more emotion than she normally showed in public. She came down off her toes and gently rubbed her lipstick off his mouth.

"You're the best, Savoie."

"I kinda made a mess of the last one. Knowing how you love fast, sexy, dangerous things, I couldn't resist."

"Yes, I do." Her gaze smoldered with promise. She kissed him again very softly and warned, "You'd better go over to the ball diamond with the boys while I can still resist you."

As she slid behind the wheel, adjusting the seat and mirrors, as excited as a kid herself, Max watched with a satisfied smile. Until Alain Babineau jockeyed by him with a low growl that sounded like, "You son of a bitch."

They sat on the first row of the bleachers watching Giles teach Oscar how to maneuver the radio-controlled car. While Babineau was sullenly thinking that here was yet another thing the boy would turn to Savoie for, Max dropped a bomb on him with deceiving nonchalance.

"Tell me about you and Charlotte."

Surprise took him like an unexpected elbow to his still-aching nose. "Say what?"

Everything about Savoie put his back up. The fact that he was a criminal and should be doing time instead of playing big brother to his son. The fact that Oscar never acted like spending time with *him* was the best gift in the world. The fact that he had to work hard just for groceries and cable, when Savoie could effortlessly conjure up pearls and a car. And the fact that Savoie had scars on his body from saving Oscar's life. Alain hated feeling grateful to him for that.

Max continued to watch the miniature car spin around the bases. "She tells me the two of you had an affair."

Alain stared, then drawled, "If she told you that much, I'm sure she gave you all the details she felt you needed to know."

Savoie's gaze slid slowly to meet his. "Let's pretend she's never told me anything and that I'm asking you, man-to-man."

"Man-to-man? That *would* be pretending."

The bastard. Who did he think he was, acting as if an answer was due him? Just because he directed the majority of illegal activities in and around the city, just because he'd stepped from anonymity into obscene wealth and power, swaggering around as if he was untouchable, as if he wasn't a monster but a real man deserving of Charlotte Caissie, didn't give Savoie the right to pry into his very personal life. Wasn't it enough that he had Cee Cee's heart on a plate and Oscar's devotion as a side dish?

"Fuck off, Savoie. What happened between me and Cee Cee is none of your damned business."

"She told me it was nothing." Max said smugly.

"If that's what she told you, then why ask me?"

"I just wanted to make sure that that's how you saw it, too."

Babineau wanted to smack that smirk off the bastard's face, but he wasn't quite *that* stupid. He settled for a gradual insinuating smile. "What we have is a history together, Savoie. It goes back a long, long way, on a lot of different levels you couldn't even begin to imagine or understand. That won't change no matter who she's sleeping with."

Chew on that, you son of a bitch. Hope you choke on it.

Cee Cee stood at the kitchen window, drying off glasses while keeping an eye on the two men across the street. While appearing cordial, Max had been in her partner's face from the second they arrived, and she knew Babineau had had about enough of it. Especially on top of everything else recently sprung upon him.

Men. Geez.

"Are you sure Ozzy wouldn't be a bother, staying with you?" Tina asked, interrupting Cee Cee's thoughts.

"No way. He's a great kid. Max is crazy about him. He didn't have any kind of childhood himself. I think he sees Ozzy as his chance to enjoy those things he missed."

Tina looked across the street with a wistful smile. "He and Max get on so well. Like they have some special sort of understanding between them. He never took to Alain like that. I don't know why—they just aren't on the same wavelength, I guess."

Cee Cee glanced at her. Could it be that she still didn't know?

Tina caught her look and smiled. Behind the perky exterior, Cee Cee sensed a weariness and worry as the other woman said, "I never got the chance to thank you personally for what you did for Oscar. Alain and I are so incredibly grateful."

She shrugged. "All in a day's work. You had the really tough job." At Tina's confused look, she said, "Raising him by yourself for so long. That took courage."

"I didn't have a lot of choice."

"Yes, you did. And you chose the hard road."

Tina blushed. "I don't have regrets. Not any."

Cee Cee hesitated, wondering how far she dare take this. Her social skills were pathetic, but she took a chance that Tina Babineau might be in the same boat.

"Alain never said much about your past, only that his sun rises and sets on you and your boy."

Tina looked away uncomfortably. "My past isn't much to talk about. I try to forget it, when I can."

"I know you stayed at St. Bart's for a time before Ozzy was born. Did you know I practically grew up there?"

"Sister Catherine talked about you all the time—though I'm not sure I believe all the stories she told about when you two were girls."

Cee Cee grinned. "Believe them." Then her mood sobered. "We went through a real ugly ordeal together. It changed everything about our lives, about who we became. I don't think I ever would've gotten past it if not for Max."

"And did you? Get over it?"

Cee Cee looked into the hopeful face and couldn't lie. "No. I'll never get over it. But I can forget about it for a time. And that's enough."

Tina's dark eyes held haunting secrets, the kind Cee Cee understood all too well, and her mood toward Alain's wife softened.

"If you need someone to talk to, someone who knows what it's like to be scared and helpless and alone and survive it, you might find I'm a pretty good listener."

Tina studied her carefully, and she was about to speak when Cee Cee's cell phone rang. She held back a curse as she went to the living room to pull it out of her purse.

"Caissie."

"Sorry to tap you on your day off."

She blinked in surprise. "Showboat?" Stan Schoenbaum of Vice was no buddy of hers, and the last person she expected to hear from after he and Max had gotten into it during a softball game.

"I need to talk to you about the case you're working on. Now."

She blinked. "Where do you want to meet? Babs and I can be there—"

"Just you, Caissie. Newton's in fifteen. Say you'll be there." There was urgency in his usually arrogant voice—and desperation.

"All right," she said slowly.

"Caissie . . . thanks."

Now she was alarmed.

She returned to the kitchen with a regretful smile. "Gotta go. Thanks for the invite. It was nice of you."

"Maybe we could talk some more. Maybe have lunch."

Cee Cee liked the idea, which surprised her. "Yeah. We could do that."

They shared a smile. Their first.

CEE CEE STOOD at the door to her new car and softly said, "Max."

His dark head shot up from across the street, and at her beckoning gesture he came to her side at a brisk lope.

"I gotta go, baby."

Used to her business tone, he didn't ask for details. "Everything all right?"

"Yeah. I'll see you at home."

He opened the car door for her, enjoying her pleasure as she slid into the black leather bucket seat and caressed the steering wheel. He closed her inside and was about to step back when she leaned out the window.

"C'mere."

Happy to reap another sweet benefit in thanks for the gift, he bent to accept a kiss that was rich and tender. And definitely not about a big-block V-8.

Her palm rested against his cheek, keeping him close while she gazed into his eyes with raw emotion. "I was never truly alive until you. I just wanted you to know that."

Then the engine roared and she tore out of the driveway, dragging his heart behind her.

NEWTON'S WAS QUIET. The lunch crowd had gone and the serious drinkers were still in bed. Stan Schoenbaum, sitting in a booth at the back, was already into his second bourbon. When he looked up at her, she was struck by his ravaged features.

"Hey, Caissie." His tone was flat, lifeless.

She slid into the booth. "What's going on, Stan?"

He fidgeted with his glass, his eyes puffy and red. "You're working that 'Tides That Bind' case, right?"

"Yeah, me and Babineau."

"You just found the third girl, a hooker like the others?"

"Yeah. That's right."

"And if this bastard follows pattern, he's got his new vic tucked away already."

"Probably." She waited patiently to find out where he was going with it.

"I think I know who he grabbed." His eyes met hers with the torments of hell in them. "I think he has my daughter."

Eight

*T*HIS IS KELLY. She just turned seventeen."

Cee Cee took the school photo and studied the face of a young girl with shining auburn hair and dimples. "Pretty."

"Our oldest. Got her daddy's pride and her mama's stubbornness. Always knew exactly what she wanted, and wouldn't let anything get in her way. She wanted to be a professional dancer. I wanted to get lessons for her when she was a kid, but then the other two came along and there wasn't a lot of extra cash for things like that. When kids got a dream, they don't want to hear about things like braces and a new transmission or their mama getting laid off at work. She had the talent and the drive, and it was just killing her, doing nothing with it. But there was nothing I could do to help make those dreams happen, you know?"

Cee Cee made a sympathetic noise, and tamped down her impatience.

"Some girl at school told her about a club where she could dance at night and make enough to pay for lessons during the day. A *club*." He snorted. "You know what kind a place we're talking here. My little girl, just sixteen then, telling me she was dropping out of school to work in a titty bar."

"I imagine you handled it with sensitivity."

He flinched at her mild sarcasm. "I handled it the way you would have. I locked her in her room and took away all her privileges. But she found a way to slip out, and she was gone. I've never been so damned mad in my life." His rock-hard jaw trembled. "Two months, we heard nothing from her. Then a call to ask for money. I wouldn't give her any. I was sure she'd come back. Sure of it."

"But she didn't."

"No. Her friend was just a hook to pull her in. There was never enough cash left over to take those classes in classical dance. And pretty soon it took more than dancing to make ends—" He broke off, his eyes dark with pain and fury.

"Why do you think something's happened to her?"

"About six months ago, her younger sister turned thirteen. Kelly called, wanted to come home and see her, but only if we'd promise not to try and make her stay. She stopped by, looking almost like my little girl, and for a little while it was like we were a family again."

"But she wouldn't stay."

He shook his head. "She gave me her word that she wasn't doing drugs, that she was being careful, and that no one was hurting her or forcing her to do anything. We came to an agreement—her mama's idea—that she'd come home every Sunday, have dinner with us, wear her old clothes, sleep in her bed. I'd slip her what cash I could and we'd try to talk, so if she was in any trouble, she wouldn't be afraid to call us.

"She was tired, Ceece. So tired and unhappy the last few times she came home. And scared. She wouldn't say of what. She started talking about getting her GED. I was sure, *sure*, she was gonna ask if she could move back in."

"And then?"

"She missed this last Sunday. No call. Nothing. I didn't think much of it until the third body surfaced, then I went nuts looking for her. She was working in the same damned club the Cole girl was, and she hadn't been at work. No one had seen her.

"That monster's got my baby, Cee Cee. I just know it." His head dropped into his hands.

"Stan, what do you want me to do?"

After a minute, he straightened. He looked terrible. "I told my wife she'd taken a trip up north for a few weeks. I didn't want her to worry; it would kill her and the other kids. The press, the waiting—I can't do that to them." He paused, then made a humbling admission. "I couldn't take it. Them plastering my little girl's face all over the place: my little girl, the hooker."

Understanding, she made no judgments. "Stan, what do you want me to do?" she repeated.

"Find my girl, but don't go public with it."

"You know showing her photo could get her home a lot sooner."

"And it'll bring the Feds in, and it'll be out of our hands. If this perv doesn't know we're onto him, maybe he'll keep her alive until the end of the month. Maybe I'll get her back in time. You can follow up on the QT, get inside."

"We'll need to talk to your wife, Stan." She waved off his protest. "Marilyn has to know. She'll hate you for keeping it from her, and you know it. You need each other's support, and we need things from her that only a mother would know."

"All right." Shaky hands threaded through his hair. "But you'll keep it quiet, right?"

"Just me and Alain until we're sure we're on to something. In the meantime, I want you to file a missing person's report. It's what he'd expect you to do. And maybe that's all it is."

"And if it's not?" His tragic expression woke an empathetic fury inside her.

"Then we'll tear this town apart until we find her."

CEE CEE FELT a stir of air, and her head popped up from the papers strewn across her coffee table. Max was standing on her balcony.

"Geez, I almost swallowed my tongue!"

"That would be a loss, considering what delightful things you can do with it. You missed supper. You didn't call." He said both things casually, but managed to make her feel guilty.

She still wasn't used to someone keeping tabs on her. While part of her liked it, another part muttered, "What time is it?"

"Almost eleven."

She slumped back against the couch cushions and summoned up a stretch. "I had no idea it was so late."

"What are you working on?"

He still hadn't come into the room. With shadows cloaking his expression, she couldn't gauge his mood. Were they still on the outs over the Tina thing? The fact that he seemed to be waiting for an invitation to join her pointed in that direction.

"Going over some old files stored in the closet. Things of my daddy's. I'm hoping to find something that ties into this case I'm working on."

"Would you rather be left alone?"

"No, please come in. I've got the rest of these to go through, though."

She went back to riffling through the thick folder in front of her.

The couch was covered with files, so he sat on the floor. "You can take this stuff back to the house, if you want. There's more room for you to work there."

She laughed without humor. "Jimmy'd roll over inside his mausoleum at the thought of me doing cop work under his roof." She wasn't wild about the idea, either. It brought the term "conflict of interest" too close to home.

After a moment, she glanced over to find him scanning the pages, too.

"What are you looking for?" he asked.

"Mentions of Manny Blu."

"Why are you after Carmen?"

"Is he a friend of yours?" she asked carefully.

"No. Jimmy hated him. Wouldn't have him out at the house. Called him a cheap hood."

"That's harsh, considering the source."

Max grinned and she relaxed.

"He owns the club where one, maybe two, of the girls worked. Maybe both were hooking for him. Maybe he gets his kicks out of corrupting and killing innocent kids. If he's involved, he's not going to wiggle away."

"Maybe I can help."

Cee Cee smiled. To think that some couples spent evenings watching reality TV together.

"Thanks, but I got it." She wanted it to be her teeth that bit Blutafino's butt. And when she took that bite, she didn't want any complications to bite her own— like Max's fingerprints on the evidence.

And maybe, just maybe, she was still a little bit sulky over the way Max excluded her from his own business. Perhaps separate but equal was the way to keep a healthy balance in their relationship.

To lead away from that touchy arena, she went directly into another minefield.

"Did you and Babs get things worked out this afternoon?"

"We're circling each other for the moment, looking for weakness so we can make a quick, clean kill."

"That's *not* funny." And he wasn't laughing.

"He hasn't said anything to Tina, Max. And she and I are going to have lunch." At his pointed silence, she said. "What? I can be pleasant and sympathetic when I need to be." Her tone softened. "And we have things in common. Some good, some not so good."

"You don't need to involve yourself."

Surely he didn't mean his words to feel like a slap, but they did. Her tone roughened. "I created the problem, I'll smooth it over. And I *am* involved, because you're involved."

Was he afraid she was going to make an even bigger mess for him to clean up? Or was this his kind, his way; no Uprights need apply? If so, why didn't he just get it out in the open so she could deal with it?

"Are you and your partner going to be okay to work together?" he asked, as if that was the issue that concerned him.

"This isn't the first tiff we've had, and it won't be the last. We'll get through it. He's a good cop. We know each other's habits, and how the other thinks."

"But you didn't have me and my monstrous clan standing between you before."

Her mood sobered. "Don't push him so hard, Max. He's got to be seeing you as his worst nightmare. You're a hero to his son and share a family secret with his wife. You're rich, you're powerful, you flout everything he believes in. And you're not human. He doesn't know how to deal with it, or with you."

"And I have you."

She nodded, then said in absolute candor, "And that's got to threaten the hell out of him on more than one level. Give the guy a break. He's afraid of you."

"I'm afraid of him."

She almost laughed until she realized that he was serious. "Why?"

His voice was quiet and grim. "He has what I've always wanted. He lives the life I've envied. He controls how often I can see Ozzy. He has information that could destroy me. And he had you.

"He shares with you things that I can't. A history, a relationship, a *species*, and that annoyingly clannish brotherhood of the badge. He doesn't bring the possibility of death by supernatural causes into your life. He doesn't . . . hurt you by turning into something horrific."

His gaze slid uncomfortably to her breakfast bar

where he'd taken her in his beast form, too lost to mating madness to care if he frightened or damaged her. Too out of control to consider the consequences of that act.

"And now he holds my secrets in his hands," Max concluded. "His whole life has been turned upside down because the woman he loves isn't who or what he thought she was. And he blames me."

The ringing of Max's cell provided a welcome interruption.

"Savoie."

Beneath the light press of her hand on his shoulder, Cee Cee felt his muscles tighten.

"I'll be there." He snapped the phone shut and glanced up at her.

"Trouble? Two-legged or four-legged?"

"That was Jacques. He wants me to come down to the club."

Not much for her to go on. *Cheveux du Chien* catered to Max's Shifter clan. His regular table in back was where he conducted his kingly business. Business that didn't involve her, or any of the Uprights that most of his kind viewed with hatred and suspicion. Because of his relationship with her, some viewed him the same way.

What was calling so urgently for his attention so late? He didn't offer any information, and she was too proud to ask for it. "Okay. I've got things to finish up here."

"I'll see you back at the house then?" The fact that he phrased it as a question said everything wasn't settled.

"Sure."

She leaned down to kiss him, losing herself in the taste of him. Letting him go before the need to cling kicked in.

After he left, she looked around for a nostalgic moment.

How many nights had she spent like this? Only instead of the turkey wrap and diet soda, she'd have been working through a six-pack and a bag of chips, lighting one cigarette off the butt of another. With no hope of a sexy lover showing up to seduce her, she'd have been deep in work until fatigue or the alcohol caught up with her close to dawn. Night after night.

For years, it had been enough. No worries about saying the wrong thing. No fear of stepping on sensitive toes. No relationship rules to remember. Just the freedom to do whatever she wanted whenever she wanted. No one wondering why she hadn't called. No one crowding into her space, into her thoughts. Into her heart.

Back then, everything she had was in these few simple rooms. Everything she was was embossed upon the badge she carried. There were no deviations from right to slightly wrong. No question of where she stood, nor doubts from those who stood beside her.

Things had been so easy then. Get up, do the job she loved, and come home satisfied. *This* home. Not a mobster's mansion where the floors were stained by blood and secrets. Where the lover who lay with her in the night wasn't human.

She leaned her head back against the couch and rubbed her eyes.

What was she thinking? She didn't want to go back to that time when she was miserable and alone, one drink from being an alcoholic, one case from burnout?

Why did the way Max Savoie filled that once-empty life suddenly scare the hell out of her?

She scowled, frustrated by her strange, restless mood. She hadn't felt so edgy and moody since she was a teenager with hormones ping-ponging all over the place.

She tried to work again, but when an hour had passed and she'd accomplished nothing, she picked up the phone.

"Savoie."

She could hear the pulse of music pounding behind his deep voice. And suddenly she didn't know what to say to him.

"Hey."

A pause. "Did you need something, Detective?" Just a touch of impatience. He was busy; it was a bad time.

"No." *Yes.* She needed him to wrap her up in his arms and kiss her senseless, until the painful throb of her odd anxiousness went away. "I think I'm onto something here. I might be a while."

"Okay." A pause. "Anything else?"

"I love you, Max." A longer pause filled by a hard techno spin. "Did you hear me?"

"Yes. Is everything all right, Charlotte?"

"Yeah. Sure. Just tired. I'll let you get back to business." She shut her phone.

She was so tired, soul-deep weary. Tension tightened the muscles in her neck and shoulders, making it impossible to focus. Because the comfort and easy camaraderie of her life was gone, changed in an instant out in the bayou when Max Savoie had let his mask fall in front of her fellow cops to save Oscar's life. And she didn't know what to do about it.

She should just close her eyes. Just for a minute.

When she opened them, it was morning.

THE UNEASINESS BUILDING like thunderheads over the past few days banked into a dark horizon over Max's mood as he pocketed his phone. Something was wrong, but he didn't have the luxury of sorting it out right now. Not with a whole other set of problems waiting to bite into his ass.

"Sorry," he murmured to the group gathered around his table.

His kind. His clan. They'd all sworn fealty to him when he took over Legere Enterprises International. Among them were the heads of the various worker organizations that kept the city moving. A silent, unnatural workforce staying out of sight, existing in the dangerous shadows. He'd made them bold promises to stand with them, and for them—but now the allegiance he depended upon was wavering.

Their panic was so thick he could smell it on them— because of the Trackers who'd come here and torn through their fragile sense of security, first by killing one of their own, and then by almost exposing their existence to the Upright world.

"What is it you want me to do?" he asked reasonably.

"More will come to replace those you killed," someone said. Others nodded at that logic.

"Then we'll have to be watchful and prepared."

"That's easy for you to say. You're the only one in this room who's ever survived them," Philo Tibideaux said.

His brother had been slain by the vicious bounty hunters who'd come in search of a rumored pureblood who would save the Shifter clans. Consensus named Max Savoie as that savior, though he had no idea why or what wearing that crown might entail. And now they were doubting their choice.

"What of the rest of us, and our families?" Philo asked. "Are you going to be there to protect us all?"

"I'll do what I can."

"They've left us alone for generations," another lamented. "Why come back now? What do they want?"

Some simply sat and rumbled, but others paced with restless growls, sliding between forms in volatile anxiety. Max watched his dangerous, violent clan work up a feverish pitch of fear that could easily culminate in attack.

Because he was the most convenient target, he remained calm yet cautious. The last thing he wanted to have to do was kill them all, but he could. And knowing he could was the only thing keeping them at bay.

"They've already got our will and our memories, and our courage. What more could they take?" Jacques LaRoche snarled. This was his club. His meaty hand ruled the docks at Max's command.

In their agitation, the others looked to him because he was one of them, a familiar blunt instrument, not a sleek outsider like Savoie.

"I'm not like most of you. I wasn't born here. I had

another life, a family that they stole from me before tossing me down here because I no longer had value to them. But they were wrong to think they had no reason to fear me. I won't ever roll over for them. Thanks to Savoie, I've found my teeth again."

Some assenting rumbles.

"Why should we suffer when it's *him* they're after?" Silence, then the quiet voice from the back said what many were thinking. "I say we need to save ourselves. To do that, we need to give them what they want."

Nine

LaRoche's head whipped from side to side. "Who said that?"

"I did," came a meek voice from the rear of the group. "You know me, Jacques. You all know me. I'm a laborer, not a fighter. I have a human wife and four children who haven't enough of our bloodline in them to howl, let alone bite. If we anger the Trackers, if they come for another Gathering, what chance would my family stand—would *any* of our families stand—with us in the city and our loved ones in another parish waiting to be slaughtered?"

A Gathering. They trembled. One hadn't occurred for two generations, but whispers of the savagery kept the New Orleans clan wary. They were cowards when alone, preferring to slink off when faced with confrontation. It was the pack that gave them strength. And the last time their ancestors had tried to organize, a terror had swept down from the north to slay the men and half-breed children, and steal the women away.

That threat whispered to them now. While most rallied around Savoie for the security and the pride he encouraged, they were also wary of the danger.

They fell silent when Max strode to where the hi-lo driver sat cringing in the shadow. The warehouse worker hadn't witnessed the initial meeting between Savoie and the clansmen here at *Cheveux du Chien*, but he'd heard it recounted too many times to doubt its savagery. Of how Savoie, with his Upright female cop at his side, had ripped through all comers like a chain saw.

Savoie's lethal hands settled lightly on narrow shoulders as Max hunkered down so they were eye-to-eye.

"What's your name?"

"Henry Durban, Mr. Savoie."

"Henry, don't ever think I take your fears for granted. I know what it's like to be alone and afraid. And I know what it means to find strength with those of your own kind. If I thought for a second that surrendering myself up to them would keep all of you safe, I would do it. But it won't. Because they have no fear or respect for us. Unless we draw a line and forbid them to cross it, they'll come and go as they please. They can do what they want, take what they want, because no one cares if they do.

"But *I* care. And I'm not going to let them continue to make us feel like we have no value. Do you believe me, Henry? Will you trust me?"

He spoke to one man, but they all felt it.

"I do and I will, Mr. Savoie. Just tell me how I can keep my family safe."

Max rose and faced the others wondering the same thing. "The Towers are almost finished. Henry Durban and his family will have the second unit available. My word on it." He'd promised the first to Jacques LaRoche.

"We'll form a new community there, a community of families who will support and take care of one another. No more crowding into dark rooms, hiding like rats. Isn't it time you lived free of fear, so your children can feel pride in who they are and you can walk among men without shame?"

This was met with overwhelming enthusiasm, but Max caught LaRoche's cynical gaze. At Max's questioning furrow, the bar owner simply called, "A round on Mr. Savoie. He can afford it."

As they scrambled for the rail to place their orders, Jacques chuckled at his puzzled friend. "Nice speech. Rally 'round me, men, and head for the castle. We can wait out any siege if we just stick together."

"Why are you mocking me, Jacques?"

A heavy sigh. "I'm not. I want to believe as much as the rest of them."

"But . . . ?"

"I've seen the Trackers, Max. Me and your fierce little female went up against them. I had to run to stay alive; they would have broken me in half. What chance does a mite like Henry have? Trackers are just the attack dogs of the monsters we fear.

"And you don't know them; you were raised in the wild. They've never Processed you. You don't know what they can do if they decide to claim what they've always owned."

Max leaned forward. "What do you mean, Processed? I don't understand."

"How could you? You're not truly one of us. A Porche and a Prius will both get you from here to there, but it's a question of power and style."

"Explain."

The huge bald man hesitated.

"Jacques, how can I protect them, how can I ask for their trust, if I don't understand the danger?" He gripped the other's forearm. "What is it?" Max insisted.

"The things you offer us . . . You bring us hope, Max, yet you have no idea what you're jumping into. If it were me, I'd run like hell and hide in the deepest hole I could find."

"Maybe I should, Jacques. But it'd have to be a pretty damn big hole for all of you to come in with me."

Jacques nailed him with a look that demanded all.

"Philo's not wrong. I wish he was."

Then Max told Jacques everything. About the Tracker who'd played games with him in the park. About the police officers who knew of their existence. About the new family he'd discovered and feared to lose. He'd shared bits and pieces before, just enough to get assistance when it was needed, but not the whole truth. If he'd understood friendship more than he understood betrayal, he would have realized sooner what a strong ally he had in LaRoche.

The big man was silent, absorbing the information.

"Knowing all this," Max challenged, "tell me you still have my back."

"First, you tell me that you can walk away from what you have. That you can turn your back on the things Legere left you. Because once you commit to this, to *us,* you can't go back. Could you give up Charlotte for us? Make me believe it, Savoie."

Objection roared through him. Give up his mate? *Never.* She was everything he'd ever wanted, and the fear of almost losing her was still fresh. He hadn't forgotten what it was like rushing her broken body to the hospital, hearing them say there was nothing they could do, that she was damaged beyond repair. Going to her apartment alone with the task of picking out something for her to wear for her funeral. Lose her? Never.

Yet he could hear Father Furness's warning that he'd have to sacrifice everything he loved.

And staring into Jacques' sympathetic face, ironically it was Charlotte's voice that goaded him. *Step up, Savoie.*

He had to know what he was, where he came from. How could he have any kind of life with Charlotte until he knew those truths? How could she continue to care for him if he backed away now to hide from his heritage?

How could he keep her safe?

His voice was rock steady. "Everything I am is yours."

FROM HIS OFFICE window, Max could see the Towers rising bold and strong against the morning sky. Legere money funded it, his ground supported its foundation. To get it built, Max had cut a deal with the devil, Simon Cummings, who had the pull to get the project approved. They'd both made concessions to get what they wanted. Cummings got the PR glory for reclaiming and repopulating a former area of urban blight. Max got a guarantee that those who worked for him would be fairly housed. And their bargain was struck and bound by a decades-old secret that would never be told.

But because Max mistrusted Cummings, he worried about the promises he'd made to his clan. He worried about his ability to protect the woman he loved from pain.

She hadn't come home last night.

He'd sat alone on the dark staircase listening for the sound of her car, yearning for the first whisper of her scent. Sick with indecision over the things he'd shared with and learned from LaRoche, he'd needed her to anchor him. He'd watched the sun come up through the transom over the door with no sign of her. No call.

The gulf between their different worlds wasn't going to go away anytime soon. He could feel the tension, the new caution when they were together, but he didn't know how to get past it. He didn't doubt she loved him. When she said it, she meant it. When she touched him, he felt it. Their feelings for each other weren't the problem, and that commitment was cemented by their bond.

But their outside lives were making it damned difficult. No matter how strong their magnetic pull, their worlds were forcing them apart. And his greatest fear was that there was no way to overcome it.

"Mr. Savoie, Mr. Petitjohn is here."

"Send him in, Marissa. Thank you."

Max swiveled his chair toward the door, his features an expressionless mask to meet the viper he kept close to his breast. He couldn't look at Francis Petitjohn without seeing bits of Jimmy Legere's brain all over the floor at his feet. Petitjohn had killed his cousin in an ill-conceived coup, and now he was alive for only as long as Max tolerated him.

Yet the things that were reminiscent of Jimmy soothed Max's soul. Petitjohn shared those beloved features, the cadence of his voice, the edges of his scent, and Max clutched at those threads of memory. He couldn't force himself to kill the only link left to the man who'd been a mentor and father figure to him.

Knowing the sentiment wasn't returned kept Max from foolish illusions.

"Whatchu need, Max? Did you have a chance to look over those cost projections for the Towers?"

"Not yet." He'd taken them home with him on Friday, but had been too distracted to open his briefcase. "I'll go over them this afternoon." T-John grimaced. "Problem?"

"I need the okay before lunch. Can't you just sign them and trust me to take care of the rest?"

Max stared at him unblinkingly. *Trust him?* Like he'd trust a water moccasin not to bite. Suspicion slithered like that undulating deadly snake. Perhaps he'd left Petitjohn in control of Jimmy's interests a bit too long. Long enough for him to enjoy the taste too much.

"No. I don't think I can."

Looking impatient, T-John shrugged. "I guess I can stall them, but it'll mean a few weeks of delay. When you stop the ball, it takes some time to get the momentum rolling again. Jimmy understood that, but I guess I can't expect you to. If you want to control the ball, I'll step aside. It's your money, your risk, after all."

Max rubbed his eyes. Was he seeing a threat where there was none? T-John knew what failure would bring; he understood what price he'd pay for betrayal. What possible benefit could he gain if LEI didn't flourish? Success was in both their best interests, and T-John was all about greed.

"These are the same figures we went over a few weeks ago?"

"A few tweaks here and there to maintain code, but essentially the same. We managed to clip a few corners to keep Cummings quiet about the bottom line, but the numbers are good, damned good."

"You're okay with them?"

"Yeah. If you want to take your time, hey, it's no big deal. I can have McCracken come up around three to do a line by line with you so you're comfortable with it."

Weeks of delay. He couldn't afford it; he needed to get his people to safety. He'd made promises, and he needed to put his energies behind his obligations to his clan.

"Have you got a copy of the paperwork with you?"

It appeared on his desk as if by magic. Max gave it a cursory glance, then, after a long, weary breath, signed it. "I want things on schedule."

"You got it, Max. Anything else?"

"Carmen Blutafino. Are we affiliated with him in any areas?"

A laugh. "Manny always wanted to get Jimmy into

bed, business-wise, but Jimmy wasn't having any. He's made a couple of moves on us since you took over, but nothing worth looking at. He's kinda like the strange uncle you keep an eye on at Christmas when the kids are around, if you get my meaning."

When Max just stared at him, he sighed. "He's got a thing for the young stuff—you know, dancers, film stars, Internet porn stars, hookers. The younger the better. Drafts 'em outta school, starts 'em off in his clubs, and farms 'em out to his other endeavors. Picks 'em out himself."

"From photos, or does he interview them personally?"

"Hell, I don't know." He frowned slightly. "Why the interest?"

"Something my detective is working on."

"And we want to help out the cops?"

"When it comes to the torture and murder of young girls, I don't mind asking a few questions. It's just plain decency."

T-John shrugged, then said philosophically, "We step on his toes, he's gonna go for our balls."

"I don't let just anyone feel me up. How 'boutchu?"

Petitjohn grinned. "I'm mighty choosy. I could talk to a few people. What do you want to know?"

IT FELT LIKE the electrostatic shock you feel after scuffing your feet over a carpet. Except Charlotte was sitting in Babineau's car when the sudden zap made her jump.

Her whole system tingled, bringing the tiny hairs on her arms and at the back of her neck up in an eerie prickle. She'd felt gut instinct before and shivers of déjà vu, but nothing like this strange quiver of awareness from out of the blue.

Awareness of someone or something else.

She glanced around the service station lot. The driver of the battered pickup truck next to them was inside the building paying for his gas. Vehicles zipped by on Tchoupitoulas Street, heading through the Warehouse District toward City Central and the Quarter. Nothing to warrant the sudden breathlessness that had her on high alert.

She scented the air, almost expecting the whiff of ozone that preceded a thunderstorm. But this was different, from some deep, internal place she didn't recognize—yet abruptly could name.

Max called it a Glimmer, the extrasensory communication between those of his clan. Was that what this was? Was she sensing a shape-shifter close by? Why here and why now? She'd been in close contact with his clansmen and women many times without the slightest spark. But maybe it wasn't the circumstance. Maybe it was the individual.

Then she got a glimpse of a dark-clad figure across the street, tucking back into a doorway. For an instant, the eyes in that shadowed face gleamed hot and bright.

Was someone following her? If so, was it for protection or was it a threat?

The sensation suddenly disappeared, leaving her empty and shivery.

Her cell phone's vibration at her hip startled her. "Caissie," she answered.

"Good morning, Detective."

The low, sexy rumble of his voice melted the tension from her spine. "Hey. Look, I'm sorry about last night."

"That's all right. It doesn't matter."

Something in his tone had her frowning. Impatience, a curt bite, the same way he'd spoken to her the night before.

What the hell was up with that?

She drew a deep breath before her attitude got out of hand. She could be bitchy at times and wouldn't apologize for it, but it was unlike her to be one without reason.

"Maybe we can meet for lunch." She wanted to look into his eyes when they spoke. And suddenly she needed to be close when she asked him about her Shifter encounter.

Silence. Then a brisk, "I'm sorry. I can't."

"Oh." Her analytical mind started spinning, connecting his cool mood to his meeting with his clan. Had they discovered her loose-lipped handling of their secrets and given Max an ultimatum? Was that why she was being tailed? *Oh, bullshit.* She was just tired, that's all. "I can't make supper. I've got someone coming in to interview."

"That's fine. Will you be free by nine?"

"I should be."

"Can you stop by my office?"

"Sure. Do you need a ride home?"

"No. I've something we need to talk about."

Her heart skipped a beat.

"Can it wait until we get home? I'm really looking forward to curling up with you."

A pause. "No. Just come here first. I gotta go."

———————

THE MEETING WITH Marilyn Schoenbaum was brutal.

They'd met at several police functions. Marilyn was a tall, sturdy woman with hawkish features and unwavering blue eyes. She'd been an EMT dispatcher when she and Stan met. They'd married when she found herself pregnant, and she agreed to overlook his occasional transgressions to raise his family. If she knew he'd tried to make Cee Cee one of those side pieces, she never gave any indication of it. Now she greeted Cee Cee and Babineau at her front door.

Alain did the talking. Cee Cee had filled him in on her conversation with Schoenbaum, and he'd agreed with the Vice detective's request that they keep it low-key. His easy manner and pleasant smile went a long way toward calming Marilyn since Stan confessed that their daughter might be missing. Alain downplayed the seriousness, holding her hand, making it sound like they weren't really concerned but were covering the bases out of friendship for Stan.

While Babineau got the necessary information regarding friends, hangouts, and habits, Cee Cee was the observer. And she saw what she'd seen in hundreds of living rooms across the social scale: terror. Pure, raw, heartrending terror. The loss of a child. The thought of that child in danger and pain. The helplessness that came with waiting and not knowing. It didn't get much worse.

Unless you were that child.

Stan Schoenbaum was a loudmouth who believed

in unnecessary roughness on the job and who cheated on his wife in an offensively blatant manner. But the man sitting next to Marilyn was a husband and father broken by emotion and regret. His arm was about his wife in support while his other hand laced though hers. The poignant unity of those interlocked fingers said far more about their relationship than his selfish acts of adultery. This was why Marilyn Schoenbaum ignored the gossip. Because that grip was both strong and tender. That was love. And trust. As basic and powerful as it got.

She stared at those hands, at their plain gold rings, and she thought of Max. Of how the simple press of his palm, the gentle curl of his fingers about hers, could steady her world and bring everything into focus.

Was that why she felt so scared, so lost? Because Max suddenly felt out of reach?

"What do you think?" Babineau asked as they got into their police car and pulled away from the Schoenbaums' home.

"I don't want to think she's the latest vic, but I can't ignore the timing."

"I'm sure Manny Blu's connected. I'd love to bring him down."

"We have to get closer. That means working with Vice."

A growl of distaste. "They're not gonna let us have a piece unless we've got some pretty convincing circumstantial evidence to stick on him."

"Then let's find something."

HER PROFESSIONAL NAME was Cocoa. Her rap sheet identified her as Tonya Michaels, and listed her bad habits as ranging from uttering and publishing to solicitation. She'd done time for nickel-and-dime distribution. Alain Babineau had helped her out when an abusive pimp had beaten her boyfriend to death and left her with a broken jaw and too many bruises to count. He'd put the pimp away without bringing her into the mix. She had a four-year-old son she'd been terrified of losing. Babineau had gotten her into a program to kick the drugs and helped her set up a decent home for her boy with a maternal aunt. She'd told him if he ever needed anything, just ask.

Now he was asking. "Manny Blu."

He and Cee Cee met her at Daisy Dukes on Chartres, close to where she plied her trade, and sat in a booth by the kitchen, trying to look inconspicuous. But then, a six-foot purple-haired hooker wasn't that unusual in the Quarter.

She picked up a Cajun fry drenched in hot sauce. "That fat fuck? Whatchu want with him?"

"We want to know what you know, Tonya."

The flamboyant black woman froze up at Cee Cee's use of her real name. "Why? You lookin' for a book deal to retire on?"

"I'm looking for the animal who slaughtered three of your sisters of the streets, before he has the chance to make it number four. Could be someone you know."

Tonya drew her straw distractedly through her iced tea. "I knew JoJo."

"Marjorie Cole?"

"Yeah. Nice kid."

"How about these girls? Did you know them?" She set the photos of the other two victims down.

Cocoa took a look, then winced away. Then looked again. "Maybe. Lordy Lord. What did he do to them?"

"Terrible things you don't want to know about. Where do you know them from, Tonya?"

"I don't know their names. I seen 'em around."

"Around where, Cocoa?" Babineau coaxed, nudging the photos closer. "You don't want your little boy to have to ID you from one of these, do you?"

"That's harsh. That's just harsh." But moisture welled up in her heavily lined eyes. "I think I seen 'em at Manny's club. I can't be sure. They didn't look like that." She shuddered and pushed aside her food. "I only worked there a couple a weeks."

"Do you still have friends there we could talk to?"

She laughed. "They ain't gonna talk to no cop."

Cee Cee leaned forward and put her hand over the other woman's. "Could you get me inside, so it'd be between us girls?"

Cocoa laughed again. "You a tad old, ain'tcha, sugar?"

Cee Cee refused to let go of her hand. "Yeah, but I've got all the right equipment."

Cocoa gave her a scrutinizing once-over. "Could be you'd do okay. Got nice perky tits."

"I'm perky all over, and I can remember a drink order."

A low chuckle. "Who said anything about drinks, sug? Manny ain't hiring no waitresses."

A very bad feeling got hold of Cee Cee. "What's he hiring?"

A huge grin. "Dancers."

Ten

CEE CEE EXPECTED to see Max in his power suit, but he was dressed all in black—a long-sleeved tee shirt, jeans, and tennis shoes. He looked as sleek as a jaguar, and too sexy for her own good.

"Heya," he said.

"Hey yourself."

"You're early."

She gestured behind her. "I could go sit in the waiting room. I'll bet you've got a better selection of magazines than we do at work."

"Sorry, no *Soldier of Fortune* or *Handguns R Us* catalogs."

"Ha-ha. Have you been sitting here thinking up funny things to say?"

"That was pretty much the only one I came up with. Sorry I couldn't be more clever."

He was plenty clever. And sly, as well as amusing, when he wanted to be. Which of those was he being now, as he regarded her with a small smile? "What's on your mind, Savoie?"

"I've got some information for you. You asked me about Manny Blu, so I asked some questions."

"This is about my *case*?"

"Maybe it would be better if I just showed you. Here, put these on."

She stared at the stack of dark clothes and jogging shoes he pushed across the glossy desk top. "Is this a date or a B and E?"

His teeth flashed. "Can't it be both?"

Curiosity and excitement warred with objection. "Savoie, what the hell are you up to?"

"No questions. Don't ask for my help if you don't really want it. Now hurry. We don't have a lot of time. Pete's waiting to drive us." He stood and circled the desk to approach her.

"A chauffeur to take us to the scene of our crime?"

He grinned again. "Why not?"

She toed off her heels, grumbling, "I must be crazy to go along with this."

"Then don't," was his mild response. "I'm not forcing you."

She scrambled to change her clothing. He was maddening, watching her with that half smile, his eyes mocking and smoldering. Getting her heart knocking with anticipation and, yes, lust. This was the Max Savoie she'd fallen for. Cagy, clever, taunting, provoking her into doing what she knew she shouldn't. And she couldn't hurry after him fast enough.

Max lounged in the comfortable backseat of the town car, as relaxed as she was edgy.

"Where are we going?"

"You'll see." He slid a glance at her from the long slant of his eyes, a look that was daring and playful and hot as hell.

She was about to press the issue when his hand settled over hers on the seat between them. His fingers threaded through hers and curled into her palm, possessive and protective. And as she remembered the Schoenbaums' linked hands, she almost lost it right there.

"What's wrong, Charlotte?"

The quiet question made her jump. "Nothing. I don't know."

"Have I done something? Tell me."

She couldn't look at him, twisting with misery. "I don't know what's wrong. I'm all balled up inside. I can't think. I feel off balance somehow."

"Is it this case?"

"Maybe. No. Not really." Ridiculous tears burned in her eyes. "I thought for a minute that you asked me to your office for The Talk."

"What talk?"

"About why dogs and cops shouldn't live together."

His blow-your-hair-back laugh burst out before he could catch it, before he realized she was serious. His other hand scooped under her chin, turning her face toward him. His voice was exquisitely tender. "Why would I want to do that, Charlotte? What possible reason would I have?"

She regarded him somberly. "A lot of them, both two- and four-legged."

A small, mystified smile. "But you're the reason my heart beats."

And she forgot everything she'd planned to say to him as emotion pooled deep and hot.

Max's fingertips brushed over her cheek. "When this case is over, we'll go away somewhere."

She eyed him suspiciously. "What do you mean?"

"You and me, on a vacation."

"A vacation?"

He almost laughed at her tone. As if leaving her city unguarded for even a week was unconscionable. "Yes. I'm sure you've never taken one. Where do you want to go? Anywhere you want."

"The beach." Her mind began to work, imagining it. Warming to the idea of lying on hot sand with her hot lover, warm seawater splashing over her toes. Nothing but the sound of waves and wind and gulls. "We could go to one of those private resorts, wear next to nothing, rub lotion on each other, and have big fruity drinks the size of goldfish bowls. You'd like Sex on the Beach."

"I like sex anywhere, as long as it's with you."

She grinned. "It's a drink."

The car stopped, and he opened the car door and got out. "I think I'll like the beach. You pick the place, I'll make the reservations."

He told the driver, "Wait for us discreetly."

Cee Cee glanced up and down the tree-lined street. The neighborhood was old money, big houses, high security. She followed Max as he strolled casually down the uneven stone walk, sticking to the deepest shadows. Then he slipped down a narrow lane behind a row of well-fortified homes.

She couldn't stand it anymore. "What are we doing here?"

"Paying a courtesy call before you go for a warrant."

"On who?"

"Carmen Blutafino."

She jerked to a stop, gripping his elbow. "You're going to break into his house? And you expect me to go with you?"

"And you didn't think I could plan a date we could both enjoy. Doesn't that sound like fun?"

"It sounds like forced entry for unlawful purposes."

"Only if we get caught. Here we are. Formidable, isn't it?"

A high iron fence made a bristling defense between where they stood and the large pre–Civil War stone house with its moody balconies and most likely haunted past. Despite herself, Cee Cee was sweeping the perimeter with a careful gaze.

"He's got cameras and motion detectors. How do you expect—"

The lights went out for a few blocks, plunging them into darkness. She could see the flash of Max's grin.

"Jimmy had some very talented and influential friends. One has a very nice job with the power and electric company. I suggest we make use of our time. Up you go."

He gripped her waist, hoisting her high enough to catch one of the branches of the giant live oak that draped across the fence boundary.

"Can you stand up on my shoulders? Hey, you're pretty good at this." He held her steady while she got to her feet. "Were you ever a cheerleader? I'd have quite an eyeful now if you were wearing one of those short little skirts."

"Horn dog," she hissed, using the top of his head as a step to boost herself up into the tree. Crouching on the branch, she put down her hand. "Let me help you—"

Suddenly the limb bounced as he landed right beside her. "Thanks. I got it."

"Now that we're up here playing Tarzan and Jane, you want to tell me what we're after?"

"Ooh, now you've got me distracted by thoughts of you in leopard skin. Keep your mind on the business at hand, Detective, and your hands to yourself." He swung around her and began to climb.

She sighed, aggravated and intrigued. And having fun. She started after him. "If you were Tarzan, I'd be looking up your loincloth."

"And enjoying it, you naughty girl."

The centuries-old oak covered the entire side yard, topping the three-storied house by a good fifteen feet. Max moved with the confidence of an aerialist to the end of one of the gnarled branches, then had Cee Cee's heart in her throat as he leaped across a seemingly impossible distance to grip the roof's overhang with one hand, then twisted to land effortlessly on one of the upper galleries. Then he beckoned.

She eyed the six-foot gap from tree to porch and the distance to the ground below. And shook her head, whispering, "No fucking way."

Max laughed at her, his hands reaching out. "Jump. I'll catch you," he whispered back.

She looked down again. Way, way down. She swallowed hard. "What if you miss?"

"I'll apologize." He beckoned again. "Come on. Jump. Don't be such a girl."

She growled and took a huge breath, then she jumped.

Time seemed to hold her aloft as she stretched her hands out to Max. His were so close, ready for her.

Then gravity kicked in, and she started to drop like a brick.

The air squeezed from her lungs as his arm cinched around her, scooping her up and tossing her as if she was weightless. Her feet touched down next to him, and her knees gave way.

Her arms locked around him, hanging on as if still in mid fall. Nothing had ever felt better than his hard, lean body.

"Safe and sound," he said smugly.

"That was easy," she wheezed, pushing away before she went all soft on him. "Okay, what the hell are we doing here? Come clean before I cross that threshold into criminal activity."

"Carmen doesn't trust anyone, so he keeps all his important papers here under lock and key. He keeps a file on everyone he's ever interviewed, complete with pictures. Including the girls who work in his clubs."

"He's got pictures?" Oh, this was too good to be true.

"Shall we take a peek and see if we recognize anyone?"

"Oh, baby, you know how to plan a date."

"You can thank me properly when we get home."

He drew out two pairs of thin surgical gloves. "I remembered protection."

"What a guy."

He disabled the security items on the door with ease, then waved her inside. "Jimmy brought a famous second-story man down from the East Coast to teach me how to gain illegal access to just about any place, for times when skill is more expedient than brute force."

"Education is a wonderful thing."

By the narrow beam of Max's penlight, they started tossing Carmen Blutafino's office—and struck the jackpot when Max finessed the locked drawer of his desk.

Cee Cee pushed him aside in her eagerness and raced through the alphabet. Cole, Marjorie. Her throat tightened. She had no names for the other two, so she hurried through the hundreds of youthful faces, trying to mentally match them to the morgue Jane Does.

Patsy Gleason.

Shawnee Potts.

"Is that them?" Max asked softly, peering over her shoulder. She nodded. "Take them and let's go."

"I can't take them, Max."

"Why not?"

"Unlawful search and seizure. They could never be used as evidence."

"Get a warrant and come back."

"On what grounds? That we saw their files while we were ransacking his house? I have to do this the right way, Max."

A way that felt almost impossible as she slipped the folders back into place.

"At least you have the names."

"Which is more than I had this morning. Let's get out of here." She moved away from the desk, feeling as if she was abandoning the pleading faces of those four girls in the drawer. Because she'd seen Kelly Schoenbaum's name in there, too.

Then the lights came on, and with them the wail of the alarms.

Max hustled her out onto the balcony. "No time for delicacy, Detective." He picked her up and threw her.

Arms and legs pinwheeling, she found herself floundering in the leafy branches. She grabbed on and got her balance before turning back to Max, who'd made no move to follow.

"Go on. Don't wait for me," he said.

"Max!"

"Have Pete take you back to your car. I'll tidy up here. Go on, Charlotte—go!"

Lights were coming on in the lower rooms now.

Cursing, she shinnied down the tree and sprinted through the shadows.

Max smiled to himself, then quickly finished up in the room. He relocked the French doors from the inside, then slipped out into the hall just as he heard rapid footsteps rounding the landing below. Putting on his wraparound sunglasses, he ducked into the room opposite where a small boy was sitting up in bed, rubbing the sleep away.

Max crossed the room in quick strides, putting a finger to his lips with a quiet, "Shhh. Sorry to wake you."

Before the child could blink Max was out the window, dropping to the flowerbeds below. And by the time Lena Blutafino rushed to her son's side, he was gone.

CEE CEE DIDN'T waste any time worrying about Max. He'd managed to evade criminal charges his entire life, and she didn't doubt he'd slip these as well.

She also didn't allow her conscience time for browbeating. Instead, she chafed at the restrictions of a job that kept her from doing it as justice demanded.

What was the chance that those files would still be there if she got a warrant? The second Manny Blu was alerted to a B and E, he'd hide every sliver of potentially damning evidence in a new location. But what could she do? She knew the rules, the reason and necessity for them.

Yet, she wondered bitterly, what rules had applied when three girls, possibly four, were being cruelly tortured?

It was late by the time Pete pulled up beside her car. There were no lights on in the building, so apparently Max wasn't back yet.

"I'll wait for him, Miss Charlotte," Pete told her as he held open the door. "You go ahead and leave."

Maybe some precedent for due cause would come to her weary mind on the drive out. If not, at least she'd have Max to work out her frustrations on.

She was fishing her keys out of her pocket when she noticed a manila envelope wedged under her wiper blade. Pete was waiting to make sure she was safely away, and there was no sign of anyone else.

She unlocked her door and retrieved the envelope

before sitting behind the wheel, where she took a minute to see what someone had left her.

And stared at the contents.

Three files. Three photos. And three job applications with notations written in Carmen Blutafino's hand.

Eleven

BYRON ATCLIFF SAT at his kitchen table in a silk paisley dressing gown and leather slippers, his hair sticking up at odd angles. But being pulled from his bed at three in the morning didn't lessen his authoritative manner as he glared at his two detectives.

"Why not just request a warrant?"

"We have the proof we need right here."

He gave a rather jaundiced glance at the files Cee Cee held. "Obtained how, did you say, Detective?"

"Someone left them on my car. No note. No prints."

"And you were where at the time?"

"I'd left my car to go grab something to eat."

"And you were with?"

"Max. We were discussing vacation plans. For when the case is concluded, of course."

Atcliff made an assenting noise. Almost like a growl. "You seem to have some kind of guardian angel of important evidence watching over you, Caissie, dropping off just what you need to get you what you want."

Her jaw tightened. A while ago, information on Benjamin Spratt had similarly appeared just in time to keep Max from going down as their prime suspect. "Is that a bad thing, sir?"

"Not as long as your hands are clean."

"Yes, sir."

He sighed wearily as he stared at the files. "So, you discovered this manna from Heaven and did what, Detective?"

"I brought Detective Babineau up to speed, and we had another conversation with Miss Michaels, whom we'd interviewed earlier this evening. She ID'd the photos and placed the girls in Blutafino's employment. We went from there to talk to Detective Schoenbaum of Vice, and checked in at the lab to see if there were any prints on the evidence."

"Seems like you talked to everyone but me first."

She never blinked. "We didn't see the need to wake you until we had a compelling package put together."

"And that would be what?"

"We want to go undercover in cooperation with Vice in the club where all three vics were working. We can be set up by tomorrow night. I have an interview with Blutafino at five-thirty. If he likes me, we're in."

"And what are you applying for, Detective?"

"An entertainment position, sir."

"I wasn't aware you could sing, Detective Caissie."

"I don't, sir, but I've been told by an expert in the field that for an old gal, I've got a decent rack."

"We're talking performance art, I take it?"

"Yes, sir."

"Is this decent rack going to end up in the news, embarrassing the department?"

"Not even my noble journalistic pals will be able to recognize me, sir." She placed her palms on the table-top and leaned in, her eyes hungry and intense. "Let us do this. It's a chance to get close to Blutafino, and possibly get to the latest vic before she becomes the next statistic."

He looked to Babineau. "What about you? Are you going into show business, too?"

"No, sir. Can't dance and no rack to speak of. I'll provide backup position as talent management and boyfriend."

"Wife and significant other have no problems with this?"

"None, sir."

Neither detective betrayed any discomfort under Atcliff's scrutiny. Finally, he sat back in his chair. "Make it happen, Detectives. Keep me updated. And, Caissie, I don't want any video showing up at future police functions."

"Soul of discretion, sir."

"Good night, sir. Sorry to have disturbed you."

On the front walk, Babineau gave her a look. "I wasn't aware you knew your way around a stripper pole."

"I have all afternoon to learn under Cocoa's excellent and expensive tutelage."

They climbed into her car, more thoughtful now that they'd gotten the go-ahead and the initial surge of adrenaline eased.

"Savoie going to be all right with this?" *With us*, was what he didn't say out loud.

"Sure."

"You haven't told him?"

"That you and I are going to be incommunicado for several weeks, sharing a sleazy hotel room pretending to be lovers, while I spend my nights prancing around almost naked for strangers? I think that's more info than he needs to have. How's Tina going to handle it?"

"She'll tell me to be careful and kiss me good-bye." And worry every second, he didn't have to add.

How *they* were going to handle it was the question neither of them asked.

"I'll drop you off, get my hooker gear together, and be back for you at seven."

Babineau nodded. That would give him time to grab some sleep and smooth things over with his wife.

Instead of using that time to do the same, Cee Cee headed to her apartment. Instead of enjoying the sweaty farewell sex her body yearned for, she took a long shower. Instead of closing her gritty eyes, she pumped coffee and pillaged her closet for props.

And when she absolutely had to, she reached for her phone.

"Savoie." His tone leaped at her, sharp edged and hard.

"Hey. Hope I didn't wake you."

"I wasn't sleeping."

Of course he wasn't. He was pacing, wondering where the hell she was.

"I came into some rather fortuitous evidence. The chief has cleared me to go undercover. I'll be out of touch for a while. Sorry I couldn't have given you more notice, but we've been scrambling all night to put things together."

"Undercover? Are you going after Carmen?"

"I can't give you any details. Don't try to get in touch with me; I'll call you when I can."

A pause. "I don't get to say good-bye to you?"

"We're saying it."

"Face-to-face."

"No time, sorry. Don't worry. I'll be careful."

Silence as he took in what she was trying shove past him in a rush. "I want to see you."

"I can't make it happen."

When he finally spoke, his words were a low rumble. "So, no kiss for luck? No packing your lunch or waving good-bye at the door?"

"Not this trip. Gotta go."

Quietly: "Shall I make reservations?"

Please don't make this so damned hard. "Not yet."

"Charlotte? I love you."

"Me, too." A pause. "I'll call you." She cut the connection before her resolve shattered.

MAX PLANNED TO concentrate on business. He thought that without anyone to come home to, he could direct all his energy to the office by day and to his clan by night. Time would go by quickly, and before he knew it, she'd be back.

He hadn't anticipated the way missing her would suck the very spirit out of him.

He found himself listening for the sound of her car, jumping at every ring of his phone. But she didn't call. It had only been a little over a week. Not that long, he told himself. He'd given her the damned evidence, after all. Had he expected her to do nothing with it?

Not his Charlotte. She was a juggernaut, making plans and plowing forward full steam ahead, with no time for a kiss good-bye. And apparently no time to miss him enough to pick up the phone.

Why didn't she call?

He'd gotten spoiled. Having her in his life filled every corner with unimagined delight. The sound of her voice, her laugh, her sighs. Listening to her grumble about her day, tease him for his sheltered ignorance, provoke him with sultry innuendo. The simple joy of watching her get ready to go to work, or undress to join him in bed. The feel of her there, beneath him all hot and infinitely greedy, next to him in the night, warm and soul-satisfying. The touch of her hand on his face.

Loneliness howled through him.

It was nine-thirty Saturday morning, and he had absolutely no idea how he was going to fill the hours of the day. His cell phone was in his hand before he consciously considered what he was doing.

Don't try to get in touch with me.

An objecting growl rumbled through him on a fierce spike of emotion. The need to have her close, under his care, in his control, threatened to consume him. She was his mate, his love, his . . . what? His possession? The instinct was so strong, he shivered with it. His to have and protect.

He was so startled when the phone rang, he almost dropped it. His hands were shaking when he flipped it open. His voice broke. "Charlotte?"

"It's Tina Babineau. I'm sorry. Is this a bad time?"

He hauled back hard on his chaotic feelings. "No, it's fine. I was expecting a call. It's good to hear from you."

"Oscar was wondering if you'd mind some company. It's been so quiet here with Alain gone, we've been jumping at shadows."

"Would you like me to send a car over for you?"

A pause and a nervous laugh. "No, that's not necessary. What time would be convenient?"

"C'mon over. I'll have Helen fix us some lunch." He was smiling for the first time in days when he sauntered into the kitchen to say, "We're having company."

TINA BABINEAU WAS soft and shy and sweet. She dressed in tender shades of peach and cream, always understated, almost unnoticeable. Invisible. The same way Max had been taught. Coincidence? he wondered as the two of them sat on the back porch steps, watching Giles and Oscar assemble a foam glider.

Lunch had been unexpectedly easy. Everything about Tina was easy and quiet. He found himself relaxed and content in her company, something he hadn't been in days. He enjoyed listening to Tina talk about her family, about Oscar, about her hopes and plans for them. Normal things so outside his experience, she might as well have been discussing life on another planet. And in the pictures she built, he saw the things he'd always wanted. Family. A place to belong. To be accepted. Things he longed to share with Charlotte.

"Thanks for letting us barge in like this. Oscar's been after me all week. He was sure you wouldn't mind."

Max smiled. "He was right. You're always welcome."

"Oscar and I both feel safe with you. Why is that?" she asked softly, as if to herself.

"Because I'm like you."

He let her mull that over while he leaned back on

his elbows and stretched his long legs out in front of him. He watched Oscar race across the grassy yard after the glider Giles launched for him.

"You must be so proud of him. I'd give anything to have a son like that."

"I'm afraid for him, Max." When he glanced at her, Tina rushed on. "I'm afraid someone else might come to take him away from me."

"I won't let that happen." He said that with such certainty, belief bloomed in her gaze. "I'll protect him."

"From what? You know, don't you? You know why they picked him, why they took him." Her mouth trembled as she turned to her son. "I asked Alain, but he says he doesn't know. Why is he lying to me?" She clutched his hand, startling him. "I don't understand. He treats me like I'm something fragile, made of glass. And lately . . ." Her voice trailed off.

"Why are you afraid to be yourself around him? Because he'll know you're different? And why do you push pills into Ozzy until he's dull and complaisant, when you know he's so much more? Are you afraid your husband doesn't love you enough to handle the truth?"

She looked away, but he caught the wildness and fright in her expression. "He'd leave us, Max. He'd run if he knew—"

"That there's something inside you that you've struggled to hide from all your life? Feelings and instincts so strong, they wake you up at night and have you prowling, restless and panting, without knowing why? Sensing that you're more than those around you?

Different, stronger, alien, dangerous." He paused, then added the kicker. "Not human."

She turned back to him, her eyes huge and bright.

"You're not crazy, Tina. And neither is Oscar."

"Then what are we?"

He smiled, a slow display of white teeth. "You're something else. Like me."

Twelve

TINA BABINEAU'S EYES glazed with panic. "What do you mean, *something else?*"

Max turned on the steps to face her, holding her hands firmly. "Don't be afraid. You're not alone. We're special. Blessed." That's what his mother had always told him to take the fear from his heart. "We look like them, and we're taught to blend in with them. But we're not human, Tina."

"What are we?" she whispered.

"Are you ready to see?"

She swallowed and gripped his hands as hard as she could, then nodded.

And slowly he let his hands change.

"Don't be afraid," he said gently as she stared at the lengthening claws, at the long distorted fingers, at the thick thatch of black hair. When she looked up in alarm and disbelief, he let his eyes glow golden. And he mentally reached out to her with that Glimmer of sensation that their kind shared between them.

With a moan, she shut her eyes; a harsh tremor shook her body. Then she cried, "Oh, thank God. I thought it was madness. I thought I'd passed something terrible on to my son."

"You've given him a gift. A valuable gift we have to protect. We're called Shifters, Tina."

"Like . . . shape-shifters?" Her hesitant question earned his smile and nod. "Does Cee Cee know?"

"Yes."

She blinked, astounded. "And Alain?" Her voice quavered.

"Yes. When he went into the bayou after us, he saw me change to kill those who were after Oscar. He knows that you and Oscar are my kind."

She slowly processed that. "So that's why he's been so distant," she murmured. Then her gaze flashed up. "And Oscar? What does he know?"

"He knows that I accept him for what he is, and that he can go to Charlotte for anything."

His hands returned to their usual form. Curious, she lifted them to examine his fingers and palms. Her brow furrowed, perplexed.

"But I don't turn into . . . into an animal."

"Our females don't change." That wasn't quite true, but he saw no need to tell her that. "But they can recognize their own, as you did me when we first met."

"I felt something. I didn't know what it was." She dropped his hands to rub her temples, as if trying to force the information to be absorbed. "And those men— if they *were* men—what did they want with Ozzy?"

"I think they want to catch us, to experiment on us and breed us. Then, if they decide we're a threat, kill us."

"Who *are* they?"

He'd been asking himself that question all his life.

His mother had hinted at the mysterious, dangerous *they* to fill a young child's mind with fear, to get him to suppress his talents, to shy from strangers, to withdraw behind a wall of isolation so no one could single him out as different. That awful, faceless, nameless threat had followed him as he grew up, making him cling to the rescue Jimmy Legere offered with a grateful, single-minded relief. Jimmy, who was indeed more exploiter than savior, just as Karen Crawford had claimed.

And he'd done terrible things for Jimmy Legere out of that deep, shivery well of gratitude, believing his mentor was keeping him safe from a far greater danger. And maybe he had been.

"They're called the Chosen," Max began.

And while they watched Oscar's innocent play, Max told her all he'd learned from his father and from Jacques LaRoche.

It was hard to tell how much was folklore and how much was fact. His father had been a notorious liar who slanted the truth to fit his purpose. LaRoche's recall was spotty at best, his memory damaged and broken. But they both warned of a controlling elite who suppressed their kind into servitude, into a brutish warrior caste used politically and economically as weapons.

The Chosen's rule was centuries old, using telepathic and empathic powers to subjugate through fear and pain. Shifters were their property, inferiors bred and trained selectively for their genetic traits. The finest lines were valued and protected, the weak and unstable discarded, often killed.

To belong to a house boasting pure bloodlines ensured favor and prestige to that entire family, and that favor was prized, stirring fierce, murderous rivalries and shrewd alliances. The Alpha male of a line was akin to royalty, a breeding-age female a treasured bargaining tool.

Dangerous, guided by instinct, and physically powerful, Shifters adhered to a pack mentality, Max told her. Challenging one another for dominance, the strong and cunning ruled within their clans, but the Chosen yoked them through mental intimidation. Each Shifter child was mentally imprinted at birth to be submissive to their rule. Once Registered, there was no hope of choice or free will. Breeding "in the wild" was forbidden. And mating in their basic forms, which was the only way to transfer their pure genetic strengths, was strictly regulated so that the breed would be improved, and the offspring were trained and tested for abilities.

"Like livestock," Tina whispered with a chill of horror.

"Yes. Bred and sold as a commodity."

"To do what?" she asked softly.

"What we do best: kill. As bodyguards. As assassins. As mercenaries."

"For whom?"

"Whoever can afford us."

Tina jerked to her feet and began to pace, her arms wrapped tight about her trembling frame. Her gaze locked upon her son. "Is that what you are? Did Jimmy Legere own you?"

"Yes. And no. He knew what I was when he bought me from my father. He knew more about them than I did, and kept me from discovering the truth so he could control me. But he also hid me, kept me safe from my own kind."

"Why?"

"Because of who and what I am. I am the product of two pure lines. I'm not imprinted. I've never been trained or judged, and my mind is my own. The Chosen can't find me; they can't control me. I'm a danger and a threat to them because of that, because of what I represent. But I'm valuable because of who my parents were." A pause, long enough to warn her. "And so is Oscar."

She froze, tense in her denial. "How could you know that?"

"Because Oscar and I share the same father."

He watched it sink in, saw the shock dull her eyes and quiet her breathing. Then she shook it off. "No! That's not possible. I don't believe you. Why are you doing this? Why are you making all this up?"

"Who is Oscar's father? Tell me."

Just then, the boy came racing up to the porch, shouting, "Did you see? Mama, Max, were you watching?"

With a tremulous smile, Tina turned to her son. "I'm sorry, honey. I missed it. Max and I were talking. What did you do?"

His features fell. "I got the glider to do five loops and come back to me. Giles said that's something nobody has ever, ever done before. Do you think that's true?"

Max put a hand on his shoulder. "If Giles said so, I'm sure it is. Oz?"

The eager face tipped up toward his. "Yeah, Max?"

"Your mama needs a hug."

A quick smile. "Sure." But when he stepped toward her Max caught him, holding him away. Oscar glanced up in confusion.

"From here."

He went stiff with understanding. "Max, are you sure?"

"Yes. Go ahead."

Anxiously, the boy looked to his mother, seeing no encouragement in her expression, but no resistance, either. He took a shaky breath and, after a moment, sent a tentative Glimmer her way.

Tina gasped. When she didn't move, Oscar burrowed back into Max for reassurance. Max gave him a slight squeeze.

"It's okay, Oz. Why don't you try that trick with the glider again. We'll be watching this time."

And as Tina looked between the two of them, seeing similarities she wanted to deny, the boy went down the stairs, the bounce gone from his steps. Leaving Max to curse himself for stripping away that spontaneous innocence.

Shaken, Tina confronted Max. "Why did they come after him if they could have you?"

"Because I was just a rumor, and he was a certainty."

"But now that they know about you, he's not in danger anymore. Is he?"

"I'm sorry, Tina."

Her eyes grew wild and angry. "If you're . . . you're his brother, like you say you are, you'd give yourself up to save him. Wouldn't you?"

"Yes. If I could."

Then do it. He could see the demand in her expression, hear it in her panicked breathing.

"Tina, we bond only once, and for the life of our mate. Charlotte is my mate. She can't have children, so my line stops with me. I can't offer them what Oscar does."

She was silent for a moment. When she spoke, her voice sounded thoughtful. "Not necessarily. If Cee Cee were to die, you could take another mate and have children of your own."

Max recoiled, and his tone cracked with a hard finality. "But I wouldn't. Not ever."

"Are you guys watching?"

Oscar's shout wedged between their tension, making them both step back.

"We're watching, honey. Go ahead," Tina said.

As the glider looped and soared, Max wondered if he'd made a mistake. Had he just done the unforgivable in trusting Tina Babineau with the truth?

"He's all I have, Max," she said quietly.

"And I'll protect him and you. I swear."

"Like you did before?"

He flinched. "Now that you and your husband know what's at stake, we can work together."

She said nothing.

"I want you and Ozzy to stay here with me until they get back. The two of you shouldn't be alone. And this summer, I want to set up lessons for him so he'll have the skills he'll need as he grows older. Meanwhile, I'll make arrangements to see that he's protected around the clock. They won't get to him again, I promise you. My life on it."

Her gaze rose to his, holding him accountable as she said, "We'll need to pick up some things."

WITH OSCAR TUCKED into bed and Tina putting away her clothes in the adjoining room, Max roamed the second-floor gallery.

Having Oscar in the house stirred unimaginable joy in him. His family. His kin. He'd felt loyalty and attachment to Jimmy, but nothing like this. Even his feelings for Charlotte, though probably more powerful and intense, weren't as deeply imbedded as those for this boy—his *brother*. Instinct urged him to protect Oscar with every shred of his being; there was nothing he wouldn't sacrifice.

He drew up, suddenly thinking of Tina's words. Then he began to pace with greater agitation.

Why hadn't Charlotte called him? Was she afraid he'd come charging into the middle of her investigation like some lovesick fool and endanger her efforts? He wasn't that stupid, that out of control.

He wasn't.

He just needed to hear her voice. Having another man's family under his roof wasn't the same as having the woman he loved in his arms.

He turned and abruptly found himself face-to-face with Tina Babineau. She was pale as moonlight with her fair skin and white nightgown. He could sense her turmoil and need to be comforted, but she wasn't his female. In a loose interpretation that would drive Alain Babineau over the edge, she was his stepmother. That made him smile, and hers was a faint echo in return.

Tina walked to the rail and leaned her elbows upon it. Max joined her there, close but keeping a wary distance.

"I never knew who Oscar's father was," she began quietly. "When I was fifteen, I did something foolish. I was looking for adventure; I left the protection of my adopted family and lost a week of my life that I can't remember. When I was found, I had a beautiful string of pearls around my neck, like the ones you gave to Cee Cee. And I was pregnant with Oscar."

Max went cold. Apparently pearls were his father's thank-you gift of choice.

"I never knew my real family," she continued, "And the mother and father who raised me are gone now. I feel like I'm losing everything I love all over again."

He laid his cheek on the top of her head, promising, "You won't. Alain loves you and Oscar too much to let you go."

"Knowing what we are? How could he, Max? How could he possibly?"

"Mama?"

They turned at the sound of Ozzy's sleepy voice.

Max freed one arm to include him, drawing them close. "I'll keep you safe, both of you."

He enveloped them with a soft, warm Glimmer, smiling as Oscar returned it like a hard squeeze. He was surprised and heartened when Tina's slipped around them both, the hesitant whisper of a gentle breeze.

A fierce obligation to them filled him. A mother like his had been. A child like he had been. His family.

And there was nothing he wouldn't do for them. Starting tonight.

Thirteen

CEE CEE ROLLED over, pulling the covers over her head, hoping to shut out the lovey-dovey sounds of Babineau's nightly call to his wife.

She was beat. Her feet throbbed all the way up to her shoulders. Even a long, scalding shower hadn't shed the ick factor from all those leering eyeballs. Her mood was raw, her body achy, and listening to kissy-kissy stuff was just about grounds for homicide. Especially when she suspected that the sentiments weren't sincere.

Alain was in over his head, drowning in avoidance. He might pretend all was well on the home front, but she could see the strain in his expression. And since it was her fault, she stayed carefully neutral.

She breathed a sigh of relief when he finally said good-bye and went into their tiny bathroom. Geez, it was like rooming with a teenage girl. All the misery. All the drama. None of the gratification. She should know; she felt the same way.

She rolled restlessly onto her back and stared at the ceiling, frustration gnawing through her. With Max. With her partner. With the case. With her lack of any life. She was grouchy, snappish, felt bloated in the skimpy outfits she shimmied in nightly, and she wanted chocolate. *Lots* of chocolate.

They'd found out nothing beyond the circumstantial. All the girls had danced and turned tricks for Manny Blu, starting at this club. But they'd yet to single out any suspects they liked from the customers. Manny himself kept his distance. He did a nightly walk-through to check the take and to feel up some of the younger talent. Either he wasn't their man or he was out of the market until the next phase of the moon. Vice was all over him, but he never varied from his routine, and there was no room in his schedule for the ritualistic torture and murder of his employees.

The girls grew nervous when the subject came up. They either knew nothing or were too afraid. They pretended nothing was wrong, as if acting that way would make it so.

If she and Babineau didn't come up with something substantial soon, they were going to get shut down.

And where would that leave Kelly Schoenbaum?

Thoughts of her colleague's young daughter haunted her sleep. She'd wake drenched and quaking from nightmares Babineau never mentioned to her. Nightmares in which she was that helpless, terrified victim, where even though she begged for him, Max never came to her rescue.

Why hadn't she called him?

Solid relationships were the exception in her profession. The danger, the hours, the stress, the temptations, and especially the worry, wore away the strongest foundations until they crumbled. Her own parents were a fine example of failure.

She was looking at Max Savoie for the long haul. That was a ride very few of her peers rode all the way, and they didn't have the obstacle that she and Max had between them.

Watching Babineau struggle shook her deeply. His love for his small family was almost deifying. To see it fracturing now made her wonder why she was so accepting. When she started considering how Max wasn't driven by the human code of conscience or conduct, that opened the door to all sorts of unpleasant worries. Especially when she kept remembering his speaking of killing her coworkers.

It's what I am.

Was she completely blinded by her lust and love? Too blind to see the truth? That Max had never changed from being what he was when he stood behind Legere, that he still ran the biggest criminal organization in the South behind his sweet promises to her that he'd reformed?

No. She wouldn't believe it. The insinuations of headline-hungry sensationalists like Karen Crawford were nothing over the word of the man who gave her life meaning. The man who would do anything to keep her.

Including hide his objectionable agenda?

That damned envelope of evidence. Illegally procured, provided without a trace. Like before. An unexpected gift presenting her with exactly what she needed to get the job done. She'd taken it that first time, smothering her misgivings, because it not only gave her what she wanted, it also gave her a clear path to loving Max Savoie by absolving him of guilt. And she jumped at it.

But that didn't change the fact that she'd covered up crimes he *had* committed.

Would you break your laws for me?

When she'd said yes, she'd given up any control she might have had over their relationship. And with her, it was all about control: of her situations, of her choices, of her emotions. All that changed the moment she'd let Max into her heart. There was no more black and white, right and wrong. And the loss of those rigid certainties upset the sturdy blocks her life was built upon.

He knew she loved him. He knew she would surrender her honor, her very life to protect him. He had her living out of his house, out of his pocket, parading before the media at his side. Though her pearl chain was very attractive, she feared she was becoming the attack dog on his porch, just as he had been for Jimmy Legere. And it was chafing.

She rubbed at the scars on her shoulder, proof that there was nothing natural about what was between them. Their union was altering her physically and mentally, making her into something not quite human.

He was swallowing her whole, consuming her heart, her thoughts, her physiology, for fuck's sake! She'd just wanted to be his lover—not the Bride of freaking Frankenstein.

And yet here she was, bound heart and soul, and considering the huge step from sharing drawer space to sharing forever.

Max had literally brought her back to life. She would be dead if he hadn't infused her with whatever weird abilities she'd received with his savage bite. When they'd battled the pack of Trackers to rescue Oscar Babineau, one of them had literally smashed her spine and internal organs beyond surgical repair. Yet they had repaired themselves.

And through the power of his devotion, he'd mended her wounded spirit.

Now she was scared to death that she was losing her identity to him, because she just couldn't help herself. She couldn't *not* fall in love with him.

So she didn't call, although she thirsted for the sound of his voice. She stayed away, but that didn't lessen her hunger for him, even if only in dreams.

Dammit, Max, what am I going to do about you?

She could almost hear his voice whispering through her subconscious.

Love me. Be with me.

A slow sensation of warmth began at her feet, so subtle and soothing, she hardly noticed it at first. By the time it reached her knees, they were moving helplessly between her sheets. By the time it scorched along her thighs to pool like lava between them, she was trembling and breathless. Her body bowed as the heated intensity gathered, quickening until an earthquake of pleasure radiated from her molten epicenter. She moaned his name, thrashing in need. "*Max.*"

But he wasn't there.

And he hadn't been invited to manipulate her psyche, any more than he'd been asked to tamper with her cases.

Her eyes flashed open, wild with upset and frustration, and she gave him a massive psychic shove. "Back the fuck off!"

Inside the bathroom, the shower stopped.

"Did you say something?" Babineau called through the closed door.

"I said make sure you turn the lights off."

She collapsed in the cold, sweaty sheets, trembling in the dark.

MAX SNAPPED BACK in his chair, reeling from what felt like the smack of a shovel against the side of his head. For a moment he didn't know where he was.

"Max?"

He blinked his eyes open, coming back with a jolt, to see Jacques LaRoche regarding him curiously. "What?"

"Your nose is bleeding."

He lifted his hand to his nose, and it came away red. *His woman packed a punch!*

He'd been someplace between a daydream and a doze when he heard her, clear as the clinking of nearby glasses on a waitress's tray.

Dammit, Max, what am I going to do about you?

He let his spirit reach for her and was startled by the unhappiness and despair rolling from her into him. *Oh,* sha. *Don't hurt on my account.*

Drawn closer by the power of her emotions, he could see her through the static distortions. Not the way he'd view her if she were sitting across the table from him, but the impression of her, her inner patterns, her signature Glimmer and unique scent.

His passions shuddered. He could almost feel her. The sleek curves, the taut skin. Could hear her quickening respirations as she grew more and more aware of him and began to respond to his presence.

Then that defensive slap that knocked him on his empathic ass as if he were trespassing.

And then he picked up other things. The scent of a man's fresh scrubbed skin, and the sound of Alain Babineau's voice.

She was in bed, under the covers, and he was coming out of the shower.

It's just the job, his intellect reminded him.

She's my mate—mine alone! his instinct roared.

"So, we're agreed then?"

Max blinked, pulling his thoughts together, but it was like scooping up sand into a single pile—everything kept trickling away.

Focus. What had they been talking about?

He looked at Jacques, a mass of muscle and brute force, the epitome of what they'd been bred to be. Powerful, fierce, linear, and loyal.

Max trusted maybe three individuals: Charlotte, Giles St. Clair, and Jacques LaRoche. Charlotte was his link to his dreams, Giles to his past, and Jacques to his heritage. He didn't make attachments easily, had never truly had a friend, and never a lover before Charlotte. But suddenly he had this unexpected trio in his life who had gotten close enough to win his affections. It made him nervous and uncertain. And grateful. They were sort of like family, too.

LaRoche frowned at his hesitation. "If you've got doubts about Philo, don't. He's like my own brother, particularly now."

Philo Tibideaux. His brother was dead, and Max was the one he blamed for it. How could he trust someone who carried that kind of pain in his heart?

LaRoche swore his redheaded friend would never strike against Max's leadership.

Philo had gathered a cadre of like-minded clansmen who would stake out an invisible perimeter around the city. They planned to watch and wait, alert for any sign of infiltration or threat.

A futile gesture, Max could have told him. Trackers wouldn't be seen or even sensed unless they wanted to be. And they were already inside the city. Max could feel them breathing down his neck.

He'd gone out trying to reestablish the brief connection with the mysterious figure from the park. His vast ignorance about who he was, and what he was capable of, was a danger to his whole clan. The need to learn more burned like a fever. He'd made himself visible, vulnerable, trying to lure the other shifter out—but nothing had happened.

It spooked him. What were they waiting for?

"I have no problem with Philo or with what he wants to do. And I wouldn't try to stop him if I did. He has a right to do what he thinks best to protect the clan."

"It's important to him, Max. It's his only way to fight back against what they did."

And Max, again, saw the hapless, harmless Tito Tibideaux as he lay in Dev Dovion's drawer, battered, tortured, and dead. Not because of Max, but because of Oscar Babineau. Oscar, who couldn't claim the same allegiance of the clan, whose only protector was Max.

If anything happened to him . . .

"You all right?"

"What?" Max responded blankly for the second

time. Now Jacques was squinting at him, certain something was wrong. He managed a quick smile. "Got a lot on my mind, with this and the Towers so close to completion."

LaRoche nodded and took another sip of his beer, then gave a satisfied sigh. "I can't wait to entertain in my new digs. Quality *femmes* shy from a fella who lives in a ratty trailer smelling of last week's socks."

"More like last week's sex," Max muttered. "At least you're getting some."

LaRoche chuckled. "Where's your little female, Savoie? Haven't seen her with you for a while."

"She's undercover with her partner."

"Oh."

It was just a twitch of the lips, but Max's gaze bore in with suspicious intensity. "What?"

"It's just that one of the day crew said he saw a new girl at the Sweat Shop that reminded him of your lady."

Max's brows lowered. "The Sweat Shop. Is that some gym?"

LaRoche choked down a laugh. "Don't you ever get out, Savoie? It's a club. A dance club."

She was out at a dance club with Alain Babineau. Very casually, he asked, "Was this girl with anyone?"

"She wasn't a patron. She was working. Maybe Charlotte's pulling down a little cash on the side by moonlighting. I'm sure she has the . . . stamina for it."

Max swiftly snapped up his coat. "Where is this place?"

Looking sorry he'd enjoyed a snicker at Max's expense, LaRoche put a hand on his shoulder to press him back into his chair. "It's too late tonight. Finish your drink, then go home. Get some sleep. I'm sure he was wrong."

THE SWEAT SHOP.

Appropriately named.

Max stood inside the dark doorway, nose crinkling at the strong scents of human exertion, smoke, and lust, glossed over by stylishly placed neon and mirrors. Behind his dark glasses his gaze swept the large room, noting a center stage that L-ed into a narrow isthmus off to one side sporting a half dozen poles imbedded in a lighted bar. Big booths offering private stages ran the length of one wall, and the rest of the floor was covered with small tables.

"Not a gym," LaRoche commented from behind him, "though you must admit there's some quality athletics going on."

Max said nothing. He was afraid the others would see his shock.

It was a strip club.

He'd never been in such a place. Jimmy was a straightforward mobster, too conservative to dabble in fleshly vices on a blatant scale. Legere's own needs had been met in more discreet establishments. For Max, there was only one female he'd ever wanted to see naked. Though he briefly admired the agility of the young ladies plying their poles, they offered no more distraction than a big-screen TV showing tennis or golf. He had no interest in skin-baring athletics unless it involved him and Charlotte.

What did interest him was the sight of Alain Babineau ringside at the center stage. He looked like a pimp with his slicked-back hair dyed black, and wearing a silky patterned shirt half buttoned. Tina would have had a heart attack.

As Max started across the room flanked by his Shifter entourage, the detective's idle gaze touched on him, and stayed in surprise. His mouth moved in a silent *Oh, fuck!*

Max nodded for his men to clear the next stage-side table so he could sit down. The quartet of businessmen took one look at the glowering black-clad tough guys and couldn't scramble away fast enough. The second they sat down, a waitress was there dealing out coasters with deference. She was just a kid, probably still shy her driver's license, tarted up in a tiny black satin skirt, red sequined tube top with platform shoes to match, and enough makeup to touch up a cathedral ceiling.

"Evening gentlemen. I'm Candy. What can I get you?"

Since he didn't know what name Cee Cee was using, Max couldn't ask for her, so he ordered a water and glanced around while his men named their preferences. He didn't see her, but could sense her nearby.

He settled back in his seat, simmering as he imagined how she'd look in one of those glittery tops. He was a little uneasy about how she'd react to seeing him there, hardly inconspicuous with his dangerous companions. He gave another quick look at Babineau, who appeared frozen in his chair. As the center stage cleared for a new performer, he continued to scan the waitstaff for Charlotte.

The hard-pumping beat of Mötley Crüe's "Girls,

Girls, Girls" revved up, accompanied by a roar as a Harley motorcycle muscled its way onto the platform. Max's gaze flicked up to its tall, redheaded rider, who wore a helmet with a mirrored half visor and black leather chaps and bolero, both edged in long whips of red fringe. His glance paused as she swung off the monstrous bike, balancing on ice-pick-sharp stilettos, her backside bare of all but the thin silver chain of a G-string. And as he was greeted by all that smooth skin, his jaw began to drop.

She spun in a swirl of fringe into her routine, working the edge of the stage, prancing, sinking low to shake her rump in the face of patrons who leaped up to tuck bills in her G-string, then whirling and strutting away. She still wore the helmet, shielding everything but the wet slick of her lips as she untied her skimpy vest and shook it down her arms.

Black leather strings were attached to silver disks that barely covered the tips of her breasts. As she circled the vest above her head, she saw him. The motion faltered for only an instant, then the leather went flying.

Right into Jacques LaRoche's face.

Hips swinging, shoulders rocking to the infectious beat of the music, she sashayed to the edge of the stage. Without looking away from her, Max passed a fifty to LaRoche, who teased her down into a crouch to let him thread the folded bill under the tie at the side of her right breast. She leaned forward to press a bright red lip print onto the top of his gleaming head.

Then she turned to Max, remaining in the crouch, her palms on the stage, her body rippling as she edged toward him, reaching out to remove his sunglasses, then flipping up her visor. Their gazes locked. Then she put on his Ray-Bans and backed away with a tempting wiggle.

Max's stony expression broke into a wide grin.

On her feet once more, she worked her way around the motorcycle as if it was a lover before sinuously sliding her leg over the wide seat and waking its bad-boy rumble. She put out her hand, pointing to Max and curling her fingers to beckon him from his seat.

He'd hopped up onto the stage before the bouncers caught his movement. Cee Cee waved them back as she handed him his sunglasses, then flipped her visor down as Max got on the seat behind her. And she carried him off the stage, heading straight for the wide-open delivery door leading to the alley.

Cee Cee drove them down a couple of blocks, turning into another shadowed alley to cut the engine. She was shaking. And it wasn't the chill night air or the vibration from the Harley. It was Max—the press of his thighs trapping her between them, the heat of his arms curled around her bare waist.

Deciding the best defense was a quick offensive, she got up on her knees and pivoted around so they were face-to-face.

"What the hell are you doing here, Savoie?"

He pulled her helmet and his sunglasses off. She heard them hit the stones before he yanked her to him, slamming her mouth onto his. Then she heard nothing but the roar of her blood and her wild, wanting moan.

They took greedily with hard, urgent gulps, tasting, sucking, mad for each other. Her hands were in his hair, tangling, kneading. Her knee slipped over his thigh so she could lean into him and rock against the massive proof of how much he'd missed her. Wanted her.

His hands were hot and rough, caressing, squeezing the endless temptation of skin offered by her arching body. With her legs spread wide, there was next to nothing to stop him from thrusting his fingers into her wet heat, driving her relentlessly to a fast, rocketing release that made her tremble and pant raggedly against his throat.

"Where are you staying?" His voice had the same deep throaty growl as the Harley's powerful engine.

"You can't be here, Savoie," she protested weakly. Then he was kissing her again, swamping her senses with waves of pleasure. And she heard herself groaning, "Don't stop. Oh, baby, don't stop," until she was dizzy, until she had to clutch his face between her palms to push him away so she could gaze raptly into his eyes. "When I saw you sitting there, my heart almost jumped out of my chest."

"It's not like there was a lot of fabric there to hold it in, *sha*."

A laugh burbled out. She kissed him, sinking into the sweet luxury of his mouth, then they were groping each other with reckless abandon. Finally, she tore herself away.

"I have to get back. Max, I have to get back."

"I need you, Charlotte," he whispered as his lips brushed over her temple. "I have to be with you. Let me be with you."

She was kneading the lapels of his raincoat, nudging her face against the frantic pulse in his neck. "I want you, too. So much I can hardly breathe."

"Where?" he repeated impatiently.

The name of her motel was on her lips when reality crashed the party, and she drew a deep breath of reason.

"Thank you," she said softly.

He touched his lips to hers. "For what?"

"Thank you for coming here."

"I haven't yet, but I plan to. Soon."

"But not tonight, Max." At his frown, she explained, "I'm on a case. Every move I make is under surveillance."

"Those were some awfully tempting moves, *sha*."

His tone was still pleasant, but the cooling in his eyes had her cautious.

"Something else on your mind, Savoie?"

"Why haven't you called me?"

Defensive irritation snapped into place over the stab of guilt. "I'm in the middle of an investigation here. Busy."

"No place for your phone in your wardrobe?"

She tried a quick flanking maneuver. "It's my job, Max. If you can't handle the fact that other men are looking at me—"

"Do they get to touch you?"

"No."

"Do you touch them?"

"No."

"Then I have no problem with them looking." His voice lowered to a spicy mix of desire, pride, and possessiveness. "Because I know you belong to me. I'd expect any breathing male with a pulse to thoroughly enjoy the show. As long as that's all they enjoy."

His hands began to move once again, coaxing her resistance to drop as he pulled her in tight. His passion for her steamed from him like fresh rain off hot pavement. The burning need to give in to everything he wanted, everything they both wanted, threatened incineration, and she took a mental step back to maintain her control.

"This isn't going to happen, Max. Not here, not now. Not while I'm on the clock."

She turned away from him and started the big bike, its roar drowning out any argument. An argument she didn't want to have with him, because she was afraid she couldn't hold her own against it.

She drove them back to the club and parked the bike in the alley. As they reached the back door, Max spun her up against it, caging her between his forearms. He lowered himself slowly to take her on a quick, reckless ride with his lips until she was breathless. But her mood was still all business.

"Don't come back here, Max. I can't have you complicating things."

"Is that what I'm doing, Detective? What if I just want to help you out while I help myself to you?"

She caught his hands and pressed them away. "No. You're too well-known. *Listen* to me, Max. I can't have you ruin all the man-hours we've spent—"

"I have been listening, Detective. And I don't like what I'm hearing. "

"What have you been hearing?" she challenged, glancing at the door then back at him impatiently. She was going to be missed, and they couldn't be found together.

"Nothing."

That got her full attention, and she felt a prickle of alarm. "What do you want to hear?"

"How 'bout, 'Heya, Max. Just sitting in this crappy motel room missing you, wishing I was home sharing a meal, a conversation, a bed with you.' That's all. That's all I wanted to hear."

"I was going to call you." It sounded lame and too damned after the fact even to her.

"Why didn't you? 'Hey, Max. I'm not shot up full of holes somewhere in an alley. I've been too busy playing house with my partner for it to occur to me that you might be worrying.'"

Her temper flamed hot, burning guilt to ashes. "Is this about Babineau? Were you spying on me? Is that why you're here?"

"Why didn't you call me?"

"I don't have time for this, Max. I can't put a case on hold to soothe your ego."

He abruptly stepped back, his expression still. "I'll let you get back to it, then."

He pulled open the door to let her slip inside to go to her dressing room, then followed more slowly. LaRoche and his compatriots were waiting and fell in wordlessly behind him to form an aggressive front as he strode through the backstage area toward the main floor. Then the hint of something faint and sweet stroked over him like an icy touch.

He paused to murmur briefly in Babineau's ear, then was gone in a swirl of his long black coat.

When Cee Cee joined her partner, preparing for an awkward explanation, she found him tense and all business.

"He was here. Just a minute ago."

Cee Cee frowned. He clearly didn't mean Max. "Who?"

"Our man."

The killer.

Fourteen

CEE CEE SWEPT the room with a quick glance, her senses on high alert. While she and Max were playing kissy face, the killer had been here, within reach.

Babineau gripped her elbow and pulled her down into the seat next to him before she drew any attention. Like that wouldn't happen. She still had on her club face, a black mask painted around her eyes like a Maori tattoo—so bold, no one looking would remember the woman beneath it. Those same dark forked flames covered the scars on one shoulder and slid down to mid biceps. With the red wig and scarlet lips, she looked like some deadly black magic princess. She'd changed into a short denim skirt and plunge front beige top that didn't conceal the lacy fuchsia bra she wore under it. Another reason for none of the patrons to recall her features.

She turned to him, a fire of excitement in her eyes. "How do you know he was here?"

"Savoie said something about a sweet smell. He said you'd know."

"Where is he?"

"Savoie? Gone. How does he know? How can he tell?"

She leaned close to be heard over the pounding

music, filling Babineau in on the trip to see Marjorie Cole in the morgue. He had no comment. Nor did he question her.

Cee Cee forced down the frustration of being so close only to have him slip away. "Babs, talk to the guys on the door; find out who just left. Get descriptions if you can, especially if they were regulars. Tell them somebody lifted your wallet or something."

"Where are you going?"

"I need to talk to Savoie. This is the closest we've gotten and I don't want to miss anything. Maybe there's something more, something he might not think is important."

If Babineau read anything into her desire to chase after her lover, he kept it wisely to himself. "I'll see if I can get one of the waitresses to go out to breakfast with me. Maybe if I play the jilted boyfriend, she'll feel sorry enough for me to make me feel better with a swap of some information."

With his smooth, unthreatening charm and good looks, the runaway schoolgirls would drool all over him. Was that how their killer did it? Lulling them into lowering their guards, into trusting him?

The clock was ticking on Kelly Schoenbaum. Cee Cee was damned sure he wasn't bothering with the sweet talk now.

SCRUBBED CLEAN OF her stripper persona, Charlotte stepped into the cavernous depths of *Cheveux du Chien*. Here the clientele didn't just act like animals, they *were* animals. And she, as an intruding human, was prey.

From out of the smoky darkness, their eyes glowed with firefly brightness, hot points of dangerous light all focused on her. She knew their secrets. She'd seen them drop their guise of humanity and let loose the beasts inside. Though they didn't trust her, they allowed her into their safe haven because she belonged to Savoie. And because she'd helped put one of their own to rest with the dignity he deserved.

And because she'd seen to his brother's burial, Philo Tibideaux approached with a faint smile of welcome.

"Evening, Detective. I hear I missed quite the show." When flashing his sassy grin, the lanky redhead was startlingly attractive. "Wouldn't care to give us an encore, would you, darlin'?"

Her tone was as cool as her stare. "Darn, I left my G-string in my other purse."

"Clothing could be optional."

"Sorry."

He sighed dramatically. "I'll just have to live vicariously off the stories I've been told."

"Greatly exaggerated, I'm sure."

To his credit, his gaze stayed focused on her face. "I highly doubt that, Detective Hot Stuff."

Her smile crept out as she looked toward the back table to find it empty. "Is Max here?"

"Haven't seen him. Jackie might know where he is. He's back in the office, *cher*." A quick wink. "You might wanna ax him what kind a stories he be telling."

"I'll do that."

He laughed and stepped aside.

The music was a wailing Buddy Guy blues tune about being too broke to spend the night. Beneath the achy beat, Cee Cee felt something else: a soft vibration that wasn't sound. A ghostly flutter stroked across her skin, along her nervous system. What was it?

"Get you your usual, Detective?"

Amber, one of the club's waitresses, regarded her through veiled eyes. Her tray was wedged just below her impressive breasts as if they were being offered up. A primitive competition over Max bristled between them.

Cee Cee nodded and smiled narrowly. "I'll be in the office."

Amber nodded and strode toward the bar with an exaggerated sway of her hips.

The office door was open. Jacques LaRoche stood by the one-way glass that looked out over his establishment, where he'd been observing her approach. When he turned toward her, she saw the faint outline of her lips still imprinted high on his brow.

"Charlotte. An unexpected surprise. If you're looking for Max, I don't know where he is. Did you need him for something?"

"Working a case," was her neutral answer.

"At Manny's place? You on loan to Vice?"

Her surprise was followed by an appraising study. "No, just a crossover from Homicide. Have you heard anything about a couple of his working girls that turned up dead?"

Amber arrived with her Jack and water, and a bottled beer for her boss. She placed them on a small glass-topped table and was about to slip away when Jacques stopped her.

"Amber, you know any of the girls over at Manny's?"

The waitress paused thoughtfully. "I used to know a couple. Friends of friends. But they took off about a month ago."

"Any particular reason?" Cee Cee asked. Clues turned up in the strangest places.

"The money was good, if you can stand the work and the boss. So that wasn't it. Can't say I know why. Just packed up their stuff and disappeared. Might be . . ."

"Might be what?" Cee Cee pressed.

Amber met her stare without blinking. "That would be your job to find out."

"Got names?"

She supplied them, and Cee Cee committed herself to finding out more about them. Starting with the obvious. "Were they your kind or human?"

"My kind. They were tight with a few of Philo's crew, but were Upright groupies. Got off on being the wild things doing the wild thing, if you know what I mean."

They both knew she did.

"And the Shifters on Philo's crew? Maybe they have some information."

Amber's gaze slipped to Jacques, who nodded for her to go on. She supplied Cee Cee with four unfamiliar names, then left before more could be asked of her.

"You here just because of your case, *cher*?"

Something in his knowing tone had Cee Cee taking a wary mental step back. "Why else?"

"I don't know. Maybe something to do with the reason that Savoie was crunching on glass when he left." He waved a hand at the table with their drinks. "Have a seat. The doctor is in."

She hesitated. It wasn't her nature to share personal stuff, especially sensitive information that Max had specifically warned her not to divulge. Yet she longed to unload her fears. And she couldn't go to her former shrink for advice on her out-of-species relationship.

Jacques patted the back of her chair with a huge hand. "Think of it as confession, and me as your priest."

She laughed at that ridiculous image, but sat down. She had to talk to someone, and Jacques LaRoche had earned her trust and friendship.

"Things are different since we bonded."

He dropped into his chair and took a long pull on his beer. "How so?"

"You were bonded, weren't you?" she asked evasively.

"Yes."

"Was there anything . . . special between you and your mate?"

"Besides the great sex?"

She squirmed a bit. "Aside from that. What made that relationship so different from your others?"

A melancholy expression appeared as he took another drink. "I've told you this before. There's an awareness of one another, a closeness, a protectiveness. It's like you become one heart, one soul. The thought of separation is like dying. Worse than dying," he corrected quietly.

He'd lost his mate, and now Cee Cee understood how that had devastated him. His earthy response to females of either species was physical, just biology, he'd once told her. What he felt for his mate was spiritual.

Was that what she now had with Max? Something greater than self, deeper than love, stronger than chemistry? If so, why was she still so afraid?

The prospect of what they could become together—one heart, one soul—overwhelmed her with its enormity.

She shook it off. "Could you hear each other's thoughts?"

Jacques stared at her sharply. "What?"

It was too late to take back the words, so she plunged on, needing to know. "Could you communicate with each other without words; feel each other when not together? I mean *really* feel each other?"

"You and Max can do that?" His words were barely a whisper. When she didn't answer, his expression closed down tight. "Don't talk about this to anyone, Charlotte. Not to *anyone*. Do you understand?"

"No, I don't." She leaned forward urgently. "Tell me why."

"Because we can't do that. None of us since the Ancients."

That was a term she'd never heard before. "Who are they?"

"Just legend. Stories for children."

"Then tell me a story, Jacques."

He rubbed his palm over the top of his head, then he got up and shut the door. He looked spooked and anxious, as if the words themselves were dangerous.

"This goes no further."

She nodded.

"This is the legend we're told when we're children, kind of our creation myth. When mankind was young and helpless, the gods mixed with beasts to create the Ancients—protectors for their people. These new creations looked like men so they could walk among them when necessary, but they could also take the shape of an animal to live unnoticed at man's side. They were fierce, loyal, and intelligent because of the wisdom given by the gods, but in time they also grew arrogant. They began to wonder why they had to serve puny man when they were the far superior beings. And in that prideful arrogance, they began to destroy those whom they'd been created to protect."

"And the gods were royally pissed off."

Jacques smiled grimly. "So the story goes."

"So"—she leaned on her elbows, attention rapt, forgetting about her drink—"what happened to these Ancients?"

"In their fury, the gods cleaved them all in two. But instead of that killing them, their spirits were divided and lived on as separate beings. One half remained beasts, able to change form, but without the courage to rise out of their role of servitude. The other half retained the mental gifts of instinct and manipulation, but were frail, without the physical ability to challenge man for control. The beasts fled to the wilderness of the Celtic shores, becoming the Shifters. The others hid among man in France, calling themselves the Chosen Ones."

He told how the Chosen Ones became spiritual advisors, sages, priests, and soothsayers, influencing with their special talents, but never having enough strength to take control themselves. Until they found their other savage halves, and used them like weapons to crush their enemies and force kings to bow before them.

Just a myth, he said. But after all Cee Cee had learned and seen, it was completely plausible in her mind.

"Why didn't the Chosen Ones and the Shifters mate? Wouldn't that blend their abilities again?"

"Even if you get beyond the fact that they detest one another, such matings always proved barren. The Chosen Ones viewed the Shifters as brutal, offensive beasts, too inferior to be worthy of their DNA. And the Shifters loathed and would devour those who had enslaved and slaughtered their kin for centuries. Once the technology was available, they tried artificial means and even gene splicing. But nothing . . . normal ever came of it."

She shivered. The same result as between Shifter male and human mate: a genetic dead end.

"So the Chosen Ones can't change shape, and the Shifters can't do mental manipulations."

"No."

"And Shifter females can't shape-shift?"

"No."

But Max's mother could. And Charlotte and Max had shared more than just thoughts telepathically.

So, what did that make Max?

"How do you know all this, Jacques? And don't tell me you learned it at your mama's knee."

"I never knew my mama. I never had a family, at least that I can remember." His gaze was evasive. There was more that he wasn't saying.

"And yet you retained this knowledge. How is that?"

Jacques regarded her through eyes dark with demons.

"Because my mate wasn't Shifter. She was Chosen."

He set down his empty bottle and got up. Discussion over.

They both retreated behind their secrets as he walked her to the exit.

"Thanks for the bedtime story." She smiled up at the big man as he paused at the threshold. "Perhaps someday you'll finish it for me."

"Perhaps." He returned her smile faintly.

"Jacques," she ventured suddenly, "what do you think Max is?"

He considered her question for a long moment, then told her somberly, "Our salvation."

CHARLOTTE PONDERED THAT as she headed down the sidewalk toward where her car was parked several blocks away. Though Max and Oscar shared a father, her guess was it was Marie Savoie who was the deciding factor. The female who could shape-shift. It had to be through her that Max inherited his unique abilities. Rollo had told his son that his mother, Marie, was of pure blood, of rare untainted heritage. Now Cee Cee suspected there was more to her history than even he had realized.

What would that make Max?

She could see her car beneath a streetlight. Though there was no one else on the one-way street, a sudden sense that she was no longer alone quivered through her. An abrupt shove of energy hit her between the shoulder blades, making her stumble. She jumped into the shadows with her back to the darkened storefront, her ankle piece in her hand.

Four shapes moved in on her, quick and low. Two on her side of the street, two on the other, maneuvering to flank her. Definitely not human, but lacking the smooth gliding menace of the Trackers. Members of Max's clan. Following her for what reason?

"Back off," she called out gruffly, her eyes darting from one silhouette to the next. "I don't want to take you down, but I will."

They'd shifted just enough so that their faces weren't recognizable. Sharp teeth and feral eyes gleamed. They were dressed like dock workers with heavy boots, jeans, and open shirts over tight undershirts. She glanced toward her car, calculating the odds of making it in time, deciding they were too slim. So she adopted a wide stance and tried to bluff her way out.

"What do you want? If you know who I am, you know messing with me is stupid and maybe fatal. I know what you are, and I'm not afraid of you. I've kicked your kind's asses before, so back off!"

She saw movement from the right and swiveled that way, shooting off a quick round. A sharp yip and the figure reeled back, letting her know she'd hit the non-vital area of his shoulder she'd aimed for. But the other three had closed fast, approaching in different directions too quickly for her to safely take another shot.

She clubbed the first one's misshapen snout with the butt of her gun, but the next hit her hard and low, knocking her to the sidewalk. Snarling as fiercely as they were, she battled back with fists, elbows, and knees, finally connecting with a throat punch that snapped the gaping jaws together and sent the assailant tumbling back to choke in the gutter. Before she could roll into a more effective position, another slammed into her, flinging her head back against the stuccoed wall. The night exploded with lights, then went alarmingly dark.

Hot pants of breath seared her throat and Cee Cee tensed, expecting a fatal slash of teeth.

Instead, her attacker suddenly backed away. As she struggled to sit up with the wall at her back, her hand groping her gun, she could hear a shuffling of footsteps, then the sound of them running away.

"Are you okay?" A woman's voice, shaky and slightly breathless.

Blinking to clear her vision, Cee Cee saw a large, blurry hand reaching for her and instinctively struck out at the massive shape looming over her.

Her blow was easily blocked, and LaRoche's voice said, "Easy, Charlotte. They're gone." His concerned features filled her foggy vision. "Someone sent out a damn strong alarm just as I heard your shot, but this brave young lady managed to scare them off just before I got here."

The woman laughed huskily. "I don't think my can of mace was all that threatening. They probably heard you coming."

The instant Cee Cee struggled to stand, Jacques's big palms scooped under her elbows to assist her. She wobbled for a moment, then focused on the woman.

She was as tall as Cee Cee. Wearing a hunter's orange vest over a black hooded sweatshirt and skinny jeans, she appeared slender as a boy. Black hair was pulled back in a heavy braid, revealing strong, angular features bare of any makeup. Piercing blue eyes, a hawkish nose, and the wide mouth were too bold for her to be attractive, until she smiled. She beamed with genuine pleasure as she passed Cee Cee her gun, holding the trigger guard between two fingers.

"I think this is yours. Quite an exciting welcome for a newcomer to your city."

"And well timed, for my sake." Cee Cee extended her hand. "Charlotte Caissie."

"Monica Fraser." Her grip was firm and as aggressive as her stare as she assessed the big bar owner. "And you are?"

"Jacques LaRoche, grateful friend of Detective Caissie's, and future employer if you're looking for a job."

Cee Cee's surprise at his offer eased when she noticed the hum of recognition between the two of them. Her new acquaintance was a Shifter, too. Could she have been the one to extend that warning push?

"I'll consider that after I've had a chance to unpack. I'm staying at a friend's condo in the Quarter House. I was looking for an all-night grocery to pick up a few things when I got turned around. Maybe you can point me in the right direction."

Jacques responded with a gallant, "There's one on Royal. I'll walk you there myself once I make sure my friend is all right." His flirtatious manner dropped away when he looked to Cee Cee. "Did you get a look at them?"

"Fangs and claws and work clothes. Not much to go on. Winged one of them in the left shoulder." Her voice lowered. "I think they followed me out of your place."

Their new friend looked nervously between them.

"Should you notify someone? I mean, you were attacked by . . . by . . ."

"I know what they were. And I won't be writing up any report. I'll leave that to Jacques. It's his jurisdiction, not mine."

Monica looked relieved and curious.

"Charlotte is an NOPD detective and an Upright," Jacques explained. "But we don't hold that against her."

"Okay." She smiled, even more confused.

"Four Shifters come after me right after Amber gives me four names?" Cee Cee mused. "A coincidence, Jacques?"

"I'll find out," he assured her. When she put her hand to the back of her head and grimaced, he grew concerned. "You want me to call Max to come get you?"

"No," she said quickly. "I'm fine. No need to worry him until we find out what's behind it. It might have been a random robbery." *Or not.* They'd shared secrets before to protect the same man. "Let me know if anything interesting turns up. I'm parked right there. Thanks again," she added, turning to the stranger.

Monica nodded. "Glad to have happened by."

But as Cee Cee climbed into her car, she began wondering about the coincidence. Had Monica Fraser just *happened* by, or was something more calculated behind her appearance?

Geez, when had everyone become suspect? Couldn't someone have done a good deed for no other reason than it was the right thing to do?

She put the car in gear. It would be nice to think so—but she wasn't an optimist.

UNDER THE COOL light of the moon, Max took a slow breath and a step of faith.

His foot touched the glassy surface of the garden's reflective pool. Focusing inward, he centered himself in the mental plane his father had shown him. He closed his eyes, imagining his physical form weightless, like a whisper of evening breeze drifting across the water without a ripple.

He breathed in, filling his lungs with air that could hold him aloft, letting him float free like an untethered balloon. The tread of his high-tops never broke the surface as he advanced, not thinking of the steps themselves, but of the destination. No substance, no weight, drifting lightly.

The sound of a door closing in the house behind him caught Max's attention, his concentration faltered, and he dropped. Water flooded into his shoes as he stood knee deep in the middle of the pool.

He slogged back to the retaining wall and climbed out. Progress, but not as quick as it needed to be. He took a savage breath of frustration, hearing his father's warning: *"You don't know who they are. You'll never know what to look for. You'll never know when they're coming. Let me do what I can to save you."*

Too late for that now. He had no one to depend upon but himself. But he knew where to find the answers, thanks to his father.

"Where am I?" he'd asked.

"Wherever you want to be. Focus. You can control it. Let down the walls around your mind so your spirit can fly."

"How far can I go?"
"Find out."

Max studied the water's smooth surface once again. Time to find out.

THE SINGLE-STORY MOTOR court was stripped of amenities, with none of downtown's slickness or the Quarter's charm. Their neighbors came and went, often several times nightly, and no one paid attention to the flashy redhead and her greasy boyfriend who pulled in near dawn and slept all day.

It was one A.M., and the hourly clientele were slipping in and out with furtive regularity. Her wig in place and head tipped down so it swung forward to shield her features, Cee Cee assessed those she passed and saw no threat to their operation. Just sad, lonely people trying to steal away from their sad, lonely lives for a moment of artificial happiness.

The door to one of the rooms opened, revealing a slouching figure with a cold cigarette.

"Got a light?"

Stan Schoenbaum looked like shit.

"Sorry. Trying to quit."

"Where's your better half?" he asked, glancing behind her down the empty walk.

"Looking for some action on his own. Was hoping to get a little privacy for the next half hour or so."

Stan cocked a brow as she asked him to shut down the surveillance in her room. It was strictly against procedure, but he shrugged. "Can't blame a girl for needing a bit a downtime between one and two."

He was giving her an hour.

"Sorry I couldn't help you out with the light. Maybe you could do *me* a favor." She cocked her hip and shoulders into a suggestive pose in case anyone was watching, then asked softly, "Run some IDs for me."

His tired eyes brightened. "Something to do with the case?"

"Don't know yet." She repeated the names Amber had given her, and at the last moment added Monica Fraser's to it. "That info is for my eyes only."

"Introduce me to your friend."

Cee Cee took a startled step back at the unfamiliar voice. Schoenbaum jerked his head toward the other man. "Silas MacCreedy, Charlotte Caissie. Silas's from up Baton Rouge way. One of our vics, Shawnee Potts, has family up there. He was working the missing person case and asked if he could step in with us."

Cee Cee gave their fellow cop a shrewd once-over. He was a good-sized guy with close-cropped brown hair, steely eyes, and burly good looks. "We could use the company," she told him with a nod of greeting.

"I won't get in your way," he answered, knowing how territorial districts were about their cases.

Stan's shoulders heaved. "I don't care if we invite snake handlers and Mormons in, as long as the job gets done."

"That's the plan," Cee Cee agreed, and told them good night.

Breathing a sigh, she locked herself into her shabby room, kicked off her shoes, tossed the fright wig onto the dresser, then flopped down on the bed. Her head ached meanly, foiling her plan to close her eyes and shut down for a minute or two first. Finally, she took out her phone.

Two rings and an answer.

"Heya."

"Hi. I'm calling you."

"I noticed."

In the silence that ticked by, all the things she wanted to say tumbled about her heart. *I love you. I miss you. I want you. I wish you were here.*

"You wanted to know about the killer," he said matter-of-factly. "He was there in your club tonight. He's been there before. Not out front as a customer, but behind the stage, behind the scenes. Someone who knows their way around. Someone the people who work there are used to seeing.

"I didn't pick up any trace of that scent at Blutafino's home," he continued. "He's not your man. But that doesn't mean he's not involved. If you get close to Manny, you'll get close to who you're looking for."

She'd shifted automatically into professional mode, her mind spinning ahead toward her next move. "What else?"

"I wish I could tell you more, Detective. It was good to hear your voice."

He was saying good-bye. "Max, are you still angry? You understand why you have to stay away. It would destroy my cover if anyone put the two of us together. That would be bad for both of us."

"I'm not stupid, Detective. I got that. Was there anything else you needed to tell me?"

Over the phone wasn't how she wanted to ask

about his parentage, or her strange new abilities. "I miss you, baby."

A beat of silence. "Stay safe, Detective."

MAX HUNG UP the phone, and sat pensively in the darkness of Jimmy's study. Desire and anger warred for a moment, but practicality won out.

When she made up her mind to trust her heart in terms of their relationship, he'd be there for her. He couldn't force her choices before she was ready, so he'd wait. But, when it came to her safety, he couldn't stand aside. And wouldn't.

He settled back into the big leather chair that was the throne from which Jimmy Legere had run his empire, from which he was now doing the same. He picked up the phone again and called Petitjohn. Closing his mind to her plea for independence, he said, "Set it up for me T-John."

"You sure?"

"Yes. Time to let Carmen know I'm ripe for courting."

Fifteen

Babineau showed up with beer, and they sat in silence until the first two were almost gone. It took that long for their recent tension to ease into the remembered pattern of trust. It started where it always did, with work.

Charlotte told him what Max had said about their killer being someone familiar, not a stranger unknown to the vics.

"I think we're closer than we realize," she concluded, sipping her second bottle. Enthusiasm for her work filled her up, making her whole. "Now we need a way to nudge up against Manny Blu, but I'm about fifteen years past my prime where he's concerned."

"The waitress I plied with over easy on toast said that Blu makes his working girls get regular checks at a local clinic to make sure they're clean. Judith Farraday— Dr. Judy, they call her—is something of a saint, a psychologist, mother, and best pal to them. She'd be a good source to tap. She'd know the vics, might have some insight into the latest disappearance." Babineau added somberly, "Word has it, Kelly had an appointment with her the day she went missing. She never kept it."

"I feel an STD coming on."

"Be careful there. I hear she's a smart cookie.

Worked clinics in some pretty hot zones, with a no-bullshit bedside manner." A pause. "And speaking of bedside manner, what's with you and Savoie? Surprised the hell out of me to see him show up tonight. Is he going to make trouble?"

"No, he won't. I'll handle Max."

"Savoie isn't exactly an easy-to-handle guy."

"Max is my business—just like what's with you and Tina is your business."

He gave her a cool look, then nodded. "Fair enough. Off-limits."

"Has to be while this case is ongoing. Gotta stay focused, and we can't if all the personal stuff is dragging on us."

"Even if she and Oscar are living out at his house with him?"

That hit her like a sucker punch. Why hadn't Max said anything? But then, she hadn't exactly given him any time to discuss current events, had she?

"They'll be safe there. Maybe it's for the best. It's all about the job, Babs. It has to be."

The words helped her build that impenetrable wall back up around her. All she could do was hope it would hold strong and firm for the days or weeks it would take to bring the killer to justice.

That would give her time to think of what to say when the gates on River Road opened to welcome her back home. Maybe the words would just come to her when she saw Max again. If he wanted some groveling, okay, she could bend a bit. If he needed some TLC, she'd be all over that in a second.

All she knew was that the angry words they'd exchanged couldn't escalate into silence, that cold, unforgiving silence that echoed between her parents when she was a child. Just before they split for good.

ONE THING T-JOHN could say for Max, he'd picked himself a damned fine-looking female.

Francis Petitjohn sat front and center for the nine o'clock show, enjoying every minute of it. He'd never shared his cousin's puritan aversion to rawly displayed sexual content, and watching Detective Charlotte Caissie gyrate through a striptease was highly entertaining.

He almost didn't recognize her beneath the bizarre Kabuki-style white face. He wouldn't have if he wasn't sitting so close, studying her so intently. Something about her strong, swaggering rhythm made it impossible to look away. She'd made changes to her appearance, but then who'd look past that acre of gorgeous legs and the one-two punch of tits and ass. Her hair was a stick-straight red wig. She'd used a tanner or bronzer to deepen her skin tone from creamy café au lait to rich mocha. Under the white pancake, her cheekbones looked sharp enough to chip ice, and her eyes a gun-muzzle black. Chili Pepper: a stage name fitting the act. An act he'd never have seen if he'd simply done as he was told.

Had Savoie really thought he'd follow his dictates and make contact by phone instead of in person? T-John was an up-close-and-personal kind of messenger who liked to be seen as well as heard, and it had paid off big this time. Plus, curiosity over his mission had been too hard to resist.

What was Max up to?

He saw recognition make the dancer pause, and her gaze flew about. Looking for Savoie, no doubt. Then she continued her routine with no less enthusiasm, making it hard to look away. Making it just plain hard.

"Mr. Petitjohn."

He glanced up to see Carmen Blutafino wearing a shit-eating grin.

"Manny. Nice place."

"You should have told me you were coming. I would have made you feel more welcome." He eased into the next chair, settling his bulk with a surprising grace, noting the well-armed goons at Petitjohn's back with a quick glance. "Here for business or pleasure?"

"Definitely the second, leaning toward the first."

Beady eyes brightened with anticipation. "On your own behalf?"

"No."

Greed had his chins trembling. "Jimmy would never deal with me."

"Savoie isn't as conservative in his tastes, shall we say."

"I wasn't aware that I had anything he wanted."

T-John let his gaze linger over the voluptuous dancer. "You do now."

That obviously surprised the corpulent man. "I thought Savoie was keeping house with some lady cop."

T-John smiled wide with nasty insinuation. "There's only so much one can do within the limit of the law, if you catch my meaning. He has some rather rough-edged inclinations he can't express with her. But something about Ms. Pepper there reminds him enough of his detective to make him consider exploring those things with her. He'd be very appreciative."

"I'd like to oblige him, but she's not mine to bargain with."

"Oh. Too bad." He put his palms on the table and was halfway out of his chair before Manny gripped his elbow.

"Maybe we can work something out. I don't deal with middlemen. No offense."

T-John's smile never faltered over his gritted teeth. "None taken. Be thinking about what he can do for you, and he'll be here himself, later tonight."

ALAIN ENTERED BLUTAFINO'S office cautiously. He'd seen Manny talking to Francis Petitjohn. Had the petty mobster blown their cover? He'd had no chance to warn Cee Cee before she went back to change her costume, so he'd have to play things by ear.

Manny Blu was smiling as he waved him into an overstuffed zebra print chair. "I'm sorry. I've forgotten your name."

"Al Babbit, Mr. Blutafino."

"Just call me Manny. My friends do."

"Are we going to be friends?"

"That depends on you, Al, and your influence over your lady. I have a potential business partner who's taken a shine to her."

"She's not a whore, Mr. Blutafino."

"Manny. I'm not asking her to be one. I've got plenty of whores. What I need is a favor. And I'm very, very generous to those who do me favors."

Alain sat and listened to Blutafino's proposal, an unbelievable opportunity dropped right into their laps.

But at what cost? And to whom?

When he was finished, the mobster looked to Alain Babineau and asked reasonably, "What do you want for her?"

"To work for you," he answered smoothly. "Something here in the club, and not just a shit job."

"Done." He nodded toward the door. "Talk to her. All she has to do is keep him satisfied, and we'll all get what we want."

CEE CEE LISTENED without a change of expression as her partner laid out the new turn of events. She sat amid the crumpled wrappers of their fast-food meal and voiced the same question that was on his mind.

"What the hell is he up to?"

"Ask him."

That got a spark behind her flat stare. "I can't. We've taken a step back from each other for a while."

Babineau snorted. "Some step back. By asking Manny to pimp you out to him? Sounds pretty hands-on to me. What's got him so pissed off that he'd go to such extremes to get in the way of our investigation?"

"That's not what he's doing at all. If he was torqued, he'd just let us swing. He doesn't need to barter with the likes of Blu. But the creep's hot to do business with LEI."

"Then why, if not to control you?"

"He's using his rep to get us in close to Manny," she concluded, not quite sure how she felt about that.

"Why would he indebt himself to that element?"

"Because it means so much to me," she told him quietly.

"What do you want to do?"

Her features tightened, her mood toughened. "We take what he's given us, and run with it as far as it can take us. Like I said, I can handle Savoie. Are you up for Blutafino?"

Babineau's smile was fierce and humorless. "Oh, yeah. If this pays off, I'll have to send Savoie a personal thank-you for making my career golden."

"Send him flowers later. Let's get our game plan together. I'll worry about Savoie's motives later."

"CHEAP HOOD" WAS too high an assessment of Carmen Blutafino.

Max sat in his office amid the glossy furnishings, glittery accents, and endless reflections, and felt the need to wash his hands. Manny's attempt to cover the sleaze with sophistication was as glaring a failure as his shiny suit was next to Max's sleek charcoal gray Prada pinstripe.

But appearances weren't everything. Blutafino was blatantly fawning, but Max didn't mistake him for harmless. A feral savagery in the tiny dark eyes told him Blutafino would peel him like a Gulf shrimp if motivated. Max would have to be careful to see that he wasn't.

Coming into the man's establishment with only his driver waiting outside pegged him as either so sure of his power that he didn't see a need for caution, or fatally stupid. As long as the man believed one or the other, Max figured he'd be relatively safe.

"I appreciate your hospitality, Carmen, inviting me into your place when I haven't been very receptive to your offers of friendship."

"It's nothing, Max. Just business. You didn't hurt my feelings." An insincere smile spread just as the door opened.

When the two undercover detectives entered the room, Babineau was a blank slate, meeting Max's stare with a pretended humility as he pushed Cee Cee toward him.

The sight of her cleaved Max's tongue to the roof of his mouth.

Her long-sleeved stretchy black dress clung to her curves, leaving her shoulders and all but the top inch and a half of her legs bare. Naughty cutouts at the hip and cleavage-exposing décolletage seemed held together by the magic of thin rhinestone-studded strands. On another it might have seemed vulgar, but because it was Charlotte he couldn't look away. Lust growled through him in a hungry wave.

The shoes were black, like the dress. Four inches of stiletto held on by a band across her toes and a buckled cuff at her ankle. Desire tore through his groin like razor blades.

"Mr. Savoie, my name is Chili Pepper." Her voice was a deceptive purr. "I understand you want to get better acquainted."

She held out her hand to him. He took the tips of her fingers, letting her draw him from his chair and lead him into a smaller room off the office, a room made for only one thing: quick no-frills sex, with a round bed in the center and mirrors covering every surface.

And if he knew Manny, cameras behind most of them.

She turned to him once the door was closed, and she met his eyes without betraying a thing.

"Where would you like to start, Mr. Savoie?"

"Not with conversation."

She flinched when his palm fit to that bare skin at her hip bone. Her eyes glittered dangerously with a confusion of warning and emotion. To prevent her from giving anything away, he jerked her up against him hard enough to smack the air from her lungs. She stiffened at the feel of his mouth against her ear until he whispered, "Smile for the cameras, *sha*. There's a good chance you're in the movies."

"I've always wanted to be on film," she murmured.

He leaned back to look deeply into her eyes as he cupped her face in his hand. "You are very beautiful. I would spoil you outrageously if you'd let me."

Charlotte was lost in his gaze. Was he speaking to her, or to Chili? She answered as both. "I'm not used to being spoiled. Would I enjoy it?"

A slow, confident smile. "Oh, yes. But I expect to get back as much as I put into it. How would that be?"

Relaxing into the game they were playing, she trailed her fingertips over the lapels of his jacket. "This is a very nice suit. I like men in suits. I like men out of them even better."

"And I like women of discretion. I'm involved with someone who means everything to me. Be very clear about that. What she and I share is separate from this. This is just—"

"Biology," Cee Cee supplied. "I understand. Biology can be fun."

His smile spread, slow and sexy. "Yes, it can. Lucrative for you and enjoyable for me."

"Enjoyable for both of us." She turned her head, catching his thumb in her mouth to suck on it before giving it a sharp little bite. "I've heard there are things men like to do, disgusting, naughty things. Are those the things you want to do with me?"

"If they are?"

"I'd like that, too."

His teeth flashed bold and bright. Then his grip tightened, his fingers and thumb clamping onto her jaw, startling her. His expression was harsh, alarming her as he leaned in close.

"One thing you must understand. I don't share. What's mine is mine. I'm generous, but I'm also selfish. And I can be quite unpleasant if you need to be reminded."

She smiled up at him. "I have a very good memory. I don't need to be told more than once."

He released her and stepped back, all business once again. "I'll come for you tomorrow night."

"I think you can count on that." With that husky promise, she slipped back into the office and left the room. Babineau scrambled after her.

Manny Blu looked to Max expectantly.

"I want her exclusively," he told Blutafino.

"She's not mine."

"I'll be very grateful."

Manny smiled. "I'll make arrangements."

Sixteen

Was there any more vulnerable position for a woman than flat on her back under a paper sheet with her heels in the air?

Cee Cee closed her eyes and tried to relax, focusing on why she was here rather than what was going on beneath the sheet.

"Those bruises on your face look like fingerprints. Get a little rough with you, did he?"

"No, he . . . not really."

"An unfortunate occupational hazard. You deal with it or find another line of work."

Judith Farraday's tone was as direct as if she were discussing blisters on the feet of an athlete. No judgmental comments, just straight truth.

Cee Cee liked that about her.

She also liked that the doctor donated her time to work for next to nothing in the worst section of the city, seeing to its invisible population.

As a well-respected private practice physician with a wealthy clientele, Judith Farraday had signed on to do a humanitarian tour in Central America that left her party slaughtered. One of the dead was her husband, another her sister. Instead of rebuilding her practice after returning to the States, she became a trauma doctor in Chicago, trading tennis elbow for gunshot wounds. After that, she followed a wandering path across the country wherever the need was the greatest, establishing clinics like this one before leaving them in good hands to move on. There was no sign of her numerous awards on the bare walls of her office, just a photo of three smiling people against a jungle back-drop.

"Any unusual bleeding? Cramping? Abdominal pain? Nausea?"

"No. I'm good." She stared up at the acoustic ceiling tiles and tried to think of it as a casual conversation over coffee.

"Everything looks healthy. Monthly business on schedule?"

"I haven't had one of those for twelve years."

A pause, then rustling under the sheet and more invasive sightseeing. "Why not? Everything seems in good working order on this end."

Cee Cee gave a faint, bitter laugh. "Nothing's in any kind of working order. The result of one of those occupational hazards."

"Hmmm. I don't have the best equipment here and I'm not a specialist. Maybe you should see one, be-cause I'm not detecting any gynecological problems. No scarring, no lesions, no abnormalities. Everything in the proper place." She wheeled her stool back and snapped off her gloves. "Go ahead and sit up. I should have the results of the STD tests in a couple of days. Standard precautions. You on any particular type of birth control?" she asked, reaching for her prescrip-tion pad.

Clutching the rough paper about her, Cee Cee slowly absorbed what she was being told.

Everything was fine. Normal.

"I'm not on any birth control."

"Are you stupid? You don't look stupid."

"I—I've never needed it. I can't get pregnant."

"When was the last time you saw an ob-gyn?"

"Twelve years ago, when I was told there was too much internal damage for me to ever conceive."

The doctor regarded her unblinkingly. "Get another opinion. And get on birth control in the meantime. I'm not seeing anything but a healthy reproductive system in its prime years. Maybe the initial diagnosis was wrong. Maybe your treating physician was a negligent asshole." She wrote down a name. "Here's a referral. A good man. He'll put you up on the rack and check under the hood."

The paper shivered in her hand. What if it was true? *Don't think about it now. Concentrate on the job.*

"I heard Kikki Valentine saw you regularly."

"*She* wasn't a stupid girl," Dr. Judy told her. "Do you know Kikki?"

"I know her dad. A cop. Got me out of a nasty situation once and I told him I'd do him a favor if he needed one. He's looking for Kikki."

"I haven't seen her for a couple of weeks. She was on some antibiotics and asked me if she could pick them up on a Sunday morning. I came in special for her, but she never showed. I was running a little late and figured she didn't want to hang around. Never heard from her after that. Kids come and go on a whim. Exciting new guy, bad old guy, trouble with the law, trouble with family, restless. You name it. She was a nice girl. Hope she's okay."

"Me, too. Some of the girls at the club are kinda nervous, you know, with what's been happening."

The doctor looked up, perplexed. She was a strong-featured woman with good bone structure, serious dark eyes, and close-cropped auburn hair. She wore a baggy tee shirt over chinos. Quite a change from up-scale Chicago. "What's happened?"

"You know, two of the girls turning up dead. That 'Tides That Bind' killer."

"Is that what they're calling it? I don't have a lot of time for the news. Or for gossip. I keep telling you girls to take extra precautions. To stick together, to watch out for each other. You're the only family each other has. You just don't want to believe it's a bad, bad world out there."

"Were those girls who died your patients, too?"

"I don't know. I never heard that their names were released. I look after a lot of them but most don't use their real names anyway, and I don't ask. That way, they're not scared away from getting the care they need. Call me for the test results, and make an appointment with that specialist. And for God's sake, be smart."

Cee Cee didn't feel smart. She felt a numbing panic that got bigger as she returned to the club. What if all her recent crazy up-and-down emotions were caused by her hormones kicking back in after a twelve-year hiatus?

What if it was true?

———

BABINEAU WAS AT his new position as security. And sitting in a private booth with Carmen Blutafino was Max Savoie. His stare honed in on her the second she entered the room, but there was no change in his expression. He had his game face on, reminding her of their new roles.

"Everything all right?" Babineau asked as he studied her pale features. "You look a bit under the weather."

"I'm fine. What's going on over there?"

"A lot of flirting. A lot of smiling. I think they've decided to date. Manny wants you to join them when you're looking your best."

"I've got a set—"

"I think you've got a *new* job."

MANNY BLU FOLLOWED Max's distracted gaze across the room. Interesting. He was accustomed to using a man's weaknesses against him, but hadn't expected sex to be Savoie's Achilles' heel. Watching the heat and intensity bank in the unblinking stare, he couldn't doubt it. Lust of the flesh would never have tempted Jimmy Legere, but his young protégé was ripe for the plucking. And soon he'd be all his.

"She's lovely, isn't she?"

"Yes."

"She'll be joining us in a minute, so let's get business out of the way, shall we?"

Max returned his attention to the table with some difficulty. His tone was curt, impatient. "What do you want?"

Blutafino chuckled. "No need to go right to the bedroom when you can enjoy the drinks and dancing first."

"I don't dance with other men. I don't consider business a pleasurable form of foreplay. What can I do for you, Carmen? You've been after LEI for years, so you must know the answer."

It was hard to keep victory from his expression as he leaned in. "You control the transportation networks. I need to move some merchandise without any interference. You can make that happen for me."

"I won't traffic drugs. No negotiation there."

A sly smile. "This is a more delicate commodity that requires special handling. Sometimes in bulk, sometimes just one special item. Perishable and valuable."

Max took his meaning without a flinch. "Human cargo."

"Female. Do you have a problem with that?"

"No."

"Good. Then let's talk arrangements."

"Mr. Savoie, I'm flattered that you'd want to see me again so soon."

The husky voice brought his head around in surprise. How had Charlotte gotten so close without him sensing her? He inhaled. Her scent was disguised. Perhaps by the smoke and the sweaty aroma of lust. Perhaps by the heavy musk weighting down her new perfume, or the lotion that had her newly dusky-colored skin shimmering. Something. He didn't like it.

It unsettled him almost as much as the caution in her eyes. The broomstraw red hair, the geometric faux tattoos in glittery scarlet that ringed those wary eyes and trailed down to her left shoulder to conceal his marks, all made her a stranger to him.

She was gorgeous in a flauntingly careless way that wasn't her. Not aggressive, in her usual fashion, but sly and flirty in a petal-hemmed top with sparkling spaghetti straps. Sheer wisps of dusty pink fell from molded cups that presented her breasts to their full, nearly overflowing advantage. Chevrons of sequins and ribbon gave flash to every movement, skimming over a tiny black leather skirt.

Finally, something familiar. He'd been mesmerized by the twitch of that skirt atop killer legs since the moment he'd first seen it. He put his hand on her hip, palming the supple hide over toned muscle, steadied by the contact.

"Sit."

Instead of gliding into the booth beside him, she leaned down first, her mouth pressing to his, her tongue slipping deep in what should have been a sizzling hot kiss—but wasn't. Because it wasn't personal. Max sat still and cold until she lifted away. Then she settled on the seat beside him, and he could breathe again.

"Chili, Mr. Savoie wants to make seeing you a regular thing," Manny purred out. "Starting tonight."

Her gaze lifted to Max's and she smiled. It didn't reach her eyes. "Again, I'm flattered." Even her voice was different, a husky rasp.

"I told him you'd be appreciative and accommodating."

"I will. I'll be whatever he wants me to be." Her hand glided up from his knee to his crotch, and for the first time ever, Max didn't surge to attention at her touch.

He turned to Manny, impatient and gruff. "Are we done here?"

The fat man chuckled. "Businesswise, I believe so. If you're in a hurry to renew your acquaintance, let me offer one of my rooms."

Max didn't smile in return. "When I have sex, the only one I want to be entertained by it is me. Thank you, but I think I prefer to go somewhere a little less compromising."

Not insulted, Manny waved his hand toward the door. "I'll be in touch, Max."

With a nod, he bumped his hip against Cee Cee's, encouraging her to slide out of the booth. He was in a hurry to get away from this place, from the strange vibrations he was getting from her.

She was professionally irritated by his interference. He understood that; she had a right to be. But something else was going on. Something anxious and jumpy as they stepped out into the steamy night.

"Where to, Mr. Savoie?"

She spoke without looking up at him, her tone betraying nothing.

"I could get us a room."

Her snort almost made him smile in relief. "I wouldn't trust any of the sheets you'd find around here. Let's go to my motel. It's across Basin, just a short walk."

"Whatever you like. You're the one wearing heels."

They moved down the crowded street. Though forced close to each other to avoid the garbage bins and bags put out for pick up, they didn't touch.

Trying to pinpoint her mood, Max said, "For someone who's supposedly bought and paid for, you'd look rather standoffish to any paparazzi who might be following."

Her posture stiffened. Then she bumped against him so they were hip to hip. Her arm slid around him, her hand going low to palm his butt for an ungentle squeeze.

"Just checking the merchandise," she growled.

With her head tucked into his shoulder, he couldn't see her expression, but he could picture her scowl. He smiled at her combative tone and took a chance, letting his fingertip trace the soft skin spilling over the cups of her glittery top. "Then you won't mind me sampling what I've bargained for."

"I wouldn't call it a bargain, Savoie. I hope you paid dearly."

"Oh, I did." Apparently more dearly than he'd anticipated.

By the time they reached the motel, their moods were chafed raw by anger, lust, and uncertainty. By the time she shut the door behind him, Cee Cee was about to boil over.

"Stan, turn off the tape. This is a private conversation."

"Does that mean I'm not going to get my money's worth?"

Max's cool drawl cut the tether to her temper.

"You son of a bitch, you're not going to get anything but a black eye if you get within arm's reach of me!" She stormed by him, threw her purse on the bed, and toed out of her shoes, sending them flying. Only Max's quick reflexes kept one from knocking over a lamp.

"Warning taken. I'll keep my distance."

"Is *that* what you call this? Keeping your distance? Pushing your way into my investigation, jeopardizing——"

"What am I jeopardizing? You wanted to get close to Manny. Babineau is in his pocket. Isn't that what you wanted? Why the tantrum? We're both professionals here."

"No, we are not. This is *my* job, *my* business. What kind of deal did you make with him?"

"That would be my business, Detective, not yours."

Her eyes flooded and the fight blew out of her.

Seeing that envelope he'd left on her car. Hearing Babineau's taunting jab: *Puppies.*

The instant he put his hands on her, she tried to lunge away. He spun her into him and anchored her close, her head to his chest, one arm controlled while she pummeled his back with the other. He caught her wrist before she could effect any damage.

He held her as the aggression drained out of her. "I'm sorry if I hurt you." His words were twofold.

He heard her swallow hard before she replied, "I've survived worse things."

He almost smiled because the toughness was back in her voice. But with it came the bittersweet knowledge that he'd have to release her. And he didn't want to let go. Ever. Things were too raw and volatile between them for explanation or conversation. Hurtful feelings, harmful words were just aching heartbeats away. But he feared distance more than he dreaded the confrontation, so for the moment, he hung on to what he had, no matter how risky. He had no sense where she was concerned, none.

"Let's just sit for a while. Can we do that, *sha*? We don't have to talk. We don't have to do anything."

He took her silence for agreement and steered them to her bed, drawing her with him until he was half-reclined on the bank of pillows and she was resting on his shoulder in a warily neutral pose. She felt oddly fragile to him, so he took care to soothe her. His hand stroked her cheek, her shoulder, her arm in a slow, repetitious loop.

"I ask you to believe one thing."

"What's that?" she whispered.

"I never do anything—never make a decision, never take a step, never voice an opinion—without thinking of you first and foremost. Nothing comes before you."

She remained still and silent for a long time. Then she said quietly, "I believe you."

His eyes closed.

Finally. Progress.

She'd accepted so much, so readily, he often forgot the enormity of what he asked of her. She was so exceptional in every way that he sometimes took his phenomenal good fortune for granted.

Not tonight. Tonight he knew the importance of what he held close. He understood the tenuous balance of what they shared. It was killing him not to speak it aloud, to bare heart and soul to her after so many weeks of doubt, but that would just pressure her before she was ready to choose. He'd tried that before and it had backfired. She was as stubborn as she was prideful.

For now, he'd just have to be patient.

"It's not you," she said quietly. "And it's not this case."

"What do you mean, *cher*?"

"I don't know what's wrong with me. I'm angry and edgy all the time. I'm afraid to let you close, afraid you won't like what you see. I don't like what I'm doing—to you, to Alain and Tina—but I can't seem to get a grip on it. I jump into things I know I shouldn't; I hide from those I should trust. I'm all upside down."

"What can I do?" he asked.

Her hand covered his. "This. Be here with me like this. I'm so scared I'm going to push you away. I'm so afraid you won't want me enough to see this through with me."

"You may have noticed I'm not easily pushed. I tend to stay where I'm planted. What did your boss call me? Chokeweed?"

A small laugh. "I hope he was right." Her voice caught on a sob. "I don't want a future without you in it. I'd rather die than lose you."

He squeezed her, tight. "Don't say that, *sha*. Don't ever say that."

"I love you, Max. I know I'm not good at showing it, and I forget to tell you sometimes when I know I should. I know I suck at relationships and I disappoint you by being more cop than girlfriend."

"I've never been disappointed in you. I'm the lucky one, Charlotte. *I* am."

He bent his head to press a light kiss on her brow. His hand cupped her chin to lift her face, so he could kiss her lips softly, gently. Again with more intensity. Then with the engaging tease of his tongue.

She turned away, catching the hand that stealthily traced up her thigh. "Don't start."

Not a strong objection. He could have easily overcome it, but not tonight. He guided her cheek to his chest.

"Just doing a little tasting, *sha*. My appetite is under control."

His promise would have been more credible if not for the erection pressing against her hip. The presence of that bold interest comforted Cee Cee. Because he wanted her body, but needed her love more.

"Could you stay with me tonight, Max? Just lie here with me tonight?"

"I can do that."

She smiled as an incredible weight let go inside her. Finally, she could close her eyes.

Seventeen

SHE DREAMED OF pearls falling like bloodstained tears, raining down into stagnant water as a crushing sense of horror built and built and built within her chest until she couldn't breathe. Until her heart didn't have room to beat. Until the only sound that could escape that awful press of shock and disbelief was a despairing whimper.

Grief, simple and raw.

Cornered, terrified, panting wildly as something huge began to swell inside. Stark and vicious beyond understanding, uncontrollable rage ready to explode.

Her eyes flashed open to meet Max's. In that instant, as they lay nose-to-nose, surfacing from that same black dream, she saw through him to all the violence and pain that still banged frantically inside him.

His bad dreams. His memories of the child he'd been when his mother had died.

She took an anguished breath, pulling away from the remnants of a lost boy's fright and tears, jerking free of the lethal power snapping along her body like a downed electrical wire. And she knew this was what seethed at the center of Max Savoie.

She also realized at that heart-stopping moment that whatever he now saw through those wide glittering eyes, as they swirled red and gold, wasn't her.

A menacing growl rumbled low in his throat. His lip curled back from teeth sharp as daggers. As the bones in his face began to elongate, she felt a sudden alarm. He could kill her. Kill her in a second without even knowing what he'd done.

"Max. Max, wake up. It's Charlotte. Baby, it's Charlotte. Max, look at me. *Look* at me."

When she put her palm to his sweaty cheek he lunged back, shoving her away hard enough to knock her onto the floor between the two beds while he scrambled off the other side. Her temple and cheekbone hit the night table, and she heard him cry, "Don't open the door. Don't open it!"

Max hit the thin rug hard on knees, elbows, and forehead, crouching there, rocking back and forth. Sickness swelled inside him, not just from the shared dream, but from the invasion of his consciousness and the abrupt separation that left him confused.

He didn't know where he was, *when* he was, trapped in a writhing limbo of shadows between the past and present. Instinct leapt up to scramble over rational thought. Threat crowded from all sides. He could smell the swamp, thick and rank; could taste its foulness and the coppery flavor of blood in his mouth. And then a sweet, sweet smell, cloying and deadly.

Fear, hunger, and pain punched through him. Emotions, feelings that were his own, but were someone else's, too.

No, please. Please don't. A young woman's voice.
Run! Hide! Find safety. His mother's screams.

Disoriented, breathing in quick hard thrusts, he

lurched forward on all fours toward the door. He dimly registered a red-haired female of unfamiliar scent, unfamiliar look struggling to her feet, reaching for him, mouthing his name. He couldn't hear her over the roaring in his head.

Hesitation. A brief tugging whisper that he go to her for comfort, for shelter, was quickly overruled by deeper, ingrained caution.

Humans harm what they fear. Run. Protect yourself. Survive at any cost.

So he ran, chased by ghosts from a past he couldn't escape.

"WHAT THE HELL happened to you?"

Cee Cee looked up from the edge of the bed, a washcloth filled with ice pressed to her throbbing cheek as she fought down the dizziness that delayed her pursuit of Max. By the time she'd gotten to the open doorway he'd disappeared, and she had to find him, to make sure he was all right.

"Did that son of a bitch hit you?" Babineau sat beside her, lifting the cloth to inspect the damage, his features thunderous. "He's dead. He's fucking dead."

She growled, "No, he didn't hit me. I slipped and hit the nightstand."

"Is that why you're wound so tight? Why you toss all night and call out his name? How long has this been going on? I'm going to kill him, I swear to God."

She clutched his elbows as he started to surge to his feet. "It's not Max. It's *not*."

"You expect me to believe that after listening to your

nightmares, after hearing you scream in your sleep?" His voice thickened and broke. "Listening and not being able to do anything while you plead with him to stop hurting you?"

"It's not Max who's hurting me. It's Max who saved me," she said quietly.

"From what?"

"From becoming just another statistic on Dovion's table."

And she finally told him. She and Mary Kate Malone kidnapped at seventeen while on their way home from a high school basketball game, held captive for four days to pressure her father not to testify. Abused and repeatedly raped during those endless, awful days and nights, scarred physically and mentally beyond repair. Until rescue arrived from a most unexpected source.

"Max saved us. I don't think we would have survived another day. Maybe not another hour. We wouldn't have wanted to survive. He saved us from those monsters Legere had hired to hold us, and he never told me. It wasn't until recently that I . . . I was able to recognize him."

Babineau understood. Max Savoie's rescue had come while in his beast form. "So these nightmares . . ."

She looked away from him; her eyes shimmered with tears. "Are memories."

"Did he kill them?"

"Yes. Horribly."

"Good." And Alain understood something else at that moment. "So this was why you and I never . . . Who else knows?"

"Just Max, Dev, and the chief."

"Why didn't you tell *me*? You didn't think you could trust me with something that important?"

"That personal," she clarified. "I thought—I thought it would get in the way. Because I never wanted you to look at me the way you are right now."

"You think I pity you, is that it? That I think you're weak or flawed? Christ, Ceece, don't you know me at all?"

She had no reply, just that challenging look of pride underscored with fragility.

He put his arms around her and drew her close, holding her tight.

She sagged limply against him, her tremendous strength at an ebb. After a long minute passed, he chuckled to himself.

"What?"

"Just thinking how different things might have been if you'd told me before that 'affair' we supposedly had. I recall too many drinks after a long case, fumbling around on your sofa like teenagers until your right hook kept me from sliding into home plate. Not exactly the torrid romance Savoie imagines when he dreams up ways of killing me."

"Sorry."

"About the right hook or misleading Savoie?"

"Both."

"I deserved the right hook. We're too good as partners to let sex with the wrong person screw things up. Then and now," he added sadly.

She leaned away, and now she was the one with pity in her eyes. "You're right about us, Alain. But dead wrong about Max and Tina. We're with the ones we were meant to have."

His voice filled with torment. "They're not like us, Ceece. They don't fit into our lives, into our world. They're alien." He paused, then he just said quietly, "They're fucking monsters."

She gripped his face between her hands, angry and anxious. "They're the people we love."

"They're *not* people. They're not human, Charlotte." His expression crumpled and his eyes filled with anguish. "What am I going to do? She and that little boy were my life. They were everything I dreamed of. Now that dream's a nightmare and I can't seem to wake up from it."

"Because you love them." It was that simple. And that complex.

A rapid tap on the door brought their words to an end. While Cee Cee went to answer it, Babineau wiped away his vulnerability and had his gun at the ready. Stan Schoenbaum leaned in, shadowed by MacCreedy.

"Hey, neighbors. What the hell hit you?"

"Reality, with a hard right cross. What are you doing here, Stan?"

"Picked up a strange call I thought you might be interested in. Two DBs a couple of blocks from here. One missing his heart."

Max.

"Babs, let's take a walk."

"We can't get involved," he warned.

"But we can take a look."

———

THE NIGHT WAS thick and damp, making him labor for every breath. He moved unsteadily down the crowded street, fingertips to the walls for balance, senses spinning, emotions pinballing out of control.

Home. Get home. Safe there. Jimmy will keep me safe.

But Jimmy was gone.

He reeled into one of the narrow, stinking alleys, leaning against sweaty stone, closing his eyes to shut out the light and chaos. For some reason, he wasn't wearing shoes. He remembered. He'd been in bed with Charlotte. *Charlotte.* He tried to breach the confusion with a shake of his head.

The dream.

He took a gulping breath and pressed palms to the wall as panic swelled in a threatening tide, pulling at him, drowning him in half-remembered horror. Images swirled through cold, anxious nightmares from a past he couldn't bear to relive. He couldn't go back there. Didn't want to see. Didn't want to know.

Run. Protect yourself. Survive at any cost.

Dread and sickness swept him as he saw those bloodied pearls falling . . .

"You okay, podna? You get chockay with too much drinking?"

The voice shocked him back to his senses. Max didn't open his eyes as he rasped, "Fine. I'm fine. Go away."

"Naw, we can't just go off and leaf you here like dis. Dat wouldn't be right. Give you a hand, take a reward."

Laughter, low and coarse.

"I don't need any help."

"Then maybe we just help ourselves."

His eyes slitted open. There were three of them, dark-skinned, hard-eyed, and determined. He shook his head at the ridiculousness of their planning to rob him.

"This is a mistake you don't want to be making."

The flash of blades appeared in the hands of the two flanking him, but the third held a squat revolver. A knife was a respectable weapon, up close and personal. Max didn't like guns, didn't like the savage way they allowed even a weakling to snatch away another's life. There was no fairness in a gun. No honor.

"How 'boutchu make nice and pass over your wallet."

"I've got nothing you want. Walk away while you can," he warned a second time, his voice deepening.

The speaker sneered at him. "Case you didn't notice, there be three of us and one of you."

A dark, cool fire kindled as Max shifted his balance from his heels to his toes. His mind was clear now, clear and sharp as those blades and twice as deadly, as what he was inside whispered for release. He exhaled deeply, almost like a satisfied sigh. And he smiled. "You should have brought more friends."

"That right? What makes you think so?" The gun poked at him with a belligerent bravado as the street tough assumed an intimidating posture. "Who the hell you think you are?"

"The last thing you'll ever see."

The gun leveled. As the finger on the trigger tightened, Max had the man's wrist, twisting quick and hard. The revolver discharged beneath its owner's chin, the bullet tearing through his neck as his gaze widened in surprise at the sight of his blood splashing Max's face.

As their leader fell, the two others hesitated. Then one ran; the other lunged.

The blade scissored along Max's side, then slashed across his forearm and jaw in decisive motions, missing anything vital as Max feinted aside. Max barely registered the pain as an energizing flush of power poured into his veins. His response was immediate and brutal. A snarl distorting his bloody features, he tore through the other's tee shirt and rib cage to rip free a grisly trophy he devoured like the animal he was. As he closed his eyes in near rapture, the lifeless body collapsed at his feet.

After wiping his sleeve across his mouth, Max drew in the scent of the one who'd thought he'd gotten away.

GASPING FRANTICALLY, THE small-time hood dodged down a dark alley. His lungs about to burst, he ducked into a dark doorway to catch his breath so he could think of what to do, about what he'd seen and *still* couldn't believe. But before a single idea came to him, he turned and shrieked at the sight of the gruesome figure confronting him, covered in the fate of his friends.

"Please. Please," he babbled in terror. "I got me a wife, two bebes, another on de way. I lost me my job. I only threw in with dem for some quickie cash. Dey said nobody would get hurt. I just needed the money. It weren't for me. Please."

The ghoulish figure reached out and he flinched, but the man only took his wallet. He trembled, watching strange eyes flicker from unnatural gold to cool green as the man studied the pictures he carried and the name on his driver's license. Then he drew out four bills from his own pocket, tucking the fifties into the empty bifold before returning it.

"Feed your family. Go to Legere Enterprises in the morning. Ask for Giles St. Clair. He'll give you work."

He started away.

"Hey . . . hey, who you are?"

A flash of strong white teeth in the gory face. "You'll know soon enough."

"I KNOW WHAT I saw. He was right there—right next to the other one."

"Maybe he just got up and walked away."

"With a hole the size of a saucer in his chest? I don't think so."

Cee Cee, Babineau, Schoenbaum, and the transplanted Vice detective, MacCreedy, edged into the crowd at the mouth of the alley. Careful not to catch the eye of the officer trying to calm a furious tourist whose clipped East Coast tones were growing louder and more insistent, they checked out the scene. One body remained sprawled on the ground, victim to the pistol still clenched in his hand. There was enough blood on-site to validate the woman's claim of another victim, but no evidence that another killing had been done. Of course, that would change when two blood types were found. Or three.

Cee Cee's gut clenched. A robbery gone wrong, most likely. But where was the intended victim?

MacCreedy moved in closer, crouching down near the blood-soaked stones, intense in his study. Cee Cee gripped her partner's arm and towed him out of the circle of voyeurs.

"Time for us to go see if those home fires are still burning."

MAX STOOD IN the shower fully dressed, letting the hot water wash the blood down the drain. Giles hadn't said a word about his appearance when he'd picked him up and driven him back to River Road, while a group of Jimmy's trusted cleaners slipped in to dispose of the corpse with its all-too-telling cause of death. They hadn't had time to retrieve the other body and completely sanitize the scene.

All that remained of his own wounds were the stains on his clothes. All that remained of what he'd done was the taste in his mouth and the jittery hum of adrenaline.

A high like no other: that's how his father had described killing. Max had denied it then, but he couldn't now. Not while it trembled through his system. The excitement, the danger of confrontation, the thrill of domination. There was nothing like it.

He leaned into the spray, letting the water fill his mouth so he could rinse and spit. But the taste lingered. The taste of death. He understood now that this was in his genetic makeup, what he was bred to be. But that made it no less appalling—or the fact that he liked it, savored the strength flooding through him.

He cranked the faucet to cold. With palms braced against the tiles, he let the chill beat the quiver of savagery from him until all that was left was weariness and remorse.

How could Charlotte love him? How could he ever hope she'd accept all that he was when he couldn't manage that himself?

Dressed in slouchy sweats, he peered in at Oscar, emotions crowding up. His brother. His father's other son. Oscar had progressed so quickly during their lessons, already able to conceal the essence of what he was, able to unerringly find Max even from amazing distances during their games of hide-and-seek. Simple tricks compared to what they'd be facing.

He knew next to nothing about the nature of what they were. How could he fulfill his promise to protect the boy when he didn't understand his enemy? They were going to die, horribly, and he didn't know how to prevent it.

The Shifter king. His features contorted briefly with irony. The blind following the blinder. Jacques was right to mock him; he didn't know what he was doing. The only thing he could do well was protect himself. Even now, looking down upon the innocent sleeping boy, he could hear that instinctive whisper.

Run. Save yourself. Survive. Don't look back. You don't owe them anything. You don't owe them your life.

But what would his life be without them? His clan, Jimmy's people, this boy. Charlotte.

Restless, moody, lonely, he went out onto the front porch to settle into the old glider, wishing he was still small enough to tuck under it until rescue came. But there was no rescue for him now. He rocked, letting the movement soothe his troubled mind, his heavy heart.

Then he became aware of someone nearby. "Don't you ever sleep, Giles?"

Giles St. Clair came out onto the porch, standing at the top of the steps to stare out into the night. "I'll sleep when you sleep. When I'm sure you won't be getting yourself into any more trouble."

Max smiled at the faint censure. "If you think loyalty will encourage me to pay you more when you're too tired to do your job, you're mistaken."

"Don't worry about me, boss man. I'll keep up."

"A fella by the name of Peekon Williams should be coming to you about work tomorrow. See that he gets a job. If he doesn't show up, let me know."

"Some more of that same trouble?"

"I hope not." He closed his eyes, moving the glider back and forth. He could feel Giles's pensive study.

"It's nice having the boy here."

He waited for the other shoe to drop.

"But I think you've got the wrong woman upstairs."

Max tensed. "I don't recall asking for your opinion."

"You didn't. Figured you'd want to know it."

"We need to sort some things out between us, is all."

"And that's gonna happen by you moving another family in while her back's turned?"

"That's not what I did."

Then Max caught the unmistakable rumble of a big-block engine, and his spirit settled. And as the vehicle approached, he hoped no regrets were coming his way.

Eighteen

THE TWO PARTNERS approached the porch as a team. Max's expression was inscrutable. Giles broke the standoff with a friendly overture.

"Charlotte, this is a new look for you. Very, pardon me for saying so, hot."

"Hello, Giles."

"Here for a professional or personal visit?"

Max coolly said, "It's always business first. What can I help you with, Detectives?"

"Doing some off-the-clock follow-up on a witness statement," Babineau stated with equal chill. "One vic dead at the scene with a gunshot wound a few blocks from our motel. The witness claims there was another DB minus a heart that somehow managed to disappear before the police got there. Plenty of blood to suggest she was telling the truth."

"If you're asking to search the premises for your missing body, I'll want to see a warrant first, and to have my attorney present. But perhaps I can save you some time by telling you there's no one on site without a pulse."

"You must have walked right by that alley on your way back to your car. Right about the time the DB was bleeding out. Did you happen to see anything, Savoie?

Like some kind of freak with fangs and claws yanking the beating heart out of some guy's chest?"

"No, Detective. I didn't see anything like that. If those are your only questions, your family is upstairs. They'd probably like to see you."

Babineau hesitated, then he went in through the door Giles held open, the bodyguard following on his heels.

Alone, Max frowned at the sight of the bruises on Cee Cee's cheek and brow.

"Why did you kill those men?" she asked in a voice as tight as the ratchet of her cuffs.

"Are you here to arrest me, Detective? If that's what you want, here's your confession: I killed them. Their own foolishness and greed initiated it. I did one with his own gun, the other with my bare hands. And I enjoyed doing it. To the very last bite.

"It's what I am. That part of me you loathe. What a monster that must make me in your self-righteous eyes."

She said nothing, standing on the top step of the porch, keeping that neutral distance in space and attitude. And that goaded his temper up another notch.

"Oh, I'm sorry. Not enough physical evidence for you?" He surged up off the swing. "I've just the thing."

Cee Cee waited while he disappeared into the house. Small tremors began to build into seismic waves of fear. Why was he doing this? What was he trying to prove? That there was no hope for them? Instead of working to resolve their differences, why was he determined to emphasize how impossible it was to span them?

He burst from the house full of dark, forceful power. She caught the wet garment he flung at her.

"There," he said in a low snarl. "I think I managed to preserve everyone's DNA."

She recognized the shirt as the one he'd been wearing, and her heart clenched at the vicious knife slashes in the material. Her gaze lifted, shimmery with emotion. "Are you all right?"

The quavering words almost undid him, but he held tightly to his anger. "Of course I'm all right. You think a few petty thieves could bring me down when seven skilled assassins couldn't? The only one who's ever taken me to my knees is you, and you know it."

She fingered the torn fabric, her hands shaking, then stepped onto the porch and crossed to him. She touched his side, his arm, in gentle exploration.

"Self-defense," she said. Then her eyes were all glittery again. "They attacked you, hurt you. I'm glad they're dead."

As her arms slipped about his waist and her head rested on his shoulder, the tension ebbed from Max in relief. He rubbed his cheek over her false red hair; his hands came up to knead her strong shoulders. He took a huge, satisfied breath—and his body stiffened.

Cee Cee heard the quick snuffles and the rumble of his growl vibrate through him, and she held tight to ride out the whiplash of his discovery.

He gripped her chin and thrust her head back so that her face tilted up to him. Her gaze held his firmly, her expression open without the regret, guilt, or the defiance he'd expected as he leaned close to sniff her. She watched possessive rage and tortured pride build in his tough features, and she locked her hands behind his back as if to form a circle he couldn't break.

"It was nothing, Max. Trust me."

"Trust you," he repeated in a toneless whisper. "The only reason my fist isn't breaking through his rib cage right now is because he's sitting upstairs with his wife and child."

"Max, listen to me," she petitioned quietly.

"Listen to you. Trust you. You come to me, to my home, with the smell of him all over you, and ask me that? You ask me *that*?" he roared as he shoved her away then paced the porch fiercely

"Don't be stupid, Savoie. You know there's nothing going on. He's having a difficult time dealing with what he found out about his wife."

He faced her with a deadly chill in his eyes. "Did you convince him to accept his animal bride? And what happened to your face?"

Her hand rose to her cheek, her eyes darkening with dismay, and a stark realization struck Max. He'd been with her in her motel room. What had happened there? He couldn't remember. He didn't know what he'd done, only what he was capable of: hurting, *killing* the one thing most precious to him without being aware of it.

"Maybe he's right, Charlotte. Maybe it's madness to think you can mingle with monsters without things ending badly."

"Max." She gripped his arm, but he jerked away.

"Don't try to rationalize what we both know is true. Not now. Collect your lover and go—it's dangerous for you to be here right now."

"Dammit, Max, don't push me away!"

"If you won't leave, I will."

In two gigantic strides, he vaulted over the rail and disappeared into the night.

She stared after him, furious. "Don't you run away from me," she shouted.

She plunged into the night in pursuit. She crossed the back lawn knowing it was stupid, but pride and panic kept her going. She'd plowed through fifty yards of the thick woods before her ridiculous shoes failed her, snagging on ropy vines to send her sprawling, rolling down a steep incline into a mossy ditch far below.

Once she'd recovered her breath Cee Cee tried to stand, then collapsed onto the ground with a cry of pain.

Damn shoes. Damn Savoie.

She lay there on the cold, boggy soil, cursing them both, cursing the need to crawl back to the car to slink off in shame, when she hadn't done anything wrong. She sat up to take off her shoes, but the agony knocked her down onto her back with a groan.

"Max! Max, I know you can hear me. Don't you just leave me out here, you son of a bitch."

"You should speak a little more nicely to someone if you want them to help you."

"To hell with you," she grumbled. "Don't help me, then. I'll just lie here and let you explain why you have a decomposing police detective in your backyard."

He was suddenly crouched at her feet, and his hands were warm and soothing where her ankle throbbed. He removed her shoe and began a light massage.

"You shouldn't have come after me."

"I shouldn't have had to." Pain gave her words an extra sharpness. "How could you be so . . ."

"Stupid? I'll carry you to your car and let your *partner* take you for x-rays."

"Why, that would be damned decent of you."

"Or I could just tell him where to find you, and let him drag your thorny ass out of here."

She winced at the harshness of his tone. "Whatever unruffles your vanity."

"Vanity?" His head came up and moonlight bathed his incredulous expression.

She reached out to bracket his face between her palms. "How many times do I have to tell you, there's only you? Alain Babineau is my partner, my friend. Nothing more. He's *never* been more."

She sighed. "We were never lovers, Max. We never had sex. I only said that to provoke you, and I shouldn't have let you continue to believe it. He's no threat to you, or to what we have. He needs to get back to his family. And I need to get back to you."

Relief was short-lived in his expression. He shook free of her touch. "So I've been imagining that you've been having reservations, that there's a sudden uncertainty between us? Tell me I'm wrong, Charlotte, and I'll believe you. I want to believe you." He handed her the shoe and lifted her easily into his arms.

Outrage and indignation hit hard. "Reservations? What about your cozy little business deals with Manny Blu? And your new family here." Here, the only place besides St. Bart's that had ever been home. Pain pinched her heart. "Put me the fuck down." She gave him a hard elbow and he opened his arms, letting her plop to the ground on her rump. She glared up at him, jealous and upset beyond reason.

"At least they accept me for what I am. Why shouldn't I want that, Charlotte? Why shouldn't I expect that from those I love?"

She spat, "I accept you for what you are, Savoie. I'm your mate. I wear your mark."

He shook his head. "It means nothing. That ties me to you—not the other way around. You're not bound by my rules or to me."

"Not bound to you?" She glared up at him through the haze of her tears. "What about what *I* want?"

"Tell me."

"I want you. I want you to chase after me and claim me. I want you to fight for what we have. I want you to say fuck our differences, and take me right here on the ground in your beast form until we both howl at the moon."

When he said nothing, she added more quietly, "What do *you* want?"

A hint of a smile. "You've pretty much covered it, *sha*."

Relief poured out in a soft laugh. "Come here to me, baby."

He dropped down over her, straddling her hips, hands splayed on either side of her shoulders as she reached up for him, lacing her fingers behind his head. She lifted up to meet his mouth, gripping hard when he started to rear back at the reminder of where Alain Babineau had been. She wouldn't let him go, kissing him fiercely, licking his lips, his chin, his cheeks, then rubbing her face against his.

"I want the only scent on me to be yours."

With a lusty growl he pressed her into the loamy earth, mouth devouring, hands impatient as he tore through the gauzy bits of sequin and ribbon. She arched into his palms, and cried out as he feasted roughly from her unusually sensitive breasts. She had his sweatshirt and pants shucked from him like she was peeling a crawfish and dinnertime was long overdue.

As her lips and hands moved hungrily over him, an eerie heat began to rise, heightened as they touched, prickling along the surface of their skin like static electricity. Arousing, hot, feeding their urgency for the other like a battery charger. So their bond meant nothing? she thought wildly. He was so gloriously mistaken.

She clutched at his dark head as his hands slid over her tight skirt, caressing her hips, the slight mound of her sex through the supple leather. When her legs began shifting restlessly, he reached under it to coax her silky panties off. She was making incoherent sounds of encouragement by the time he pushed up the skirt and wedged her thighs wide open.

The flicker of his tongue sent her hurdling over the edge. His insistent mouth kept her at that urgent pinnacle, at the junction of pleasure and an intensity so sharp it was almost pain. Making her writhe and finally beg for him to stop so she could breathe.

He raised over her on all fours as she sprawled on the ground, panting, shivering, mad for him.

She stroked his face, his shoulders greedily, and smiled. "Now," she purred, "let me have *you*. Show me, Max. Show me all that you are."

His eyes began to change, the cool jade heating to

molten gold. Beneath her hands she could feel his bone structure strengthening, angling into bold, more lupine contours. Her touch adored him, because it was Max. As she felt him shifting, that strange energy played havoc with her senses. Through the lusty heat, in a hazy sort of double exposure, she saw the features she loved beneath the beast he'd become. She laughed in amazement, the sound filled with dizzying joy and a relieved abandonment as she gave herself to him.

Because of the bond they shared, everything was different and new. Desperately exciting, richly dimensional. Touch, scent, even the sound of his hurried breathing, were all erotically textured.

Overwhelmed by the colors and layered images, she closed her eyes to simply feel. Trembling at the long strokes of his tongue over her skin, quivering as he nipped at her with sharp teeth, never fearing he'd harm her. His huge hands made rough circles over breasts, hips, and thighs, his nails scratching lightly, causing dangerous thrills of sensation.

She said his name, a low, awed whisper. Or at least she thought she did. She was completely out of touch with her surroundings, floating in that timeless, dreamlike state where only Max existed. Max, her lover. Max, her mate.

She didn't resist as he rolled her over and hiked her hips up high. The need to be one with him was an intoxicating drug, making her rock back against him, rubbing, moaning in instinctive female heat.

She'd never wanted anything as much as the feel of his hands, his breath, his mouth on her skin. She'd never yearned for anything as feverishly as that first probe of him between her spread thighs. That relentless pressure searing, spreading, invading. She encouraged him to fill her, backing into him until he seemed to touch the door to her womb. And she began to move, building those brilliant shivers of delight that went on and on. Tears filled her eyes in sheer wonder.

Vaguely she could feel him plunging, faster, harder, making harsh, rough snatches of sounds like snarls, until finally, with one massive shudder, he let go in a tide so strong it swept her under. And as it roared in her ears, she thought she heard him howl.

The steadiness of his breathing eased her back into awareness. She opened her eyes to see stars overhead, to feel the silky rush of warm water all around her. When she gave a start, strong arms tightened about her.

"Shhh. It's all right. You're with me."

She tried to sit up, but her muscles were ridiculously relaxed and wouldn't support her. She became aware of Max's sleek nudity beneath her, and realized they were soaking together in the big claw-footed tub.

Max nuzzled her neck. "We were all dirty and sweaty. I thought this might be nice for you to wake up to."

She sighed and sank into him while her thoughts slowly gathered. "How'd we get here?"

"I carried you."

Her eyes snapped open. "Is Babineau still here?"

A slight testiness crept into his tone. "He wouldn't leave without you. I told him we had a spat, that you twisted your ankle and fainted."

"Fainted? Hmmph."

"It was the best I could come up with, considering you were unconscious and we were half dressed."

"Oh. Nice story."

A pause, then a quiet, "Are you all right?"

She made a satisfied sound and snuggled into him. "That was quite a ride."

His lips touched her brow. "Thank you for taking it with me."

"Anytime, my king."

"Do you mean that, Charlotte?"

She twisted so she could look up into his eyes. Her fingertips brushed over his cheek as she whispered, "I meant every word, and more."

He caught her hand and pressed a kiss to her palm. She felt his smile against it and said, "I want to come home to you. Unless you think it would be too crowded." She regretted the tense codicil the moment it escaped her.

He continued to hold her hand, but his stare grew guarded. "We can discuss it when your case is over. While we're enjoying Sex on the Beach somewhere warm and sandy."

"Okay." She sighed her disappointment. Not quite the declaration she'd wanted, but maybe more than she deserved. "I need to get out before I slide down the drain."

They dried off quickly, not looking at each other. Cee Cee found her underwear, skirt, and one shoe.

"Can I borrow a shirt?"

If he noticed the strain in her voice, he didn't react to it. "Take anything you like."

She wanted to take back the last three weeks.

She shrugged on a black tee shirt that hung almost to the hem of her skirt, and, with her back to him, said, "It was just once. We'd been on a really tough case, long hours and some pretty intense gunplay. It started with drinks at Newton's with the team, then ended up at my apartment with a case of longnecks. We were drunker than skunks and just glad to be alive, which had us thinking, Why the hell not?"

"You don't need to tell me this, *cher*," he said quietly.

"Yes, I do. In fairness to you and what we have together."

"Then tell me."

A lot of sloppy kissing and clumsy groping ended up with half their clothes off and his impatient hands on her skin, seeking entry to places her mind slammed shut in panic. And plans for an uninhibited bout of sex suddenly became something altogether different. He hadn't noticed when her movements went from grasping to objecting. She'd been on the edge of a scream when that desperate right hook stopped him. After his awkward exit, she'd lain there for the rest of the night, paralyzed with shame and dread.

They'd never spoken of it for fear that it would jeopardize their working relationship. And she never would have admitted to it until it threatened hers and Max's.

"And that disaster was my most successful sexcapade until you."

He drew her, slowly, against him and whispered softly, "You have nothing to be ashamed of. I'm sorry. I should have believed you. Something about this bond between us gets me so territorial when I even think about someone else near you. I can't seem to control it; I can't think straight around it. It's there under the surface all the time, making me crazy." He sighed deeply. "I've never had anything, Charlotte, and now I have so much, it overwhelms me. The most amazing female for my mate, a clan and all those dependent upon Jimmy now looking to me to lead, a brother expecting me to show him the way."

He was silent, then asked quietly, "How am I going to keep Oscar safe if they come for him again?"

"What if it's not about Oscar, Max?"

His brows puckered. "What?"

"What if it's about you?"

"What do you mean?"

"LaRoche thinks it's what you inherited from your mother and father that makes you so different—that makes you their promised one."

He laughed. "LaRoche believes in fairy tales. But the danger is real, no matter who's the target. If I could have my way, you'd be locked behind these walls with nothing to keep you busy except attending to the two of us. Our own family."

Puppies.

She stepped away. "I'm afraid you'll be disappointed," she said in a tight voice. "I don't have Tina's domestic talents. I was raised stripping handguns, not separating eggs for soufflés. Our Home Sweet Home was so awful that it sent my mother into a bottle until she finally ran away. And though my father stayed, he found his own way to escape me. So you see, I'm a bad bet."

"Charlotte, you're my one sure thing. I'm not wrong about that."

"Just something for you to think about, Max. Because there's no guarantee I won't let us both down."

She bolted. Running from a pain and panic she couldn't understand or suppress.

MAX STOOD IN the parlor, staring out at her dust cloud in the driveway.

A soft sound made him turn to see Tina Babineau in the doorway. She looked as miserable as he was trying not to feel.

"Alain was so very polite—like we were strangers to him. Oh, Max, what are we going to do if he doesn't want us back?"

His answer came without conscious decision. "You'll stay here, of course."

Nineteen

CEE CEE STARED down at the packet of pills in her hand and listened to Dr. Judy explain the use and risks of birth control. Something she'd never had to consider before.

"What if there's a chance I might be pregnant?"

"Your labs all came back clear." Farraday's eyes narrowed. "Have you been stupid and had unprotected sex since you were tested?"

If she only knew. Not only stupidly unprotected, but outside her own species. "Let's say I had."

"Taking birth control could irreparably harm the fetus or cause spontaneous abortion. If there's a possibility, I'd suggest you wait a few weeks then get tested again. Or I could prescribe a morning-after pill, then there would be no worries."

Killing anything she and Max might have created between them.

"I'll wait," she whispered.

"And try practicing a little self-control. You're not a ragingly hormonal fifteen-year-old, you know."

But as Cee Cee walked toward the front door instead of the back, where she usually entered, she felt like one—as confused, scared, and alone as the young girls seated in the lobby. She could hear LaRoche's voice telling her the only way to pass on the pure genetic Shifter code was for a male to mate in his natural form. Had Max given her DNA that would make whatever they might have created into some kind of hybrid oddity?

She could see again the poignant longing in Max's face when he'd told her he wanted what Alain Babineau had. The pain in his eyes when she'd revealed she could never give him a child.

What if she could now give him those things? A child to bind their love into a permanent commitment? A quiver of longing tightened low in her belly. The possibility thrilled and terrified her. Because she knew that wanting and having the dream of family were worlds apart.

She was so steeped in her dismal brooding, she almost walked right through the crowded waiting area without noticing. The reflection of the pale neon glow in the barred front windows caught her attention, and she turned to stare.

Half the wall was covered by a huge saltwater aquarium.

"HOW ARE THINGS going tonight, Al?"

Alain Babineau smiled amiably at his pseudo-employer. "Good, Mr. Blutafino. No trouble. Good door take, nice crowd."

"That's what I like to hear. Walk with me."

Babineau fell in step with him as he made his nightly pass through the club. "Mr. Blutafino, there is one thing."

"Manny. Call me Manny."

"Manny. Some of the girls are skittish about this 'Tides That Bind' crazy. They're saying he has something to do with the club, and it's stirring up a lot of nervousness. A couple of our headliners are even talking about quitting."

"Who's spreading that horseshit around? I want them canned. Now. That's all I need—some hysterical stripper taking out a good customer who just happens to like bondage."

"Maybe they'd feel better if they thought we were taking it seriously. You know, looking out for their best interests."

"Stupid whores." He stopped and sighed heavily. "Oh, hell. Any ideas?"

"I could make a show of checking out some of our more . . . peculiar customers. That ought to quiet them down some."

"Good idea. Quick thinking. I like that."

"Do you keep any kind of list of particular requests by client name?"

"It's all about knowing your clientele, Al, my boy." He gave a sly wink.

Blackmail. Big surprise. "Yes, sir."

"Ask Nick. He'll get it for you. Just be discreet. Let the girls know, but don't scare off the customers. We don't want them to think we discourage naughty fantasies here."

Manny opened the door to his office, and Babineau almost walked right into the last person he expected to see.

From the blank expression on the other man's face, the feeling was mutual.

"Right on time, I see. Simon, meet my new man, Al Babbit. He's the kind of fast thinker who gets things done."

"Mr. Babbit, nice to meet you."

The detective shook Simon Cummings's hand and murmured, "Likewise."

Manny slapped him on the back. "Go on and get started on that project, Al. Keep me posted. Simon, how 'bout a drink?"

The door closed, and Babineau wondered if mayoral candidate Cummings was now blowing the whistle on him.

"Caissie."

"Heya."

Cee Cee's heart fluttered. "I can't talk right now. I'm at work."

"I'm looking at the stage. She's a nimble little thing, but she's not you."

"At. Work."

"Ahh. News?"

"Big-time."

"Shall I make reservations?"

"Not just yet—but soon. Our clock's running down on Kelly Schoenbaum."

"As in Detective Schoenbaum?"

"Yeah."

"Why didn't you ever mention that to me?" His gritty tone reflected his shared animosity with Stan Schoenbaum.

"Because this is about her, not him. Or you."

"I'll let you get back to it. Let me know when I

should make that phone call. Until then, I won't bother you."

She sighed. "Max? It's no bother."

A pause, then a low, warm, "Good night, Charlotte."

"And I found the aquarium. I owe you big-time."

"I intend to collect."

She smiled for a moment after hanging up, then dug into her research for the rest of the evening hours. She was so involved that she gave a startled jump when Babineau and Schoenbaum cast a shadow across her desk.

"I hope you brought coffee and something greasy," she said.

Babineau set a jumbo cup of java and a bag of burgers and fries on the desk in front of her. She inhaled the scents rapturously.

"Good man. Sit down. I'll fill you in while I feed the brain cells."

Between bites, she told them what she'd discovered while they'd finished out their shifts.

Judith Farraday, physician to the millionaire set, had established an exclusive practice with her husband, Dean, and her sister, Carol Lamb, along Lake Shore Drive, Chicago. A tour with Doctors Without Borders opened her eyes to true suffering and she donated more and more time to clinics serving the poor. She signed up for visits to underdeveloped countries where medical care was nonexistent. On her last trip with her husband and sister, disaster struck in the form of rebel uprising.

The fact that they were doctors and Americans

kept them alive after the initial slaughter. Their three months of captivity in steaming jungles, in the hands of crazed men, was an unimaginable horror—especially for the women.

As negotiations for ransom broke down and government reprisal grew closer, the three American doctors became a liability rather than a bartering tool. Dean Farraday, a respected plastic surgeon and rehabilitation specialist, was found dismembered. A grainy film of the carnage performed in front of the traumatized sisters was sent to various international concerns with demands for money and guns. When they got no response, Carol Lamb's grisly murder was the next film sent out. That sparked an even greater uproar in medical and humanitarian circles.

A battered, nearly catatonic Judith Farraday was rescued by a team of Special Forces and rushed to an exclusive hospital in the States. After seven months, she returned to the public eye giving interviews and speeches about human rights, and began founding clinics in the name of her slain loved ones.

During that missing seven months, Cee Cee discovered after laborious digging, Judith Farraday had a son. A child born of the rape and horror she'd suffered. A son who would be about twenty-six years old now.

Donald Lamb was a secret hidden away by Farraday money. In foster homes for the first eight years of his life, then institutionalized for the next ten, Donny Lamb was a dangerous mix of uncontrollable psychosis and mild retardation. His fondness for setting fires and hurting playmates as a child pushed him into a roller coaster of rapidly revolving care and intensive therapy.

Judith Farraday paid the bills and stayed away until Donny was eighteen. When he was ejected from his group home for the attempted rape of his therapist, Dr. Judy stepped in to assume responsibility. And there the trail ended as she moved from state to state establishing her clinics.

Until eight months ago, when Dr. Farraday opened the doors of her facility in New Orleans and Donald Lamb showed up as an employee at a Cajun Life reenactment park doing simple jobs.

"He has Kelly," Schoenbaum said.

Cee Cee pressed a staying hand over his clenched fist. "I'd put money on it." She looked up at her partner. "Match the cities where she set up clinics to any similar unsolved murders. I think our boy has a bad habit Mom's been trying to outrun. Stan, you set up surveillance on the doctor. Let's see where she takes us."

Stan looked past her, eyes narrowing. "Speaking of bad habits."

Cee Cee glanced around, surprised to see Max striding down the aisle of desks toward them. His stare knifed between the two detectives before settling on her, heating her with an unmistakable fire.

"Detective, I thought I'd stop in with sustenance and news." He glanced at the crumpled wrappers and empty cup. "I see I'm too late for the first."

She snatched the paper bag from his hands. "What did you bring me?" She buried her nose in the bag and sniffed. "Chickory and chocolate. Oh, baby. The way to my heart." Her hand reached out to curl around his. "Thanks. And the news?"

"Ahh, the second half of what makes me useful. Information." His hand eased out of hers. "That scent. It's not from a man. It belongs to—"

"Doctor Judith Farraday."

He gave her an admiring smile. "Yes. She came into the club to check a girl's twisted knee. I looked for your partner, but he'd already gone."

Cee Cee smiled. "She has an aquarium in her clinic."

"Nice work, Detective."

"Good information, Savoie."

Schoenbaum snarled, "Kissy face later. I want my little girl back."

"Let's get to it then." Cee Cee became all business. "We want to move fast but carefully. We don't want to spook them." She looked up at Max again. "Do you know where LaFont's Living Cajun Life Museum is?"

His posture tensed. "Over by Rayne. Why you want to know?"

"Because we're going to pay a little after-hours visit."

CEE CEE CALLED the caretaker for the museum so he could meet them when they got there. It was already after two A.M. and he wasn't pleased about being dragged from his bed for reasons she wouldn't discuss over the phone.

The Camaro's headlights cut through ribbons of fog as the drive grew more and more desolate. With every mile, Max withdrew into an even deeper silence. He nearly cleared seat leather when she touched his knee.

"You didn't have to come with me," she said.

"Worried I can't cover your back as well as your partner?"

"No. No one covers my back the way you do." After she earned a faint smile with that naughty insinuation, she added, "What's wrong, baby?" She could feel his tension as she rubbed his thigh.

"I don't know." Then he added quietly, "I don't like being out here after dark."

"Because of your mama?"

"I guess." He stared out the side window at the gnarled shadows of the bayou.

"The dream you had, the one about the pearls." At his surprise she soothed, "I shared it with you at the motel. Do you want to tell me about it?"

He inhaled slowly, then his breath shivered out. "Nothing to tell. I don't remember much of what actually happened."

"Just what Jimmy told you?"

"Pretty much."

"Did he tell you about your mama's pearls?"

"I don't recall that he did."

"That must have been something you saw, then."

"Must have been." His tone was as taut as his posture. His fingers started picking at the piping around the edge of the seat. After listening to the repetitive sound for one minute too many, she put her hand over his and held it tight. His skin was clammy and damp.

"You don't have to talk. It's okay."

"She used to wear them all the time. They were the only nice thing she had. I remember reaching for them when she'd rock me to sleep, remember the feel of them between my fingers. My father gave them to her."

"Did she tell you that?"

"No. She never told me anything about him. He gave Tina Babineau a string just like them."

A cold knot balled up inside her. "Family tradition?"

He followed her uneasy logic and explained softly, "I didn't know about what he'd done when I gave them to you. I wanted you to have them because they reminded me of someone else I loved."

The knot loosened. "She was wearing them when she died?"

"I caught them as she was falling. The string broke and they fell into the water. I remember standing there, just watching them drop."

His eyes squeezed shut.

Mama! Mama, please don't leave me!

"Did they hurt you, baby?" Her voice was rough with care.

"I don't know. I don't think so. I don't want to remember."

"It's okay. You don't have to."

He turned to her. "That girl on Dovion's table. That same smell was on her—the one I remember from those days and nights alone. And when I looked into her eyes, I could feel her last thoughts. She was so hungry and scared and hurt. It threw me back there again, Charlotte. It threw me hard and shook me up something awful. Made me start to remember things that I wanted to believe were just bad dreams."

"Why didn't you tell me, Max?" She held his hand tight. "You said, 'Don't open the door.'"

He kneaded her hand, his breathing unsteady. "It was something Jimmy taught me. He told me to push all the bad things into my closet and shut the door. As long as the door was closed, they couldn't get out. They couldn't hurt me."

"No wonder you have such a big-ass closet."

A hoarse laugh. He'd been so terrified, he'd slept under the bed at night, peering out from under the drape of the spread to keep a watchful eye in case that door came open and all the horrors he'd hidden away came spilling out. He still couldn't rest easy if it was ajar.

She was silent for a time, eyes on the road, warming his hand with her own. "Maybe some doors need to be opened."

He went still as she continued to muse.

"Maybe that's our problem, Max. Both of us spend so much energy trying to hold back the past, we can't enjoy the present and we can't consider the future. I didn't make that up—I'm not that profound. Dr. Forstrom, my shrinkologist, told me that. What in our musty old closets can hurt us if we open them together?"

"You have no idea what's stored away in there."

And he had no idea what she'd been hiding.

"I'll show you mine if you show me yours." She hoped her light, teasing tone would coax him into considering it, even though the very idea scared her spitless as well.

"Right."

"You bet your sexy ass, I'm right."

"No, I mean turn right."

"Shit." She cranked the wheel, sending the muscle car into a two-wheeled hop as she whipped around the corner.

"It should be coming up here on the left."

She steered into the big parking lot that would fill with tour buses in a few more hours. At three A.M., just one small pickup was sitting close to the entrance gate. She pulled in beside it and stopped.

"I like having sexy shoes in there," Max said.

"What?" She turned to him in question.

"In my closet. I like having your shoes in there. So I guess I'd better clear out some room."

"Happy to give you a hand any time you're ready, Savoie. I love taking out other people's trash—though I'm not so good with my own."

"We can work on that, too."

"Deal."

A voice called out, "Hallo in da car. Dat be you, Detective Cass-A?"

She slid out from under the wheel. "Mr. LaFont?"

"Dat be me."

"Thank you for coming out here so late to meet with us."

"I always try to make nice with the polezze. Dis be about Donny Lamb? Da boy gone and done sumpin cross the law?"

"Just here to ask him some questions."

LaFont was a wizened peanut of a man, bent and wrinkled, but with a snap of vinegar in his tone and a flash to his smile that said he had one or two *fais do-dos* left in him.

"He been a good worker, always on time, never

complaining. Kinda slow, not real talky, but dependable. He gots a way wid the animals. Dey lak him. He doan get in nobody's way and is po-lite to the visitors. Been here 'bout eight months. Works for just a little bit and a place to stay."

"Stay? You mean he has a place here?"

"Just a little shack. Nothing fancy. Gots to fit wid da look of da place, but he doan mind not having no satellite anten nor de air conditioning."

Her pulse began a quick, aggressive beat as she unsnapped the flap over her service revolver.

"Show me."

Twenty

THE VILLAGE CONSISTED of a cluster of rustic buildings around a pond. Solar lights were spaced along the gravel walkway as a liability precaution. LaFont led them in a large loop past the dark abodes and shops, then over a simple bridge, where the path narrowed to hard-packed dirt that wound between various types of animal pens.

Cce Cee glanced at the row of coops and exchanged a look with Max.

Chickens.

The only light now was the sweep of LaFont's flashlight. With Max slightly behind, moving so quietly she couldn't detect the sound of his feet on the loose stones, Cee Cee scanned the shadows, alert, ready, heart pumping, mind cool. Her internal clock ticked with the days, hours, minutes left in Kelly Schoenbaum's life. There was still time left to save her.

Lamb's cabin hunched down between a spread of live oaks. Wisps of moss trailed along the roofline like gauzy mummifying wraps. No light, no sound from within.

Cee Cee put her hand on their guide's arm to stop him. "This is as far as you go, Mr. LaFont. There'll be more officers arriving. Bring them here. Quietly."

He nodded and pressed the light into her hand

before making his way back along the familiar trail.

Tamping down her eagerness, Cee Cee woke up Byron Atcliff and made her report in a hushed voice. While she gave the details, she followed Max's sleek silhouette as he circled the building, then disappeared, one with the night.

Tucking her phone away, Cee Cee began the most difficult part of her job: waiting. First the warrant, then the search, then the stakeout, while somewhere, Kelly Schoenbaum was enduring the unthinkable.

But it wasn't unthinkable to Cee Cee. She could think of nothing but the fear, the pain, the helplessness, and finally the hopelessness.

Make them stop! Please, Lottie, make them stop!

"No one's home, Detective."

Max's voice filtering softly out of the darkness was like the jolt of a Taser, and it took a long second to calm her jittery nerves.

"You're sure?"

"He had company. Female. His is the other scent I picked up from the girl on Dovion's table. Unfortunately, that's not exactly admissible evidence."

Shit. Shit, shit, shit. And here she sat on her thumbs, waiting for protocol to work its way through the red tape.

She stared at the blank front of the building, with its papered-over windows. She needed to get inside. She needed to see how he lived, to get a feel of who she was after.

"Detective, don't say I never gave you anything."

She glanced down at Max's extended hand. "What's that?"

"Probable cause."

It was a watch. She shone the light across the childish face. A smear of something dark blurred the crystal. Blood.

"Read the back," was his quiet suggestion.

She turned it carefully with the nudge of the flashlight. There was an inscription, brief but enough.

Kelly, Happy 14th. Love, Daddy.

"Where did you find this, Max?"

"Must've fallen through a crack in the porch by the back door."

Probable cause for entry.

"I love you, baby."

His smile flashed white as he stepped out of the way to let her work.

For such a simple structure, the cabin had an amazingly complex lock system. After a few frustrating moments, Max leaned over her shoulder to whisper, "The back's easier."

She straightened so fast they nearly collided. "How do you know? Dammit, Max. Have you already— No, don't tell me."

She shoved him aside and stormed around the shabby building to the back door, which, as he'd promised, was much easier to breach.

Donny Lamb had been here recently. No thin layer of undisturbed dust topped the spartan furnishings. The dishes piled into the chipped sink were from a recent meal; the scent of grease was still fresh upon the water they soaked in.

From the threshold she made a slow sweep with the flashlight over the single room, stark and uninvit-

ing in its utilitarianism. Above the sink hung an open
cupboard stacked with mismatched dishes, Mason jar
glasses, canned goods and canisters. A row of medi-
cations she'd bet were prescribed by Dr. Farraday. A
doorless closet held two coats, coveralls, and muddy
waders. A pair of study boots sat beneath them next to
a stack of jeans and tee shirts. A lidless tuna can filled
with hand-rolled cigarette stubs sat atop a café-sized
table flanked by two metal chairs. The only other thing
in the room was the bed.

Her light wavered over it.

A twin-sized iron-framed bed with rounded head-
and footboards. Attached to the four corners by short
lengths of chain were thick leather cuffs, wide enough
to have made the abrasions found on the wrists and
ankles of each victim. Its thin mattress was covered by
a rubber sheet. The rusty splotches staining the rum-
pled material over it could only be one thing.

Max's voice intruded into her dark thoughts like a
brilliant halogen beam.

"That container on the floor is a cleaner used to
keep down the bacteria in animal pens. He probably
uses it in his job. And he used it on that girl on Dovion's table. The same chemical smell was burned into
her skin."

Had Lamb sat there calmly smoking at the table,
thinking up new atrocities while he watched her twist
and silently plead for release through freedom or
death? Her mouth would be bound or taped. Above
it, her eyes wide and wild with terror and tears that
would have no effect on a monster who had no conscience, no heart. He'd scrubbed her down until the

harsh solution began to eat away at her skin, stripping away the evidence of his repeated rapes or maybe just for the pleasure of watching her squirm.

And suddenly she wasn't seeing Kelly Schoenbaum lying there battered and abused on that bed.

She saw Mary Kate Malone.

I don't want to die. Lottie, don't let me die here like this.

A soft sound escaped her as she took a quick step back from that memory. Bumping into Max, whose arms quickly surrounded her. Feeling the tremors racing through her, he rubbed his cheek against hers and murmured, "Let's wait for your team outside."

The next thing she knew, she was on hands and knees throwing up in a patch of ferns. Then Max was crouching beside her, his strong arms pulling her into his lap to cradle her like a child as he sat on the rickety back steps.

"It's all right. No one can hurt you now. I've got you. I've got you, *sha*."

She clung to the steadying comfort of his words, spoken in the same low voice that had woven through her dreams for twelve years. She curled into him and pressed her face against his neck, desperate to fill her nose with the scent of his skin instead of the remembered smells of concrete and oily machinery, blood, fear, and the stale sweat of brutal men and brutal sex. Her fingers held him tight to keep from falling back into that pit of pain and despair.

"Don't let me go," she whispered.

"Never," he assured her. "Never."

"I have to find her, Max. I *have* to find her."

"You will, *cher*." He glanced over her shoulder then stood. "Your men are here," he told her quietly.

They approached quickly and silently, led by the ancient caretaker: Babineau, Boucher, Hammond, and several others who moved to secure the perimeter. Back in full professional mode, Cee Cee filled them in. Max stood off to the side, out of the way, as still as one of the ghostly statues in Jimmy Legere's garden.

"Boucher, I need you to find Schoenbaum. He'll want to be here. Give Savoie a ride back with you. This is no place for a civilian." She didn't glance Max's way; her focus was on her job. "Junior, secure that door. Mr. LaFont, it's business as usual. You never saw us."

As her team kicked quickly and silently into action, Cee Cee and Babineau stood with heads together, discussing strategy. Her momentary weakness was gone as adrenaline began to percolate through her.

As Max moved to follow the young officer, she looked his way to mouth, "I'll call you." He smiled faintly.

DONNY LAMB FINALLY appeared just before sunrise. After they let him walk through their perimeter and into the cabin, every one of them restrained the need to rush in and pummel Kelly Schoenbaum's whereabouts out of him. They held back, sticking to procedure while Cee Cee slipped away to inform the chief that the suspect was within their circle.

She located Babineau in the thick brush surrounding the cabin. "Status?"

"Still inside. No sign of the vic."

"What's he doing?"

"From the really inviting smell of it, cooking breakfast."

She crouched down beside him, her gaze cutting between the two doors. "LaFont tells me he's never missed a shift of work. He should be feeding the animals in about a half hour. We can't spook him, or he won't take us back to his hidey-hole."

Babineau nodded. "The park opens at eight. Let's get some plainclothes in here mingling with the tourists. Get the K-9s ready."

Then they heard a low growl of impatience from behind them. "Get the fuck outta my way."

Stan Schoenbaum looked like he'd been working on a hangover for the last twelve hours. The whites of his eyes were webbed with red. His expression was an anguished twist of rage, frustration, and pain as he struggled with one of the officers and Silas MacCreedy, who were trying to hold him back. Cee Cee waved him through before he created a disturbance.

"Where is he?"

Babineau gripped one arm, Cee Cee the other. He was shaking and unsteady, a volatile combination.

Cee Cee's tone was a bracing slap. "Inside. Get a handle on it, Stan, or get the hell out of here."

"Okay." He took a big breath and let it out in an alcohol-laced gust. "I'm okay. Let up, will ya."

Babs gave his partner a nod and they slowly relaxed

their hold. Stumbling, weaving, Schoenbaum glared at them.

"Why aren't you doing anything about my girl? Are you sure? Are you sure he has her?"

Babineau showed him the watch he'd bagged for evidence. "Is this hers?"

The Vice detective focused his gaze on the blood-smudged watch face with its sad-sack blue donkey, and his features crumpled. A low wail tore through his throat just as the cabin door opened.

Donald Lamb stepped out into the morning light. He had the same deep auburn hair as his mother and soft, unlined features. He wore his work coveralls, a lightweight jacket, and carried a handcrafted rake in keeping with the museum's simple setting. With the in-stincts of a predator, he froze, his attention snapping toward the spot where they were hidden. For an in-stant his expression went blank in surprise as he took a wary step back toward the open door. Then his free hand darted beneath his open coat.

Stan Schoenbaum surged forward with a roar, yanking his gun free, emptying it before the startled partners could stop him. The first round ended Don-ald Lamb's life. The rest were exclamation points of fury.

Before the others could take a breath MacCreedy had his arm hooked about Schoenbaum's neck, wres-tling him to the ground a second too late. He had no trouble securing the weapon or subduing the grieving father.

"Kelly," Schoenbaum was moaning. "Let me go to my daughter. I need to see my daughter."

"You stupid son of a bitch—she's not here."

He looked up at Babineau in shock. "What do you mean, not here? Where *is* she?"

"We don't know! We don't know where he was keeping her, dammit. Goddammit!"

Cee Cee assumed a brusque command, calling in the shooting, bringing up the dogs to backtrack Lamb in hopes of finding where he been overnight. The dogs led them to a pirogue tied up at the edge of the swamps. From there, no trail was left to follow. Kelly Schoenbaum could have been anywhere. The only one who knew was dead on the ground, his fingers wrapped around his cell phone.

Stan took the news with teetering control. "What now? What do we do now?" His hands trembled around the cup of coffee MacCreedy had procured for him.

"How many boats do we have?" Cee Cee demanded.

"Eight," Joey volunteered. "Two ready, six on standby."

"We need three times that if we're going to cover much ground before dark. I don't want that little girl out there another night. Babs, you talked to LaFont. Does he know of anyplace Lamb might have gone? Did he talk about some hideaway?"

"No. He said Lamb kept to himself about his off hours."

"Think. Think. What are we missing?"

"We know the vics were all hookers," Babineau mused. "How does he pick them up? LaFont said he didn't drive. He never went into town."

"Did anyone ever visit him?"

"His doctor came out to bring his meds."

"His doctor . . ."

"Once a month."

It hit like a brick. The hand on the cell phone. He'd been calling his mother.

Twenty-one

"DO YOU MIND if I smoke?"

Cee Cee pushed an ashtray across the table. "Not a very healthy choice for someone in your profession."

Judith Farraday shrugged, lit up, and pulled in a long drag.

"Tell us about Donald," Babineau began after he'd prefaced their taped interview.

"Donald was a product of the violence of his conception. It wasn't his fault. He couldn't help what he was."

"The same kind of animal who killed your husband, who raped and killed your sister, who raped you?"

Farraday met Cee Cee's gaze with a casual distance. "Yes."

"Why didn't you just have an abortion?"

"Catholic. I placed him in a good home. I'd hoped for the best for him."

"Until his genetics started to show."

She smiled grimly at Babineau. "I sent him to the very best facilities. Parental guilt, I suppose—I knew nothing was going to help him. I knew it was my fault, because I conceived him, then abandoned him. How could I expect him to understand why I loathed the sight of him, the very thought of him? I tried to correct that. I tried to make him part of my life, and for a while, with some very nice psychotropics, I thought I'd succceded. He worked in the clinics with me, doing simple jobs. His IQ was stunted, probably from the trauma in utero. He wasn't intelligent, but he was quick and strong."

"When did you find out he was killing them?" Cee Cee asked.

Dr. Farraday responded with a calm sigh. "That, I'm afraid, was my fault, too. There was this girl, my patient."

"A working girl?"

"Yes. She came on to him, promising him things his sweet, simple mind wanted to believe, if he'd get her drugs from the clinic. They had sex. Sex like wild, rutting animals." She shuddered, her eyes going glassy. "She demanded money from me, saying she'd tell the police he raped her. So I had to take care of her. I underestimated Donald's fondness for her. He was inconsolable, went absolutely out of control. The only thing that would calm him was bringing her back. But that was a bit of a problem."

"Because you'd killed her."

She nodded at Cee Cee's conclusion. "Yes. The greedy little whore." That was when the detectives saw the pure madness in her eyes.

She explained with a terrible logic how they'd moved from city to city. How she would select from her patients a girl who fit the general description of Donald's lost love. She'd offer the girl money to play out the fantasy that she was the poor deceased Frankie Bell, and for a week or so, the masquerade worked.

Donald was a functioning person and Judith wasn't eaten away by guilt and shame. And then, he'd figure out the deception. And his punishment upon the poor girl was terrible.

"I'd tell him how sorry I was, that I'd made a mistake. That I would find the real Frankie for him."

"So you pimped women for him to kill."

Her glare slashed through Cee Cee. "They had a chance. About as much chance as they had on the streets. They were warned. I warned them over and over to go home, to be safe. But they wouldn't listen."

"Like your sister wouldn't listen when she was told it was too dangerous to remain in a war-torn country?" Cee Cee asked softly. "The way you wouldn't listen when you were told to go home?"

She nodded vigorously, almost gratefully. "Yes, just like that. Too much pride to listen. Too much self-importance to think bad things can and do happen. They do happen, Detective. They do."

"Yes," Cee Cee agreed quietly. "They do."

"So you took him the girls," Babineau interjected. "What was with the moon cycle?"

"I don't know. Some nonsense he picked up from one of his many wardmates. It calmed him—the ritual, the cycle. It gave him a beginning and an end, so his frustration never got a chance to spike. He could function in the world as long as he had the safety of that ritual."

"As long as he had an innocent young girl to torture and rape. Didn't that bother you just a little bit, putting those girls in the same position you'd been in?" Cee Cee couldn't keep the disgust from her tone.

"So, Dr. Farraday," Babineau cut in to keep things

civil and moving forward, "you returned each month, bringing in the new, carrying out the old."

"Yes. Ritual. Routine."

"Here in New Orleans, and before that in Las Vegas, in St. Louis, in Boston."

"You did your homework. Yes."

"But they were still alive when you picked them up."

"Yes."

"Then you killed them. Why?"

"Donald would have been very upset to think they'd died. I told him I took them home."

Babineau and Cee Cee exchanged an astonished blink. Cee Cee had to say it.

"He would torture, starve, and rape them for weeks, but just didn't have the heart to put them out of their misery?"

"That was punishment, Detectives, learned at one of those pricey institutions I placed him in. You can see the physical scars on him, if not the mental. But as far as killing, Donald couldn't bring himself to step on a bug, let along protect himself."

"So you cleaned up after him."

"He was my son. My problem. It was the least I could do for him. I'd tell the girls I'd come to take them home, and they were all too willing to cooperate. I'd take them someplace isolated and inject them first, so they'd feel no pain, no fear."

"And kill them."

"What else could I do? He was my son." That was said like it was only a biological fact, with no trace of emotion behind it. She regarded them then with interest. "What gave me away? I was so careful."

"Your fish tank."

"Fish tank?"

"The aquarium chemicals were on Marjorie Cole."

The doctor laughed. "I'd just changed the water before I went to pick her up. Such a small, insignificant thing. I never gave it a thought."

"And your perfume. We thought it was men's cologne. That threw me for a while because you don't wear it at the clinic."

"It is cologne. It was my husband's. I only wear it when I go out. It comforts me to think he's with me."

"And you think he'd want to be with you, with the things you were doing?"

No reply.

Cee Cee rolled out of her chair and paced to the far wall, unable to maintain a stoic front. She squeezed her eyes shut and concentrated on slow, even breaths as her partner continued.

"Dr. Farraday, you can do one final thing for your son and to help yourself. The last girl, Kelly Schoenbaum or Kikki Valentine, is still alive. Where does he take them?"

"I don't know."

"You don't have to protect him anymore. Save this one life, Doctor. Let her live to make better choices."

"I'm sorry, Detective. I really don't know. I dropped them off and picked them up at the cabin in the park. He wouldn't tell me where he took them. He said that was private."

STAN SCHOENBAUM WAS holding a cup of cold coffee in unsteady hands with Joey Boucher babysitting him, while MacCreedy handled the paperwork. His gaze lifted, and when he saw their faces, his features fell. They didn't have to tell him the news.

"What am I going to tell Marilyn? That because of me our daughter is going to die?"

The other three exchanged uncomfortable looks, not knowing what to say. Boucher took a deep breath and got out of his chair, crossing over to Cee Cee. He kept his voice very low, for her and Babineau alone.

"You know there's hardly any chance of them finding her. Maybe there's another way. He brought back Babineau's little boy. Maybe there's something he could do—considering what he is and all."

MAX SAT ON the porch, rocking slowly in the glider, dressed in slouchy jeans, a black tee shirt, and his red high-tops. He couldn't rest until he knew she was safe.

Giles came up the steps, back from dropping Oscar off at school and Tina at her home to take care of some household matters. He took a look at the figure slumped on the glider, then settled against the porch rail to light a cigarette.

"Playing hooky today, boss man?"

"I don't know what that means."

"Taking the day off."

"Yes. That's what I'm doing." He closed his eyes, rocking.

"Want company?"

"No."

"Want my opinion?"

He slit on eye open. "No."

He waited, but Giles just smoked in silence. Max brooded, unhappy, dissatisfied, not knowing what to do.

"What do you see when you look at me?"

"Whaddaya mean?"

Max waved his hand to encompass himself from head to toe. "What am I?"

"The fella who pays me damned good not to answer questions like that." At Max's scowl, he sighed. "At one time, that would have been an easy one. A seriously scary bogeyman creeping around at Jimmy's back, threatening to eat my eyes for breakfast."

Max didn't smile at the reminder. "And now?"

"Someone I trust enough to march up to the doors of hell and knock if you sent me."

"Why? I don't understand. Why would you do that for me?" He shut out the sound of his mother's voice. *You're special. Blessed.*

No hesitation. "Because you care, Max."

He blinked. "About what?"

"Everything." Giles made an expansive gesture. "Every damned thing, like it's your responsibility, your problem. Jimmy, now Jimmy was a good man to work for, fair and generous. But there was no soul to Jimmy Legere. He didn't trust nobody. He wouldn't have gone out of his way for the needs of another living being unless there was something in it for him." He waited for Max to nod in reluctant agreement before going on, his tone a bit tougher.

"You could learn something from that, Max. You need to take a step back and ask what's in it for you before you go giving everything away, a chunk of you at a time, to all them that's got their hands out. You have to save something for yourself or you'll be no good to any of them. You need to prioritize, to learn to say no."

"I have responsibilities. I want to do what's right. How do I choose? How do I pick one and let the others fall away?"

"What's closest to your heart?" A chuckle. "Don't answer. I can see her in your eyes. And that's the problem, isn't it: Why isn't she here? Why aren't you asking her these questions instead of listening to some dumb wiseguy?"

"I'm not what she needs right now."

Giles laughed then, a big insulting laugh that had Max thinking about eating eyes on toast again.

"You wouldn't say that if you'd seen her come plowing in here after that business with your daddy, ready to cut me off at the knees if I tried to keep her away. She may not know what she needs, but it's you she wants."

Max's posture straightened. His head came up, his eyes grew bright. The very air about him seemed to vibrate.

Giles flicked the remains of his cigarette onto the lawn and came away from the rail with a grin. "Why don't you ask her?" he drawled, then went inside.

Max waited for the orange and black vehicle to skid to a stop at the bottom of the steps. His initial anticipation took a plunge when he saw she wasn't alone. Another unmarked cop car pulled in behind hers.

Business first.

Babineau and Boucher he could understand, but the sight of the third man getting out of the second car with the young officer had him bristling with outrage. He snarled, "What are you doing on my property?"

Cee Cee motioned the others to stay put while she climbed up onto the porch.

At first Joey's suggestion had shocked her, but then she thought perhaps it was exactly the bridge needed to bring these two sides of her world closer. She knew from experience that working together to right a wrong was the quickest way to erase differences. Teamwork. Loyalty. Trust. Things all of them understood and respected. So she'd brought her side to Max's door.

She'd known it was a risky idea bringing Schoenbaum, but he refused to be left behind. The others thought the sight of a father's grief would overcome Max's objections, but as his eyes narrowed into glittering slits, Cee Cee feared they were wrong.

"Max, I need to talk to you."

When she touched his arm he took a denying step back, bumping the glider, sending it banging against the house. His breathing was fast, his tension palpable.

"Max, I don't know what's between you and Schoenbaum, and right now I can't afford to care. I need you to do something for me. For *me*, Max. Not for him."

"What might that be?" So wary.

"Donald Lamb, the killer we've been after, is dead. His latest victim is still hidden away. We don't know where she is."

"She's in the swamps, Mr. Savoie." Joey Boucher spoke up. "I—we thought maybe you could help find her."

"You thought wrong." He started to turn away, but Cee Cee gripped his elbow and put herself in his path.

"Max, she doesn't have much time."

"She's seventeen years old." Schoenbaum's voice quavered. "He's had her for twenty-five days. I can't even begin to imagine . . ."

"I can." Max flung off Cee Cee's hand. "Would you like me to tell you? Would you like me to tell you about the cold that burns into the bones, and the hunger that cuts like knife blades until you'd eat anything you thought you could keep down? About fear so huge it's a suffocating hand around your throat, so tight you can't even pray to die? Imagine that, you son of a bitch. Imagine that while she's out there and you can't do a damned thing about it."

"Max!" Cee Cee's tone reflected her dismay. "Stop it."

But all the impotent horror and fear of that child who'd once crawled underneath the glider was too excruciating to bear.

"Imagine what it's like to be young and helpless in the hands of monsters. To suffer for their hatred, their drunken viciousness, to beg and cry and plead while they cut you, kick you, and hurt you until your mind goes blank from the shock."

"Max, please." Charlotte pressed her palms against his chest. His heart pounded with an explosive force. "Stop."

"That's what I said to them. To *him*"—Max glared down at Schoenbaum—"and his two partners." He caught her wrists and yanked her hands down as he looked past her into a man's eyes that had been cold and merciless then.

"Then put yourself in the place of the man who has to look at what's been done to a child he loves, to a child who never did anything to deserve such cruel abuse. To have that child look up through no-longer-innocent eyes and ask why, and you have no answer. Then you'll know what Jimmy Legere was thinking while he watched the pieces of your friend, Detective Peyton, bleed out onto the ground. Get the fuck off my property."

Shocked speechless, Cee Cee put up a staying hand to her colleagues and followed Max into the house as he stalked into Jimmy's study.

"Max!"

He stopped at Jimmy's desk, his hands gripping the edge of it. "Go away, Charlotte. Don't ask me to help that man."

"You can't blame a child for the deeds of the father."

"Can't I? He didn't have a problem doing it. He didn't have any problem stomping on my hands, breaking my bones because he couldn't get to Jimmy. He and Peyton and another of their pals didn't have any problem smashing my nose and mouth with a Jim Beam bottle, then forcing me to swallow the whiskey along with chips of glass and teeth.

"They used a Taser. It scrambled me somehow so I couldn't shift, couldn't protect myself. I couldn't stop them. When they were done, I had to crawl home. I was eight years old."

His breathing was raw. "Now he knows how

Jimmy felt when he couldn't find me in town. He'll know how Jimmy felt when he finally came home to find me curled up and whining like an animal under the porch glider, so beaten and broken all I could do was lay my face on his shoes."

Oh, Max. Poor little boy. Her eyes were damp and she placed her palm between his tense shoulder blades, rubbing gently, wishing there was a way to erase the pain she was forcing him to recall.

"Baby, I'm so sorry. But this isn't about Stan Schoenbaum and those others who hurt you. This is about a teenage girl who'll die alone if we don't find her. It's *got* to be about that girl, Max."

"Why? Why does it have to be? Why can't it be about me? About a little boy in the brutal hands of those who should have protected him. Policemen, Charlotte. Your colleagues. Your friends. None of you gave a damn about me. None of you would have cared if I had died in that ditch, bleeding and alone."

"I would have. I would have cared."

He turned to face her, his eyes flat and unblinking. "Then don't ask me to do this, Charlotte. It's too much. Not for him."

"For me."

"It's not about you! Don't make it about you." Yet even as he shouted that, a part of him realized that it was. It had everything to do with two teenage girls in a warehouse, suffering at the hands of monsters. The anguish of that tore through the last of his composure.

"I saved you, Charlotte. I rescued you. Don't make me into someone who can save them all. It's not what I am. It's not what I do. I'm a destroyer, not a savior.

I don't care about that girl. I don't care what happens to her. I just hope it's something so awful, he won't be able to close his eyes for the rest of his life without seeing the horror of it and remembering what he did to me."

She had to stop those awful words from pouring out of him. Cruel, hate-filled words so searingly vicious, they were a knife to her heart. Words that said a bridge between their two worlds could never stand.

Her palm dealt out a silencing blow, with just enough force to stun him, and bring his hand up defensively to cover his mouth before he turned his back on her.

"Detective," Giles said softly. She hadn't known he was in the room. He put his hand on her arm. "Time to go."

When she balked, he tugged insistently. She shook him off at the hallway and continued on with her shoulders squared to the front door.

Sighing, Giles turned back to face an equally combatant posture and waited. A second. Two.

With a roar, Max grabbed the edge of the heavy wooden desk and flung it, computer and all, through the French doors, across the porch, and out into the yard. As shredded lace curtains settled over the broken glass, Max sank down slowly to his knees, rocking forward, lacing his hands over the back of his neck to begin a soft wailing howl.

The low, mournful sound made the hairs stand up on Giles's arms as he placed his hand on Max's shoulder.

"That's not quite what I meant, boss man. Not what I had in mind at all."

———

"HE WON'T DO it," she said tightly as she came down the front porch steps.

"Damn him, that selfish son of a—"

Her hard shove drove Schoenbaum down to the ground. "You fucker," she growled as she stepped over him. "Stay the hell away from me. Boucher, with us."

Babineau and Boucher exchanged glances as she got behind the wheel of the car. They climbed in wordlessly and were thrown back into the seats as she stomped on the gas, kicking up loose stones to shower the downed detective.

"SAVOIE. LEAVE A message."

"Heya, Max. I'm just sitting here in this crappy station missing you, thinking about you, wishing I was home sharing a meal, sharing a conversation, sharing a bed with you. Just wanted to let you know that, and to tell you that I'm sorry I pushed so hard.

"I should have been thinking about you. I shouldn't have asked. I do care, and I do understand, and it's okay." A pause while she drew in a shaky breath. "Talk to you soon."

As the last hours of the workday wore down to a miserable end, Cee Cee knew she couldn't let things go until she made contact with him. She had a mountain of paperwork chaining her to her desk, following their booking of Judith Farraday, but she took another minute and dialed the house.

"Helen, is Max there?"

"No, Detective."

"Do you know when he'll be back? I need to talk to him. I need to . . . I need to talk to him."

There was a long pause, then Helen's crisp response. "He said he had some business to take care of out on the bayou. But then, you'd know about that—and what it's going to cost him, don't you?"

Twenty-two

MAX HATED THE smell of stagnant water and decay. He didn't mind the damp, the cold, or the filth. But the stink that called up his half-remembered fears unsettled him. Donald Lamb's scent kept him going, following the faint hints Lamb left when he'd pull a branch out of the way so his shallow pirogue could slip through.

Max kept to the paths and boggy surfaces where he could skim across, trying to avoid the chilly plunges up to his knees, sometimes to his waist. He kept his focus on the scent of Kelly Schoenbaum from her leather watchband, and the traces left by Lamb's careless touch. He knew the area well enough to have a general sense of where he was going. After that it would be luck rather than skill.

He kept a nervous eye on the edge of darkness pushing daylight closer to the tree line, where soon it would be out of sight. The very last thing he wanted was to spend the night in the bayou, and precious little could push him to it.

Just one thing, actually.

He felt his phone vibrate but was busy leaping from branch to branch, tree to stump. Once he had solid ground beneath him, he checked his calls and saw Charlotte's name. What could she have to say that he would possibly want to hear at this moment? This woman he loved. This woman he would do absolutely anything to please.

Still angry and feeling more than a little bit guilty over his behavior, he put the phone away to continue on at a hard, punishing run. He'd go another hour. Maybe by then he could put his ego aside to listen.

At the end of those sixty minutes, the sun was gone and he was treading carefully on unstable physical and mental ground, spooked and anxious.

There were no more paths, just deceivingly quiet patches of green over black glassy waters. He was deep inside the treacherous swamps, with so much area still to cover. Soaked through, weary and chilled, he leaned back against the scaly trunk of a cypress tree, his gaze sweeping the gathering blackness as if it hid all sorts of unseen dangers from him. He took out his phone and felt water run out of it.

"No. No. Charlotte."

He needed to hear her voice to keep from going under. Sinking fast, he shook the phone until the display lit up and, with a whisper of thanks, keyed in her message.

Heya, Max.

He squeezed his eyes shut and the terror fell away as her voice stroked him in a soothing caress.

Missing you, thinking about you, wishing I was home sharing a meal, sharing a conversation, sharing a bed with you.

Emotion rose fast and thick; images of her danced behind his eyelids. Charlotte smiling as she dropped into his lap with her cup of coffee on the wide veranda.

Her feet in his hands as she spoke so passionately about the details of her case. The sound of her sigh, the weight of her palm rising and falling with his breaths as she curled close to him in the night.

I do understand, and it's okay.

The screen flickered as the signal wavered and died. And he was alone.

Charlotte, don't leave me. Don't leave me here.

He projected the words like a wounded cry, and almost at once sensations of heat brushed over him, around him, through him. The teasing scent of her *Voodoo Love* filled his nose, driving away the odor of dank waters. And he could hear her voice stroke across his mind.

Come back, baby. Don't open the door alone.

I love you, sha.

I want you, Savoie . . . I'm wearing new shoes.

He wouldn't have thought anything could wring a laugh from him under the circumstances, but it burst out so loud and sudden, it scared up a noisy flutter of wings from unseen night birds. Then the darkness settled once more. And his soul settled into a saving calm.

After that, he had no idea how long he waded through the chest-high muck. Time only mattered as it applied to the frightened girl awaiting rescue. He no longer noticed his own fatigue. He was pure power now, tough and fierce concentration. Lamb's trail was stronger here, brushed across dangling leaves and hanging moss, imprinted on bark and lily pads.

Then, finally, a different scent.

The metallic bite of blood and suffering and fear.

Of Kelly Shoenbaum, and the girl on Dev Dovion's slab. And of dying horribly.

He shut his eyes as the rain of bloody pearls began. *Run! Run! Don't look back, Max. Don't look back.*

Then it was gone. The shivery nausea, the shadowed memories. Trapped behind a closed door.

And he moved on.

The stilt house was so covered with moss and vines, it seemed organic. Nothing about it suggested it held a living being, but Max could sense her there, could hear her faint respirations.

The door held another of Donald Lamb's exceptionally sturdy locks. Max tore through the wood panel with the rake of his claws and punch of his fist.

She was on the plank floor, blindfolded, her mouth taped, hands cuffed, ankle shackled to the wall. Her nude body was ravaged by abuse, bug bites, and starvation. She huddled, alarmed by the sound of his entry, too weak to do more than whimper.

He'd claimed not to care about this girl, but there was no way he could look at her and not be moved.

"Kelly," he said in a low voice, "my name is Max. Your daddy sent me to bring you home. Don't be afraid. No one's going to hurt you ever again."

CEE CEE PACED the parking lot at the Cajun Life museum for at least an hour. Max had telegraphed that single image to her, but nothing about what it meant. Giles had picked her up at Oscar's insistence that Max needed them and that they should hurry. They waited with her, along with an ambulance and Kelly's anxious father, in hopes of a good outcome.

She stopped suddenly. Max.

She could feel him. Could feel his fatigue and the chaos of his emotions, but that was all. He wouldn't let her get closer. So she waited and worried, and nearly wept when he emerged from the trees carrying a blanketed figure in his arms.

"Kelly!"

She put up a hand to halt Stan Schoenbaum when Max jerked to a standstill. "Wait, Stan. Just wait here."

Let her be alive. Let her be alive.

She couldn't read anything in Max's face except weariness. He looked terrible—scratched, filthy, and exhausted.

"Are you okay, baby?"

"Yeah. And so is she."

Uttering a soft thanksgiving, Cee Cee gestured for the gurney. Schoenbaum raced ahead of it to take his daughter from Max's arms, weeping unashamedly. When he'd assured himself that she was breathing, he looked up at Max, relief and gratitude twisting his features.

"How can I thank you?"

"Don't mention my name as being part of this." He took a step back, his eyes going flat and cold. "I found I couldn't blame the daughter for the father's sins." And he turned away, walking toward Giles and Oscar where they waited by the car.

As Kelly was placed on the stretcher and her vitals quickly taken, Cee Cee hurried after Max. He turned when she called out to him, his glance lowering to her Doc Martens.

"Those aren't new, and they're not terribly sexy."

"I wanted to give you some incentive." She embraced him tightly, complaining, "Geez, you stink." That didn't keep her from running her fingers through his hair, from tipping his head down so she could kiss him softly. "Thank you. I gotta go with them."

"I know. I need to go home and shower for about two days."

"I'll see you later, Savoie."

She moved back so he could continue to where Giles and Oscar waited.

THE NEXT TWENTY-FOUR hours were a media circus.

All business, wearing a sober jacket over dark jeans and an elegant string of pearls about her neck, Detective Charlotte Caissie, with Stan Schoenbaum, gave a press conference concerning the rescued victim whose identity was being protected. They cited the teamwork of their two units for their success in ending the Tides That Bind killer's spree. Schoenbaum's voice betrayed only the slightest tremor when he relayed that the young victim's status was guarded, but that a full recovery was expected. Neither could be lured from their statements when Karen Crawford asked for the name of a mysterious citizen who carried the naked girl out of the bayou, protecting her own source for that leak as confidential.

Watching the press conference from the overly bright showroom floor of the Sweat Shop, Alain Babineau smiled.

Good for you, Ceece.

"Mr. Babbit, isn't it?"

Babineau turned to regard Simon Cummings in surprise. "Yes, that's right. You remembered."

"There's very little that slips by me."

"Mr. Blu isn't in yet. And I was just leaving."

"Then maybe you'll let me buy you a meal, and we can discuss people and things we might have in common."

"All right. Hey, Barry," he called to the bartender. "Heading out. See ya tomorrow night."

"Laissez les bons temps rouler."

Babineau waved a hand and followed the businessman outside.

Cummings picked a place several blocks away, where the light was low and the scent of grease and hot sauce was part of the ambiance. "I love this kind of food. It's worth the morning jog through Audubon Park to pay for the occasional indulgence."

While they waited for catfish and fried okra, Babineau said, "Thanks for not giving me up to Blutafino."

"Babineau, right? I remember you as being the cooler head of the partnership. I thought you were Homicide."

"On loan to Vice."

"After Manny?"

"I can't discuss an ongoing investigation."

"Integrity. Good. I've heard positive things about you, Detective, and I checked. I like to know as much as possible about people before I make an investment in them."

"I'm afraid I'm not following."

"I remember my friends and reward them. When I get into office, I'll be making some significant changes. Those who stick by me will benefit from them. I'm not stopping at mayor, and every administration has a place for men of integrity."

"I have a job, Mr. Cummings, but thank you."

"And you have a modest paycheck that demands more than it returns, and a partner who garners all the attention and commendations because of who she's sleeping with and who her father was partnered with on the streets a long, long time ago. That has to annoy even a man of integrity."

Babineau placed his palms on the table and began to rise. "Thank you for lunch, Mr. Cummings."

Cummings laughed. His hand pressed Babineau back into his chair with surprising strength. "Loyalty. That's another quality I'm looking for. I have nothing against your partner. She's a fine officer, but her career is becoming a bit too . . . compromised for what I'm looking for."

"And what are you looking for?"

"Stepping-stones to a senate seat—and beyond. The right people: good, decent people in the right places who remember who helped them get there. The commissioner is a close friend. My opinions carry weight with him. I could fast-track a career for the right individual."

Babineau leaned back in his chair, suspicious and tempted. "And what would this individual have to do?"

"His job. I want to make a strong stand against crime, Detective. I want people with me who will be assets, not roadblocks. You're in a position, should you decide to stay undercover, to be one of those assets. I need to bring down an element in our city that's had free rein for too long."

"Blutafino?"

"Him, and those he associates with. If you're interested I'd like to share my plans with you, starting with what I was doing at his club when we bumped into each other. But first, let me ask you something, Detective. Would you have any problem helping me tear down Max Savoie and that crooked empire built by Jimmy Legere? If you have reservations because of his relationship with your partner, I'll understand."

For a moment all Alain Babineau could see was Savoie's smug face as he drawled, "She said it was nothing."

"No, Mr. Cummings. I'd have no problem at all."

Twenty-three

MAX STOOD AT the edge of the skeletal wall, twelve stories up, with nothing between him and an open view of the city.

"Not going to jump, are you?"

Charlotte could hear the smile in his voice when he answered, "Not today. How did you get up here? This is supposed to be off-limits."

"Not to the long arm of the law."

"Why don't you come over here and put those long arms around me?"

"Why don't you take a few steps back first?"

A chuckle. "Afraid of heights, Detective, or just the fall?"

"Actually, it's the sudden stop. If I were afraid of falling, I wouldn't be here."

He turned toward her and the wind caught his raincoat, flaring it out behind him like black wings on a dark angel. Her breath caught, partly due to the danger, partly to the delicious drama of that pose. This was the way she always thought of him: alone, arrogantly braced before the elements, powerful, and harshly gorgeous. Once he'd been hers—now he belonged to many.

He waved his arm wide. "What do you think of the Towers?"

They were called the Trinity Towers, three bold spires rising from bleak surroundings with bold hopefulness. The unifying three-floor triangular base would boast trendy shops and offices, the two outer eight-story towers, plush condominiums. The central spear, jutting like a defiant middle finger to flip off an uncaring city, would house those Max protected and now would be able to shelter. She thought the concept was magnificent. She thought he was, too.

"I'd prefer some glass between me and that long fall."

"This floor is the last to be closed in. I was thinking I might like to have it."

"For what? Offices?"

"No, I like to keep my feet on the ground for business. I was thinking I'd like to have a place to stay in the city."

"And you need a whole floor?"

"So I can see both the city and the river. Close to work for those late nights. What do you think?"

"About what?"

"Living here."

Was he asking her to live here with him? Her heart jumped to a quick yes, but her mind was cautious. She made a point of looking all the way down the long, long distance to the far end of the building.

"I guess it would be all right if you wanted a bowling alley or a shooting range."

His smile unfurled slowly. "I'd planned to put up a few walls, but if you want a bowling alley or a shooting range, it's not too late to talk to the architect."

Here she was, at the cusp of taking that next frightening step. As much as she wanted to go forward, part of her still wasn't ready. So she took cover behind her job. "Atcliff wants a decision on whether I stay with Homicide or assist Vice. Any opinion on that?"

"It's nice to be asked. This would be a very nice place for me to keep my very sexy mistress. Then we wouldn't have to go to shabby motels."

She smiled. It *would* be the perfect cover, keeping her in the game and allowing them to spend more time together. "Always thinking ahead, aren't you, Savoie? Babineau is staying on with Vice. He's gotten the go-ahead to bring down Manny Blu now that he's inside."

"Then he'll be staying undercover."

"Yes."

"I've told Tina and Oscar they can stay with me at the house."

She nodded. "They'll be safe with you."

"I saw you on the news," he mentioned. "You looked good. I seem to remember owning a jacket like that."

"Hmmm, what a coincidence."

"You wore the pearls I gave you." His tone wasn't so casual now.

"They looked good with the jacket." They'd made her feel close to him. She hadn't been back to their room at home since he'd moved Tina and Oscar in with him.

Their circumstances had changed so fast, she didn't know how to get things back to where they'd been before.

"How's the little girl?" He angled away from her, his movements restless now.

"Doing well, considering. She wants to thank you."

"Not necessary. Better she forget about my part in it."

"I can tell you from experience that won't happen. You're a hero to her—the one who rescued her from hell."

"I'm no hero," he growled. "I would have left her there, to punish an injury done to me over twenty years ago."

"The way Jimmy would have? But you're not Jimmy. You couldn't turn your back. That's not who or what you are, Max." There was no doubt in her voice, or in her mind.

He stopped pacing and turned to face her. "Why are you here, Charlotte?"

"There are some things I need to tell you, and I wanted to do it face-to-face this time. I'm taking a short leave of absence. I've got things I need to deal with before I can go forward on anything else."

"Am I one of those things?"

"I've got a flight to California in the morning. I got a call from Mary Kate's doctor. She's semiconscious. She's asked for me."

"And you don't want me with you?"

"Not this trip, baby."

"Why not? I love you, Charlotte. Why can't I make you happy? Why won't you let me make things easier for you?"

She shook her head. "You do. I'm crazy about you, Savoie. Always have been, always will be. There's nothing I want more than to just stop the world and lose myself in you."

"Then do it."

She stared up at him, her eyes full of conflict, full of yearning.

"I want you, *cher*. When I was asked what was closest to my heart, there was only one answer for me. It was you. Just you."

He slowly sank down to his knees before her, then his hands curled lightly around her ankles as he laid his cheek atop her feet, his eyes closed. A gesture so totally submissive, yet backed with such amazing strength, her heart dropped into her shoes.

Pushing her toward taking that step.

"Oh, geez. Get up, Max. Get up."

She knelt awkwardly. When she couldn't pry him up she leaned over him, circling his strong shoulders with her arms, nestling her face in his dark hair to whisper, "I love you, baby. And I need to take care of this. I'll only hurt you if things stay the way they are."

"I don't care."

"I do, Max. If I didn't, I'd just hang on tight and let you deal with everything."

"Let me, *sha*. Let me take care of you. I will. I promise."

"I don't want you to take care of me, Max. I want us to take care of each other. I'm not unhappy because of you. It's the things I can't face in my past that keep me from being all the things you need me to be. The things you and I both deserve.

"I need to open my closet and clear all that ugly shit out of there, and I have to do it now, before I damage what I care about most."

"And what's that?"

"My future with you. I haven't been able to deal with what happened to Mary Kate, but I'm ready now. All I need is for you to tell me you'll be here when I get back."

"Right here in this spot or in the general vicinity?"

A snort of a laugh escaped her, and she looked into his eyes to see the unwavering devotion there. He'd wait. Forever. "Savoie, you drive me crazy."

"And you love that about me."

The truth of that statement centered her. "Yes, I do." She touched his face, and was lost at the rough feel of him beneath her fingertips.

There was no one else for her. No one else she would ever want. Max Savoie was it, her everything. Her lover. Her mate. Perhaps even the father of her children. Thrilling. Terrifying.

"Oh, screw it," she muttered, and yanked him to her for a kiss.

Max's hands slipped under the teasing hem of her cropped shirt. "Where do you want me to touch you?"

"Everywhere. Anywhere you've been before is good. And if you can find someplace new, go for it."

He grinned, wide and wicked. "I'll see what I can do." Her shirt went flying off, followed by her bra.

She'd expected a hot, hungry feasting to match her frenzied impatience. So when his breath blew soft and moist, when his mouth suckled lightly, when his tongue flickered with a delicate finesse, he woke a startled shiver that quickly triggered an earthquake in her primed system.

As she loosened her fingers from his hair, her breath

spilled out in a wondering gust. "Wow. That *was* new. You haven't even gotten my pants off yet."

He nipped at the swell of her breast, his voice full of smug accomplishment. "But, I seem to have gotten you off to a nice start. Unfortunately, that was my only new trick."

"Good thing I like the old ones, too."

AN HOUR LATER, splayed out on her back with only a tarp between her naked skin and the rough subflooring, Cee Cee gave a contented sigh. Max eased from her with a groan, then collapsed alongside her. With the exception of his jeans about his ankles, he was still fully dressed, his raincoat spread over the both of them.

"I'm going to just lie here for a moment, then I'll call for room service. What would you like?"

She smiled without opening her eyes. Her fingertips traced intricate patterns on the heated skin of his low back. And amazingly he felt the stirrings of arousal again. Nothing he had the energy to act on, but infinitely pleasurable nonetheless.

"Espresso and éclairs. And a hot bath. And a mattress would be nice. This plywood is murder on my butt."

"It's only seven o'clock. Maybe I could find a store that'll deliver. I wonder if we have the hot water plumbed yet."

Hearing footsteps, Max lifted his head, a soft growl of warning stirring in his chest.

"Hey, Max, are you about ready—" LaRoche broke off as he came around one of the supporting walls. He continued toward them, grinning. "Hey, Charlotte.

Didn't know you were here. I'm not interrupting anything, am I?" He lifted up Cee Cee's lime green bra with the tip of the yardstick he was carrying. "This belong to you, or is the day crew having more fun up here than they should be?"

"Just christening our new apartment," Cee Cee told him, unperturbed by his presence. "Looks like we'll be neighbors."

LaRoche's smile widened. "Sorry I didn't bring champagne. Three's a crowd, so I'll catch you later on. Some things have come up that we need to discuss, Max."

"Tomorrow, Jacques."

"Okay. Tomorrow it is."

As he started to turn away, Cee Cee called, "Jacques, watch his back for me."

Frowning slightly, he nodded. "You got it."

Once LaRoche was gone, Max stood to quickly restore his clothing, his mood suddenly somber. As she hunted around for her attire, he said, "I'll ride down with you. I'm finished here for the night."

"Okay, but just to my car. I've still got to pack."

As she stood beside him in the elevator, she resisted the urge to grab onto him and hang on.

When the doors opened, Max placed his palm on the small of her back to guide her. Such a simple thing, yet it wasn't—because it was Max. Because he conveyed everything that was good and solid in their relationship with that easy gesture. The unspoken support, the confident intimacy, the sense of unity without the need to control. And even after all they'd put each other through, there was trust.

She turned into him, put her arms about his middle, and laid her head on his shoulder. His other hand came up, cradling her cheek as his lips moved over her hair. His chest rose and fell as he breathed in their mingled scent laced with her perfume, *Voodoo Love*. She depended on him to be strong, and he didn't disappoint her. When she stepped back, he let her go.

The early evening was thick with gathering humidity as a storm crept in from the Gulf. Cee Cee glanced around, expecting to see Giles or Pete waiting for Max with one of the sleek cars from Legere's massive collection. Instead, she saw a motorcycle.

Black. Something that looked like it should have the Bat insignia on the cowl. Sleek, low, with sexy contours both stylish and sinister.

Rather like Max Savoie.

"Whoa, baby. What's this?"

"BMW K 1200 Sport. Laterally mounted 16-valve water-cooled engine, angling the cylinders forward by fifty-five degrees for a low CG. Six-gear shifting with a narrow profile inspired by Formula One. It took first place at Daytona from the last row by nineteen seconds. I love a scrapper."

She blinked at his recitation. Then he grinned. "Zero to sixty in two-point-eight seconds."

"Hmmm." She refused to look impressed as her fingertips caressed the streamlined silhouette. "A Brit bike. Not exactly what I would have chosen, but at least it's not one of those horizontally mounted two-cylinder flat-twin Boxer engines."

He pushed a helmet at her. "I didn't buy it for you. I bought it because I like it. Because when I take it from a purr to a roar between my knees, it makes me think of you. Come for a ride with me. There's something I need to do, and I'd like you there."

Something in his voice spoke of importance. Her gaze traced along the black leather seat, then stroked up the inseam of his black jeans from knees to zipper with a measured heat. "Well, then. Take me for another ride, Savoie." She started to slip the helmet over her head, then paused. "Someone *did* teach you how to drive this, right?"

He grinned at her caution. "I have a full endorsement." He didn't mention the endorsement was from Giles, who pronounced his boss man looked good sitting on it. And that since the bike was just under five hundred pounds, he should be able to lift it off himself if he dumped it.

"Hang on," he called over his shoulder when they'd both settled on the seat.

Sound advice.

She'd told him she liked fast, dangerous things. She hadn't been thinking of straddling a surface-to-air missile guided by an absolutely fearless crazy man.

He rocketed through the tight traffic, threading between cars as if in a flat-out downhill slalom. His reflexes were as quick and smooth as the raw powerhouse he crouched over, ignoring the rules of the road as if they didn't apply to him. Cee Cee's fingers dug in so deep, she thought for sure they'd gone through skin and muscle to cling to the bottom of his rib cage.

Then they shot out onto the open road and Cee Cee found herself delighted the way only an adrenaline junkie could be.

Fast, exciting, and hot—both bike and rider.

Then she recognized their surroundings. Why was he taking them back into the bayou?

IT WAS A small house, just a notch above a shack, set back off the road at a shunned distance from the mostly abandoned village. Weeds ran rampant and paint was a faded memory, but the structure was sound. No broken glass, no signs of vandalism, but no sign that it had been lived in for a very long time.

Max hesitated at the gate of the sad fence that circled the yard.

"Whose place is this?"

He held up a key. "Mine. I was born here. Jimmy bought it, kept it for me. I didn't know about it until after he died. I couldn't make myself come here . . . until now."

He struggled with the gate for a moment. It had settled at an angle, sinking into the soggy ground. He closed it behind them, then knelt down to peer between the slats.

"What are you looking at, baby?"

"Everything I knew about the world I saw through this fence. We had no television, no radio, no newspaper. We never went into town. I couldn't go out of the yard except to church, and to stay with the neighbor when my mama . . . when she had company. I remember wondering what it would be like to ride by on a bicycle or run up and down the road the way other kids did. But then they'd yell things at me, and I was glad there was this fence between us."

She touched his shoulder, not saying anything.

He shook off the sadness by covering her hand with his, then held it as they walked up to the porch.

As they started up the solid steps, a voice called out from across the road. "Max?"

They turned to see a black woman in her seventies with wiry gray hair and thick plastic-framed glasses. Her head was cocked to one side on a skinny neck in an oddly birdlike fashion.

"It *is* you. Marie's boy."

Max froze. "Do I know you?"

"You probably don't remember. I'm Mrs. Pelletier from across the way. Haven't seen you since you was just a wee one, but I'd knows you anywhere. You look just like your daddy."

Twenty-four

HE SAT RIGHT where you be sitting now, and made me tell him all about you."

Only the comforting weight of Cee Cee's hand on his thigh kept Max from leaping up off the raggedy sofa to pace in agitation. He remembered the musty scent of the room, with its mountains of soap opera magazines on the floor by the nineteen-inch portable prominently displayed on a metal TV tray. The television was new. The old rabbit ears had been replaced by a satellite dish outside.

He took a calming breath and another sip of the lemonade the old woman had provided. He remembered that, too: the way its sour bite turned the mouth inside out and made the eyes sting. As his were burning now.

"Did he come for me?"

"No, child. This was a day or so after you and your mama disappeared. He seemed to expect to find you gone, but was worried about her."

Because he'd already sold his son to Jimmy Legere, and he didn't know Marie Savoie had been killed in the transaction.

"What did he want?"

"To hear about you—every little detail I could come

up with. Seems him and your mama had a lover's quarrel and she ran off 'fore telling him about you. He sat there and had hisself a good cry over not being daddy to you whilst you were a bebe."

Rollo? Max imagined big crocodile tears, but said nothing.

"He'd wanted to see your mama, but couldn't stay more than a few hours. He gave me a number where she could reach him if either of you needed anything, and he gave me a package for her. She never come back for it."

"Do you still have it?"

"I gots to confess, when she didn't come back after them first few months, I gots curious. I tried to call your daddy at the number he gave me, but there was never no answer. So I open the package, thinking he might have left some kinda address."

"What was in it?"

"Money. Woo wee, so much money! For the house, he said in his note inside. So his boy would have someplace to come back to. 'Bout den, Mr. Legere's fancy lawyer done come to my door, axing what I know about the empty house. I tell him about the money and dat I ain't seen your mama for a long, long time. He tole me your mama had died and he axed if I could look after the place, 'cuz someday you'd be coming back with questions about it and about your mama. Tole me to keep the money to use for whatever needed fixing, and to call if I needed more. So me and my boys, we look out for the place and we watch out for you. We put dat money in the bank. Only used about half of it, most of that for a new roof. The rest, dat be yours."

Max didn't know what to say in response to her goodwill.

"I boxed up all your personal things and brought them over here. Didn't want to leave them in that empty house case somebody gots ideas."

It hadn't occurred to Max that there might be anything left. Anxiety and anticipation combined in a taste more bitter than the lemonade.

"The furniture's still in there," Mrs. Pelletier continued. "I put covers over it and check now and again to make sure no varmints get in. Seem to remember you having a real nice rug in the front room. Don't know what happened to it."

It was at the bottom of the swamp, weighted with stones, wrapped around the Shifter he and his mother had killed over thirty years ago.

"Oh, did I mention your daddy's letters? One to your mama. One for you. I'll get them." She was up before he could stop her.

"A nice woman," Cee Cee said quietly, her hand gently rubbing.

"Yes. I remember her now. She was always good to us. The only one who was." He stood when Mrs. Pelletier reentered the room, taking the two envelopes with reluctance.

"I'm right sorry about your mama. She was a quality lady, doing her best for you, and don't you let anybody tell you different. She loved you."

It took him a moment to manage simple speech.

"Thank you, Mrs. Pelletier. For everything. I'll stop back soon to pick up the things you have stored and pay you for your kindness."

"Pay me?" She waved a dismissing hand. "You'll do no such thing. Just stop by for a visit. I'd like to hear all about how you done for yourself. Seen you and your pretty lady on TV. And that was a right nice shot in the newspaper." She winked saucily to indicate the picture of Cee Cee's hand on his ass. "If you want to bring something, bring your lady here. And maybe some rum. It makes the lemonade go down smoother."

CEE CEE WATCHED from the front door as Max took a slow tour about the vacant house, giving him time with his memories, but staying close should they overwhelm him. She couldn't tell anything from his expression. It was blank, no emotions visible.

He went from room to room, in and out of the two little bedrooms in less than thirty seconds, as if they held nothing for him. Or he was afraid to linger. He circled the kitchen. She could hear his low snuffles as he searched for a trace of scent. Then he rejoined her in the front room.

"There's nothing here," he said in a toneless voice. She couldn't tell if it held disappointment or relief. "I can't find her here. I thought maybe . . . Charlotte, I can't remember what she looks like."

She took a step toward him as his features crumpled, but he stopped her and gathered his control.

"I can see her in my dreams, or I think I do, but the impression doesn't stay with me. Her scent's lost to me, too. Jimmy, why didn't you tell me about all this?" He closed his eyes briefly and took a slow, deep breath.

She could have answered, but didn't. The truth would only hurt him. Jimmy had kept the existence of this place a secret so Max would have no attachment to the past. So there would be only him when Max thought of family. The old bastard.

"Let's go," he said at last, his voice heavy. "It's getting late and you have to—"

He broke off as he bumped one of the shrouded bits of furniture and set it rocking. Max took a quick hop to one side, his posture alert and edgy as he followed it's motions with a guarded gaze. He pulled the dust cover off, then he touched the tapestry back of the platform rocker, tracing the raised pattern. He slowly bent to press his cheek to the faded material, his eyes closing as a whisper of a smile touched his mouth. He circled to the front of the chair and sank down to the planked floor, resting his head on the seat and swaying with it in a slow, comforting motion.

"We'd sit together in this chair in the evenings. She'd rock me until I fell asleep. She'd read to me from one of my books. Or we'd just rock. Just rock."

He was silent for long minutes. When he finally spoke, his words were hushed.

"I asked her how long I'd be gone. She didn't answer right away and I got scared, because I'd heard her crying and she never cried. She told me I'd like it there—that I'd have everything she'd ever wanted for me, everything I dreamed of. And I begged her not to make me go. I promised I would never, ever ask for anything again if I could just stay. She said, 'Stop your crying. It won't help. You have to go with them. You have to be good and be quiet and do everything they tell you, so they'll keep you safe. That's all that matters.' "

But he hadn't been able to stop crying, pleading until she'd given him a hard shake, her eyes fierce and angry.

"Stop it," she'd snarled. "You will go and you will behave, and you will not give them any reason to send you back here. Because I can't take care of you, Max. I can't protect you.

"They'll come for you. They'll come like before, only more of them. They'll kill me, then they'll take you and hurt you. Is that what you want, Max?"

No, it wasn't. He remembered the one who'd come to their door, who'd hurt his mama, who tried to take him, who was now nothing but bone wrapped in their living room rug.

So he'd promised her he'd be good. He'd do whatever he was told. Because he didn't want her to die. It would be his fault if she died.

"She held me in this chair all night, just rocking. I must have fallen asleep, because she woke me and told me they were here, and that I was to wait in my room while she talked to them. I could hear them arguing. I'd never been anywhere with strangers before, but I didn't want anything bad to happen to my mama, so I pretended I wasn't afraid.

"They were two very big men and I was happy when Mama told me she was going to ride along with me to make sure I was all right. We rode for a long time, out into the swamps. 'This isn't the way,' my mama said. 'Change of plans,' they told her. Then Mama reached over the seat and grabbed the steering wheel. 'You won't take him. I won't let you take him. We had a deal,' she was yelling. 'But they paid more,' one of them told her.

"And she opened the car door and threw me out. I could hear her screaming for me to run. 'Run, Max! Don't look back. Run! Save yourself.' "

Tears running down her face, Cee Cee stood helpless to do anything but let him finish. Let him recite how he'd run and run, until one of the men shouted that if he didn't come back they'd shoot his mother. How he'd stood knee-deep in muck, four, maybe five years old, and turned to see them with a gun at his mother's head.

Because he couldn't let them hurt her, he'd started back, terror jumping in his chest. Cee Cee could feel his panic and fright as Max's agitation grew, as the intensity of his emotion began to draw her into the dark nightmare of his past through the bond they shared.

"I won't let you take him. I won't let you hurt him."

Marie Savoie's voice rang clearly in her mind with such desperation, such anguish. Such determination.

And she saw Marie plainly through Max's eyes as she turned to him, smiling as she said, "I love you, Max. Run. Save yourself. Run."

Charlotte knew what she was going to do. She would have done the same, without thought, without hesitation. Marie Savoie stepped between her son and the two armed men and she lunged toward them.

"Mama!"

Max's cry came from both the child and the man.

Marie falling, a bullet in her chest. Max reaching for her, her string of bloodied pearls breaking in his clutching hands, falling along with his tears into the water.

"I killed her. I didn't do what I was told. I killed her," he said in anguish.

Is that what he thought? Was that the cruel lesson that followed him through his lonely life, that his mother had died because of his momentary act of disobedience? That a child, a scared, helpless child, was responsible for the sacrifice a mother chose to make?

As Cee Cee started toward him his eyes changed, glittering with that cold fire.

He might have been a child afraid, but he hadn't been helpless.

"I killed them, Charlotte," he whispered, trembling as she knelt to put her arms around him. "I let that monster inside me loose to tear them apart. I remember their screams." He started panting. "I can feel their blood on my face, can taste it in my mouth." His eyes rolled back as he wet his lips, and his breaths grew deep and almost rapturous. "Can taste them—the heat, the fear as I killed them and fed on them."

He was still for a long minute, then the quick, anxious breaths started up again. "They came because of the blood."

She gripped him hard as her heart lurched. Her cheek pressed to his as she whispered, "Who did, Max?"

"Not who. Not who."

Instinctively, she used the bond between them to let her consciousness sink into his so he wouldn't have to speak the horrors out loud. Let herself become one with the child he'd been out in that dark, deadly swamp. Felt the terror, the protective fury growling up from his feral soul as they came, mostly at night, to feast on what was left of his attackers. Those things that lived in the swamps, sliding silently, rustling through the trees, soft breaths, quick shadows. Drawn from the darkness by the scent of the body he held in his arms.

Cee Cee rocked with him, slow and soothing, rubbing his shoulders, his back, murmuring quietly, "It's all right, baby. Nothing can hurt her now. You kept her safe. You can let go now."

She could feel that spindly, tough little boy he'd been in her arms, could feel him shivering with cold, burning with fever and thirst as nights and days bled into each other. Hugging that putrid, bloated shape that he tried to think of his mama, unable to cry because he was too weak now for tears.

Mama, please don't leave me here alone.

And then from out of that hot, raw delirium, the beast inside began to stir. Hungry. Starving. All self-preservation instincts.

He'd tried to eat the things he found in the water, slimy, cold things that came hurling back up in a cramping rush.

Save yourself, Max. His mama's voice, a tender whisper. *Do whatever you have to do to stay alive.*

"Take my hand."

His eyes opened to the sight of an outstretched palm. To the offer of salvation and sanity.

"It's all right. I'll take care of you. I'll take care of your mama. Just take my hand and you'll be safe."

Cee Cee followed his gaze to the face of Jimmy Legere, haloed by the setting sun as if he were a saint sent down from heaven.

Max blinked—and then there was just the empty house and her arms around him.

She felt him recoil and held on tight. She spoke firmly, calmly, so he wouldn't misinterpret the importance of her words.

"It's all right, baby. You didn't do anything wrong. It's not your fault. None of it was your fault, Max. You were a little boy who's not to blame for any of it."

When he tried to turn away from her, she gripped his jaw to compel him to look back in her direction.

"Listen to me. Max, are you listening?"

A stiff nod, but he wouldn't open his eyes.

"You did nothing wrong. You did what she wanted you to do: survive. The rest doesn't matter. Your mama would have been so proud of you."

"No." That tore up from the wounded heart of him as his eyes opened, his gaze clouded with grief and guilt and pain.

"Yes. Yes, she would be. Do you know how I know? Max, look at me. Do you know how I know?"

She watched as clarity seeped back into his stare, until he was seeing her, really seeing her. "How?"

"Because *I'm* proud of you. And I love you, too."

He swallowed hard, then nodded, before he leaned into her embrace, letting her stroke his hair. Finally he recovered enough to step away from his past.

He rose to his feet. "I'll take you back to your car."

She stayed close while he locked the house and led the way down the uneven stones leading to the listing gate. As he shut it behind him, she could sense him easing back from what he'd faced so he could regard it with thirty years of objectivity.

Hopefully leaving room in his newly cleaned closet for her shoes.

NEITHER ONE OF them was eager to get back to the city. Back to the empty parking lot at the Towers, where hers was the only car waiting. She climbed off the bike and secured her helmet on the seat behind him, waiting for him to lift his off so she could kiss him. Then they simply leaned brow to brow as her fingers combed through his hair, ending at that sexy curl behind his ears.

"I love you, Max. Wait until I get back to read those letters."

He nodded.

"I won't be gone long. I wouldn't have the strength to do this if not for you. I'll call you." When his expression didn't change, she said more forcefully, "I'll call you tomorrow night at nine o'clock, and you'd better answer."

"I will."

She strode to her orange Camaro, starting it up with an aggressive roar, going from parking lot to heartbreak in less than twelve seconds.

CHARLOTTE HATED TO fly. Hated the hurry, the last-minute scrambling, only to wait packed in with other impatient people.

But Mary Kate Malone was her best and only friend. They'd survived despairing childhoods, bittersweet teen years, the brutality of fate, and the choices that ultimately wedged them apart, but that love had never faltered.

So why was she so reluctant to take this flight?

It was more than the upheavals in her life; those excuses would no longer stand. It wasn't the pain of knowing that the figure lying in that bed in the damaged shell, with a fragmented mind, wasn't the Mary Kate Malone she remembered. It wasn't the fact that there was no hope of ever getting that dear, dear friend back again.

What made the journey so difficult was the truth she couldn't face. She knew a self-inflicted gunshot wound when she saw one.

Now she had to come to terms with the reason for it. The reason Sister Catherine would commit that sin barring her eternally from the reward she deserved.

She stuffed her duffel bag in the overhead of the crowded coach section, scowling at the sight of the vacant seat between a sweaty, ill-groomed old man and a young mother with a wiggly child on her lap, who looked appalled at the gun holster bared by her reaching.

"Detective Caissie?"

She glanced at the stewardess in a surly humor.

The attractive older woman smiled. "We've got an upgrade for you in First Class."

She blinked. First Class? Then a slow smile eased the tension from her mood.

I love you, Savoie.

She grabbed down her bag, ignoring the relieved breath of the young mother, and followed the uniformed attendant to the front.

First Class: a haven of space and comfort her salary denied her. The attendant slipped her bag into the spacious compartment and said, "I'll be back for your complimentary cocktail order once everyone's seated."

Not too shabby, Cee Cee thought as she sank into the generous perks of luxury travel and closed her eyes. For all of a minute.

"'Cuse me. I think you're in my seat."

She didn't open her eyes. "There's another one next to me. I just got comfortable. Climb over."

"I've never been in a plane before. I'm not sure I want to sit by the window."

She fought to suppress her smile. "Don't be such a baby, Savoie. It's not like the aisle seat is going to give you anywhere else to run if we go down in mid-flight."

"Thanks for that image. I feel so much better."

She slit an eye open as he angled around her feet, stumbling slightly. She grabbed a handful of very nice ass to keep him from falling into her lap and gave him a helpful boost.

"Are you copping a feel, Detective?"

"So what if I am?" She was so damned happy to see him, she thought her heart would burst. Her voice gruff from the emotion filling her throat, she demanded, "What are you doing here, Max?"

"Keeping a promise."

Tears quickened in her eyes. "This trip isn't about beaches and sex, Savoie." She gave the eavesdropping man standing beside the row in front of her a double-barreled look that had him quickly sinking into his seat.

Max took her stubborn chin in his hand to turn her attention back to him, to the sincerity of his expression. "My promise that I would be there for you. That you'd never have to make another trip like this alone."

Her chin quivered. He'd made that promise after she'd gone to bury her mother. "Mary Kate's the only family I have left, Max."

"I'm not going to intrude, Charlotte. But I have to be there. In case you need me for anything."

Or for everything.

"The only family besides *you*," she whispered, choking up. "Thank you, Max."

"You're welcome." A small smile, then he turned his attention to the seatback pouch, looking rather alarmed at the air sickness bag and safety instructions. She distracted him by threading her fingers between his so she could lift his hand and press a kiss to his knuckles. Her heart shuddered gloriously.

"Don't worry," she assured him, her mood beginning to soar. "Once we're at cruising altitude, we can take off these belts and get comfortable. Maybe I'll even explain the Mile High Club to you."

"Is that some kind of perk you get with a seat upgrade?"

She smiled. "Something like that, yeah. In this case, anyway." She leaned against his shoulder and sighed, "I'm glad you're here," when he opened his arm so she could snuggle in more closely. Her eyes closed as his lips brushed her brow and stress rolled off her, allowing her thoughts to travel to the ocean. Sand, surf, hot sun. Hot man. *Her* man.

"And while we're there together, *cher*, we'll have that talk concerning our future," he murmured softly. "One that won't permit any secrets between us."

"I'll tell you mine if you'll tell me yours."

"I love you, *sha*."

"Back at you, Savoie."

And by the time the plane left the ground, they were both sound asleep. Hands and hearts entwined.

Pocket Books
proudly presents a sneak peek at

HUNTER OF SHADOWS

The next sizzling novel from rising star
Nancy Gideon

Available December 2011
from Pocket Books

Prologue

Silas MacCreedy identified certain sounds with New Orleans: the mournful wail of a saxophone on the corner of the square, the whine of mopeds darting along the narrow streets like flies needing a good swat, a hard blues backbeat and drunken laughter drifting out from open doorways.

A sharp female cry wasn't one of them.

He'd lost sight of the men he'd been following, and he couldn't afford to let the trail grow cold. But no one else on the early-evening street had reacted to the possible call for help. Either they couldn't be bothered, or the sound was too faint to reach their ears. He should continue on; he had vital things to do. Yet . . .

Aw, hell. MacCreedy shut out the city soundtrack, listening.

A scuffle on loose stone. The crack of a hand against vulnerable skin.

He sighed and turned down the shadowed side street, his tread light with caution. "Better ready than dead" was the motto that got him home safely at night.

The dark, narrow alley ahead was the perfect place for bad things to go unnoticed. He breathed deeply through his nose, drawing in a taste of what he was walking into. A female. Four males. Not human. He could separate their scent signatures, now that he was closer, and he smiled at his good fortune. These were the same men he'd been tracking.

His job was surveillance, to stay hidden and see where they'd lead him. But he couldn't just watch while they indulged their nasty habit of preying on women.

He eased into the mouth of the alley, knowing he had only a moment to assess the situation before they saw him. Not good. The woman was on the ground with one man crouching over her. The three others crowded in close, their breaths quick and raw with anticipation.

"Am I interrupting something?" Silas said politely.

All eyes flashed to where he stood in the shadow, where they could see his large, looming figure but not his face. He expected the dangerous glares of challenge from the males. In the dim alley their eyes glowed with an unnatural brilliance. They were big men, roughly dressed, smelling salty from Gulf water and exertion. Dock workers. Shape-shifters, needing no weapons other than their rough strength and preternatural abilities.

His own kind.

MacCreedy took his hand away from his holster. He would enjoy handling them as soon as he got their victim to safety. But maybe they'd just run like the cowardly pack animals they were, rather than face consequences. He could see hesitation in their feral gazes and fleetingly hoped they'd make a stand so he could teach them a lesson. That would almost be worth having his cover blown.

Fight or flee, you cowards.

He was ready for them, hands fisted, muscles loose and lethal. But a quick glance at the female caught him off guard.

Beneath a tangle of long black hair, her cheek was

red from the slap he'd heard. She was slender, dressed in a sweatjacket and jeans, nothing provocative that would draw her attackers' attention. A battered backpack lay on the dirty stones beside her. Though her face was partially cloaked by her hair, he got the impression of sharp angles and a wide mouth.

And instead of the wild-eyed plea for help he expected, her stare was steady and ice cold. Beautiful deep-blue eyes, as sultry as the twilight sky.

Her voice was a sudden slash of lightning. "Unfortunately, you're intruding on a private party."

In an instant, Silas realized he'd confused predator with prey.

Her arm made a quick arc. She must have held a blade within the loose sleeve of her jacket, for the male straddling her fell back, gripping his throat as if he could stop the sudden geyser of blood. She agilely rolled free of him, was on her feet and, just as fast, was on the next man with an inhuman snarl. Gripping her arms to jerk her away, another man sealed his own fate.

Eyes blazing hot and golden, she turned in his clumsy hold and took his face between her hands. With a sickening crack, she broke his neck.

MacCreedy's instincts finally overcame his astonishment. He needed the remaining two men breathing, so he ignored the terrified pair scrambling for their lives to deal with the female determined to kill them. The instant he grabbed her slender upper arms and felt whipcord muscles tighten beneath his grip, he realized his mistake. A possibly fatal mistake.

"What have you done?" she snarled, whirling to confront him.

Something sparked within him as he got his first

good look at her, a quick flame of recognition for someone he'd never seen before. It made him slow to respond.

"I thought I was saving your life."

The upward swing of her elbow caught his chin with a force that made him stumble. The sweep of her leg clipped behind his knees, dropping him to the ground, where his head cracked on the cold cobbles, making the world spin. Then she straddled him, her strong features and lovely eyes harsh.

"You should have stuck to saving your own," she said grimly. "Too late now."

Knowing she would kill him, he hit her with everything he had, the force knocking her head back. She simply gave it a shake, then smiled at him.

"It's not nice to hit a lady," she chastised with short jabs to his mid-section.

MacCreedy twisted, trying to throw her off, growling, "If I thought you were a lady, I wouldn't have done it."

She was quick and impossibly strong. Even though he could have taken down the four males, he couldn't get the best of her despite all his training.

When his jacket fell open, the metallic flash of his badge didn't even make her hesitate. But the sight of his inner wrist as she wrenched his hand away from his gun made her pause. Her gaze fixed on the scarred brand burned into it.

Then she eased back with a small laugh. "This is your lucky night. You get to live through it."

He *had* to know who she was.

When she started to lift off him, MacCreedy gripped her arm in a staying gesture. "Wait."

Clearly surprised, she cocked her head as she studied his face. A slight, amused smile curved her lips as she said, "As much as I've enjoyed the tussle, I'm in a hurry, hero. But I guess there's enough time for a quick thank-you."

Braced for another attack, Silas was stunned by the sweetness of her assault. She took his mouth with hers, engaging his tongue in a tangling flash of desire and cool mint.

"Thanks for the rescue, even though it was bad timing."

Then she was gone, leaving MacCreedy lying between two bodies, with the taste of her on his breath and her heat burning in his blood.

One

A QUICK GLANCE AT the clock over the bar told Monica Fraser she was twenty minutes late. Not a good start for her first week on the job.

She slipped into the small server's galley and stuffed her jacket into a cubby next to the cash register so no one would notice any bloodstains. A quick brush of her palms smoothed her hastily braided hair, then she snatched up her change pouch to secure it about her waist.

"Sorry I'm late," she began as another woman came in to ring up some drinks.

"Don't worry about it," Amber James reassured her. "We haven't been busy and I covered for you. Told Jacques you were in the back taking care of female things." She grinned. "That shut him up."

Not sure how to respond, Nica returned the smile. She wasn't used to kindnesses with no strings attached. "Thanks."

Amber shrugged it off. "That's what friends are for."

To the softhearted waitress, it was that simple. Amber had enthusiastically scooped her into that huge category titled *Friends* without knowing a thing about her, without first weighing and negotiating terms for their association. She had no idea what a foreign concept that was to Nica.

Nica should have thought her foolish for having such uncomplicated views, yet part of her was reluctantly envious. While her coworker's vision was care-free and rose-colored, Nica's was as fiercely narrowed as a sniper scope. But then, Amber's life expectancy was measured in decades, not by seconds. There was no real comparison.

"I owe you one," Nica insisted, feeling the need to pay her way.

"If you insist, I'll let you take care of table four. They're loud and seem to have no control over their hands."

"Maybe I'll have to teach them some manners." She winked with an aggressive confidence that had Amber chuckling.

Cheveux du Chien was just starting to fill up with the evening's patrons; an exclusive clientele gathering under the unsuspecting nose of New Orleans. For a city proud of its diverse cultures, discovery of this hidden pocket of preternatural citizens would have been far from welcome news. In much the same way, Nica knew she'd be ostracized and feared if these clannish souls recognized her for what *she* was. The four she'd met in the alley had. Two of them wouldn't be repeating what they'd seen; that left a pair of loose ends to deal with when her shift was over.

Blending in was how she'd managed to survive for so long in her dangerous profession. Though she chafed with urgency, Nica forced an outward calm. *Draw no attention. Break no patterns.* Even if it meant a nerve-taunting delay. The pair would go to ground like frightened rabbits, but she'd find them again. They'd been easy to lure into that alleyway, where her secret would have been successfully laid to rest if not for her misguided savior.

Suppressing a growl of irritation, she efficiently cleared the glasses and empties off the nearest table, then gave it a polish with the cloth tucked in the back pocket of her tight black jeans. *Hero? Meddler* was more like it. Bursting onto her scene with a cop's unerring instinct to be just where they weren't wanted. A cop who also wore the brand of the powerful Terriot shape-shifter clan. Interesting, but none of her concern as long as he didn't interfere in her business.

Interesting *and* a damned good kisser, she thought as her tongue touched her lower lip.

It was careless not to kill him, especially when the stakes were so high—not only professionally but personally as well. She was so close to obtaining her freedom, she could taste it.

"Leave no witnesses" was a cold but necessary practice that could mean life or death for her. But what an unfair reward for a good deed that would have been, for a stranger willing to risk all on her behalf. She stacked more glasses until her tray teetered as precariously as her reasoning . . . a tall, rugged reason clad in a dark suit coat, blue chambray shirt and tie, over snug jeans.

There was something about a man in a tie and jeans . . . She sighed. Something best left alone. A male bearing a clan mark wasn't someone to be taken lightly.

Nica slid her tray across the bar so owner Jacques LaRoche could unload it.

"Is, umm, everything okay?" he asked with the squeamish distaste males had for female matters.

She liked Jacques LaRoche, and lying to him wasn't a necessity. "I was late for work," she confessed. "No excuses. It won't happen again. I didn't ask Amber to cover for me."

LaRoche's brow lifted at her honesty. "She was being a friend."

Nica nodded. "I'm taking table four for her."

Jacques watched her walk away with a smile. Monica Fraser had saved a friend of his with her quick thinking, and he wouldn't forget that. He'd given her a job as a way to thank her, and he'd been thanking his lucky stars ever since.

It took a special kind of female to work his crowd. They had to be easy on the eye without being easy in other areas. They had to have a sense of humor to handle bawdy talk without offense, and enough sense of self to know when to say enough was enough. Nica managed both things. She wasn't beautiful or swimsuit-issue curvy like the rest of his girls, but she had her own kind of appeal, with her long, lean tomboyish shape hugged by a white knit tank top and skinny jeans. The fact that she didn't bother with a padded bra in the air-conditioned room also appealed to the customers' base instincts. The quick flash of her wide smile said she could give as good as she got, and that mass of glossy black hair made every male dream of sinking his fingers into it. She'd come out of nowhere, made his life easier, and he had no complaints.

He watched her handling the difficult customers at table four. They worked for him on the docks and would behave themselves if he stepped in. He let her take care of it in her own way, though he was ready to intercede if necessary. No one disrespected his staff, on the docks or in his bar.

She exchanged tart comments with a friendly smile, just the right balance of sass and flirtation. Two of the fellas grinned and enjoyed the teasing, but the third placed his big hand on her ass for an uninvited squeeze. Without spilling a drop from pitcher to glasses, she caught his hand with her free one, gripping his thumb for an almost casual twist that brought him to his knees on the floor in an instant. After she let go without a glance or a word of reproof, he slipped back into his seat to the demoralizing chuckles of his friends.

Jacques grinned and went back to clearing the bar.

Just then, a slight prickle of sensation disturbed him; a signal from his checker at the door that possible trouble had entered the club. His gaze lifted casually to the stranger at the edge of the room. A tall male with conservatively short brown hair and a five-o'clock stubble, wearing a suit coat and tie, and an attitude that said he could handle himself. He locked stares with Jacques, then started across the room with a purposeful stride. Maybe not trouble, but definitely something. LaRoche made a subtle gesture to stay his men, letting the visitor approach.

"Are you LaRoche?" His voice was deep and smooth, betraying no hint of his intentions.

"I am. And you?"

"Let's say I'm an interested party."

"And what are you interested in, friend?"

"I didn't say I was a friend." Very smooth.

Jacques smiled thinly. "Guess you didn't. Best state your business, then."

He stood straight and sure, with no posturing or aggression, maintaining eye contact. His manner said, *I could kick your ass, but I choose not to.* Maybe he could, maybe he couldn't. Jacques relaxed, knowing he wasn't going to have to prove anything one way or the other. At least not yet.

"I was told you take care of things around here," the man continued.

"By whom?"

He didn't answer that. "I happened upon an awkward situation a few minutes ago that needs cleaning up before questions get asked. I don't have the resources."

Now he had Jacques attention. "Explain."

"Two of our kind got themselves dead, not by my hand." He gave the location. "Maybe you know them, maybe you don't care. Just thought I'd give you a neighborly heads-up before the police get wind of it and start poking around."

Jacques signaled a couple of his crew over and gave them the necessary details, along with brusque instructions to tidy the scene. Then he put a glass on the bar. "Thanks for the tip. Drink on the house?"

Silas shook his head. "Gotta be going. Have a nice evening."

As he stepped away from the bar, Silas hoped it wasn't a mistake to make himself known to the local clan. He'd been aware of this spot since his arrival in New Orleans, and had made it a point to stay away so they wouldn't sense him. The success of his plans demanded he conceal what he was and what he was after. He thought of that drink with a brief wistfulness. How long had it been since he'd shared a companionable glass with one of his own? Too long to even remember. Too dangerous to even consider.

His mission was completed. He'd alerted them so they could protect the secrecy by which they all lived. Police involvement meant unnecessary attention. Let the clan of outcasts take care of their own, and he'd take care of himself. No need to get involved.

And then Silas caught her scent.

Just that hint, teasing like a whisper across his senses, sent a jolt through his system. His skin sizzled, his blood grew thick and hot, and his breath raspy. The instinctual response came from some unknown place deep inside.

His gaze swept the room, not pausing when it caught her tucked back in the shadows. Hiding from his notice? Perhaps.

The fact that his mysterious and fierce lone wolf chose to conceal herself amongst trusting sheep wasn't his concern, so he continued out into the sultry night. There he rubbed his arms restlessly until the staticlike sensations eased.

This female was nothing to him. Nothing but trouble.

He remembered his younger sister Brigit teasing him that someday he'd be brought to his knees by fated sexual chemistry, by an irresistible pheromone drawing him to his mate. Then he remembered how he'd laughed at her, calling her a foolish romantic.

He wasn't laughing now. But he was unbearably and probably unwisely curious.